Sweet and Sinful

Sweet and Sinful

Jodi Lynn Copeland

APHRODISIA
KENSINGTON BOOKS
http://www.kensingtonbooks.com

APHRODISIA BOOKS are published by

Kensington Publishing Corp.
850 Third Avenue
New York, NY 10022

All Kensington Titles, Imprints, and Distributed Lines are available at special quantity discounts for bulk purchases for sales promotions, premiums, fund-raising, and educational or institutional use.

Special book excerpts or customized printings can also be created to fit specific needs. For details, write or phone the office of the Kensington special sales manager: Kensington Publishing Corp., 850 Third Avenue, New York, NY 10022, attn: Special Sales Department, Phone: 1-800-221-2647.

ISBN-13: 978-0-7582-2711-9
ISBN-10: 0-7582-2711-6

First Kensington Trade Paperback Printing: August 2008

10 9 8 7 6 5 4 3 2 1

Printed in the United States of America

Contents

Just Like Candy

1

She'd finally done it. Turned her porn star dreams into reality.

Freshly showered with a fluffy white robe wrapped around her, Courtney Baxter exited the hotel suite bathroom and beamed at the naked male ass asleep on the coverless bed.

Technically, it was more than an ass. A prime, hard-bodied, and excellently equipped specimen of the male species was attached to that fine backside. And she hadn't exactly become a full-fledged porn star, or ever dreamed of becoming one, for that matter. But she had enticed Mr. Hot Buns into letting her videotape their wild antics.

To think, less than two months ago she couldn't score so much as a dinner date for her average looks and behavior. Now, thanks to a little guidance from her across-the-cubicle coworker at Pinnacle Engineering, Courtney was neither average nor lacking for men to date, dine with, or just plain do.

Thanks to Candy Masterson, Courtney was a bona fide sex diva and loving every minute of it. A sex diva that was overdue to make her exit.

The secret of having fun with sex, Candy had told her, was

getting out while things were still going good. In other words, not sticking around until Mr. Hot Buns woke up from his post-orgasm slumber and Courtney had to face that awkward "I never got to know more than your sexual preference and marital status before I laid you" moment.

The beefcake in mention shifted on the bed before rolling onto his back and trapping both the top and bottom sheet beneath well-developed calves. She held her breath with the idea she'd missed her getaway opportunity. Thankfully, his eyes never opened. He just started into some serious snoring that suggested he wasn't waking anytime soon.

Releasing her breath, she took advantage of his vulnerable state and slid her gaze along his body.

Black hair covered his solid frame, thick on his head and groin, thinner on his chest and the rest of his big body. A mustache touched against his upper lip and, oh, the wickedly wonderful ways he'd used that coarse bit of hair on her.

Her pussy pulsed with the memory of his mouth down there, his tongue inside her folds, lapping at her cream. Instinctively, her gaze drifted lower, past the solid expanse of his stomach to his cock. As if he could feel her watching him, his shaft stirred, rousing to its previously solid state. This time minus the condom so she could see every inch of steely male flesh. Plump pinking head. Pre-cum oozing from the tip . . . just waiting for her tongue to reach out and lick.

Damn, it was tempting to shake the robe off her shoulders, climb back onto the bed, and let first her mouth and then her sex gobble up his erection.

It was *always* tempting.

But tempting fate by making it seem she was after more than a little harmless sex was not the point. Having fun was. Enjoying herself, her body, her twenty-six-year-old sex drive before it started petering out and she had to face the reality of an average life all over again.

That rather depressing thought got Courtney moving as it always did.

This time making her getaway meant more than chucking the robe and pulling on the red leather pants, black baby-doll top, and four-inch-heel stilettos that had taken her the better part of a week to learn to walk in without resembling a newborn foal taking its first steps. This time leaving meant gathering up her camera, tripod, and taping supplies.

She moved as soundlessly as possible through the hotel room, searching out rashly cast-aside clothing and pulling it on. She was dressed and nearly finished storing the camera and accessories in their bag when Mr. Hot Buns' snoring came to an abrupt end.

Ten feet behind her, sheets rustled. The bed gave a creak.

Courtney swore under her breath and went deadly still, silent. Pulse pounding at her throat, she felt far too much like she had when she'd gotten trapped by a wild boar on the outskirts of her parents' blueberry farm.

Cornered, and desperate for escape.

Please stay asleep.

"You should have woken me," came a sleep-roughened male voice.

She bit her lip to keep her groan inside. With the boar, she'd gotten lucky and her dad had come to her rescue. With the beefcake, her luck had run out.

Aware the only way she was going to get out of this hotel room was with action, Courtney finished stowing the tripod and zipped up the camera bag. Hooking the bag's strap over her shoulder, she pasted on her most sensual smile and turned around. Mr. Hot Buns sat in bed, his back to the plain wood headboard and his cock at full mast and calling to her from across the room. Even more than his willingness to go along with her videotaping desire, he'd been a great lay. Eager to please, again and again.

She still had to go. Now.

This sex game was about confidence, arrogance even, so she took her smile from sensual to smug. "Not on your life, buster. The way you were snoring, it was clear that I wore you out."

A frown twitched at his lips as he nodded at the camera bag. "Going somewhere?"

She'd picked him out of all the men at the bar because of the self-assured aura he gave off. Now that aura was nowhere to be found. Now he was brooding—his cocoa brown eyes reminded her of a wounded puppy—and the country girl of her roots was threatening to resurface and make her want to jump him more than ever. "It's late."

"I have this room till morning."

Yeah, and she had a personal promise to maintain. One that meant not permanently falling into the arms of the first guy who wanted her beyond an initial screw. "Sorry, but I have morning plans that require sleeping in my own bed tonight."

"I won't be getting a number, will I?"

"You said you were after a night of fun."

"I guess the whole videotaping thing made me realize you're more than a pretty face and hot body." His frown stayed in place a few more seconds, and then he shook it off and eyed the camera bag hanging from her shoulder. "Can I at least get something to remember you by?"

Something to—Oh. He wanted a copy of her tape.

Nerves ate at Courtney's belly with the thought of truly being porn material for Mr. Hot Buns, and potentially his friends as well. She considered refusing the request. But then, it was his tape, too. And it would look incredibly insecure of her to turn him down for fear he would show it to others. She'd worked way too hard at this sex-diva thing to appear timid.

"All right." Really, she would never meet his friends or probably ever see him again either. Besides, what could one little naughty videotape hurt? "I don't have an extra tape along, but if you give me your name and address, I'll mail you a copy."

"What could one little naughty videotape hurt?" Gail Taeber's voice was a cross between disbelief and outrage. Hands on her shorts-clad hips in the middle of the living room of the downtown Grand Rapids apartment they shared, she gave Courtney the evil eye. "What, are you nuts?" She waved a slim hand dismissively. "Never mind, don't answer that. It's clear what you are, what you've become. A slut."

They'd been friends since their freshman year in college eight years ago; far too long for Courtney to be offended. And truthfully, before taking control of the more pleasurable aspects of her life, she would have felt the same way.

Now Courtney knew the value of letting life's daily stresses fall to the wayside by way of a hunk to do.

"Mmm . . . Guilty as charged." Hoping to get a laugh out of her roomie, she licked her lips exaggeratedly, then segued into a little bump and grind hip action that reminded her how tight the red leather pants were. She'd intended to come home and head straight to her bedroom to slip into something literally more comfortable, but then Gail had been up watching a movie and, from the instant Courtney stepped through the door, had started in with the grilling.

Without a hint of amusement, Gail scraped her fingers through her hair, pulling back the naturally white-blond, mid-back-length locks. "I don't get you anymore."

"You don't get 'it' at all." Courtney regretted the words the instant they left her mouth. Just because she was living her desires didn't mean she felt everyone had to do the same.

Hurt passed through Gail's eyes. Then her hands returned to her hips and her expression became one of aversion. "Is that all you think about these days? Sex?"

"Of course not!" Assuming an impish smile, Courtney gave

a last attempt at humor. "I think about all the places I've yet to pick a man up."

Gail's eyes narrowed. "You're unbelievable. Not even close to the girl I used to know."

Accepting she wasn't going to get to her bedroom and comfy clothes anytime soon, Courtney dropped down on the blue and beige striped sofa. "I was kidding," she assured soberly while removing the killer stilettos and tossing them aside. "I still take plenty of things seriously. You *are* right about one thing, though. I'm not the girl you used to know. She was average. Boring. Afraid to take a chance for fear of failure." A country bumpkin who'd nearly let the best years of her sex life flash before her eyes.

"Now you're a woman who leaps into bed with every guy she meets without a thought to looking beyond if his equipment appeals to her."

"I don't do *every* guy I meet. There have been a few this month and, yeah, a handful last month. But so what? I'm happy. And I leave them happy."

"So you think. What happens when you hook up with a guy who wants more than a single night and is ready to do *anything* to see that he gets it?"

"I hook up with guys who want the same thing I want." If they changed their mind after the fact, the way Mr. Hot Buns had tonight, that was hardly her fault. Even so, Courtney was a good enough judge of character to spot a lunatic. And smart enough to know that when she did dare to walk the line, as in the case of the promised videotape, to send her package "signature required" lest it end up in the wrong hands. "That doesn't include stalkers or rapists, if that's what you're implying."

"I'm implying," Gail started sharply. Then all the bluster came out of her on a whooshing breath and a muttered, "Oh, hell."

Wearing a contrite smile, she dropped down next to Courtney on the sofa. "I don't really think you're a slut. You know me better than that. I just worry—there's always so much crap on the news about some woman being beaten, or shot to death by an ex-lover."

"Thanks for your concern," Courtney said sincerely, "but I'll be okay. We took that self-defense class in college, and I have pepper spray in my purse, if there ever comes a point when I need it. I'm not going to live in fear of such an unlikely event. This is my time for fun, for pleasure, to be more than average. No psycho man is going to ruin it for me."

Seriously, there was nothing to worry about. Courtney was behaving just like Candy, and Candy had been behaving this way for darned near a decade without incident. She would be fine. Better yet, she would be well sexed and purring like a kitten whenever the urge to get laid struck.

After spending the last two-and-a-half months in the scorching desert heat of Iraq, overseeing the first phases of construction of a multimillion-dollar wastewater treatment system, Blaine Daly was damned glad to be back to Michigan's generally mild late-June weather. Back to his role of construction manager for Pinnacle Engineering's Eastern Region. Back to an air-conditioned office building with nearly all the amenities of home, at least on those days he wasn't required to supervise in the field.

Back to Candy.

Blaine's smile was automatic as he said good morning to Sherry, the fifty-something, bottle-redhead admin working the front desk, and then breezed on past the short fogged-glass partition that separated the lobby from the two-story building's general resources and production area. He and Candy had no sexual history and too little chemistry to consider a future fling. Still, he respected her no-holds-barred approach to sex. And he enjoyed the hell out of the way she filled her scanty clothes and livened up an office otherwise occupied by mostly stoic workers.

He'd also always enjoyed her hair, dirty-blond waves that caressed her shoulders and flowed partway down her back.

The woman rifling through the double-wide filing cabinet across the room wore Candy's risqué style of clothing. A barely mid-thigh-length black skirt hugged the lush curve of her ass. Sheer thigh-high stockings, with black pinstripe, picked up where the skirt left off, and led to dark green three-inch heels that matched her off-the-shoulder, short-sleeve top.

It was her hair that was different.

This woman was a brunette. The ends of her straight, chin-length locks tipped with a lighter shade of brown, bordering on dark blond.

Had Candy gotten a cut and dye job, or who was the woman?

Blaine joined Jake Markham, one of the construction field guys he supervised, at the interoffice mail bins a few feet away. Jake's hand held open the manila mail folder with his name on it, but his attention appeared fixed on the same spot—make that babe—as Blaine's.

"New employee?" Blaine asked casually.

Jake looked over at Blaine with far too much appreciation filling his eyes for a guy still in his first year of marriage. But then, hot women had a way of screwing with a guy's best intentions, and looking wasn't really a crime. "The new Courtney."

"Baxter?" Holy shit.

Testosterone pumping through his system like mad and his thoughts far from work, Blaine zipped his gaze back to the woman.

To Courtney Baxter. Mindblowing, yet not a total shocker.

He'd always believed she had an inner dirty girl. Her job as a technical writer responsible for the firm's local proposal efforts meant they worked together from time to time. Each time they got close, he swore her blue-green eyes revealed naughty thoughts. He'd nearly asked her about them a time or two, and if they didn't happen to involve the two of them without a stitch of clothing. But he hadn't wanted to embarrass her, just in case he was mistaken. And nothing ever came out of her own mouth that wasn't 100-percent professional.

Until now? Or was changing the way she dressed as far as things went?

Without looking Jake's way, he mused, "Wonder what brought the transformation on?"

"Knowing how women are, she probably realized she's creeping up on thirty and figured she'd better start using it before she loses it."

Doubtful. Courtney's twenty-seventh birthday was still a month away—he recalled seeing her last one mentioned in the company newsletter and the date stuck in his mind for whatever reason. As for losing it, the raw sensuality floating off her body and sucking him in from thirty feet away made it seem unlikely there was a chance of that happening anytime in the next six or seven decades.

"I wouldn't go there," Jake said, apparently keyed into Blaine's thoughts.

Or, shit, Blaine admonished himself, maybe it was the way he was eying Courtney up like a fresh-off-the-grill porterhouse. Losing the wolfish look, he glanced at Jake. "Why's that?"

"Rumor has it she's on a pleasure quest, but that she already has a man lined up for when she decides she's had enough of the hunt."

Was that supposed to dissuade his interest in her? If so, the attempt failed miserably.

Blaine had never told Courtney that he was as attracted to her as she sometimes appeared to be to him, because he believed his player reputation could be a turnoff. Now it seemed that was exactly what she was after. A guy who knew when he was wanted and had no problem moving on when that want had run its course.

His body kicking to full awareness with the knowledge, Blaine looked back at Courtney. Only, she wound up being a whole lot closer than planned. If she were taller, he would have ended up with his nose stuck between her breasts. As it was, and with her heels on, she was almost mouth level to him and he came damned close to brushing her lips with his.

For the instant it took her to gasp and step back, he felt the warmth of her breath mingling with his own. Saw the flicker of unmistakable lust in her eyes. Caught the hitch in her breathing as her response to his nearness moved from surprise to desire.

He grinned as the truth flooded him.

He hadn't been mistaken with his wonder if her naughty thoughts were about the two of them naked. She wanted him. And the rousing of his cock spoke volumes about his want for her.

An appreciative smile curved her glistening, red-painted lips as Courtney slid past him to nod at his field guy. "Morning, Jake. Love the shirt." Slim black bracelets jangled along her suntanned arm as she fingered the open collar of Jake's polo shirt, letting the wine-colored material slip slowly from her fingertips.

Jake said something in return, but Blaine could give two shits less what it was.

Courtney was back to looking at him. Her thickly lash-fringed eyes filled with those same daring thoughts he'd been sure of seeing a hundred times before. The difference was that her expression was unguarded now. Her body inclined toward him. Her breasts inches from filling his hands. With the off-the-shoulder style of her top, it wouldn't take much effort to work the material the rest of the way down her arms and then off.

"Have a good trip?" she asked in a voice just this side of seductive.

There were a lot of ways he wanted to answer that question. Vocally. Physically. Up against the duplex printer. Preferably when the top was lifted and her bare butt cheeks pressed against the warm glass.

Since this was the office and, while he never made a secret of his reputation for getting around, he had a lot of coworkers under his employ and respecting his professionalism while on the clock, he stuck with the first. A vocal, nonsexual response. "Yeah. We got a lot accomplished. I'd love to tell you about it, but it would take a while and I'm due for a conference call in five minutes."

"That's too bad."

It for damned sure was. The department-head meeting was the reason he'd returned to work on a Friday, instead of taking the weekend to recoup. The meeting, and the fact that he felt like he'd been neglecting his local responsibilities for far too long already. The work being completed abroad was under a Pinnacle contract. Still, no one had filled the bulk of his shoes while he was away. "Drop by my place tonight."

Avid interest lit Courtney's eyes. Her smile turned wickedly playful . . . and then vanished. "I wish I could, but I have a date."

"Bring him." A little competition didn't scare him, particularly since he wasn't looking for anything serious for the time being and, clearly, neither was she. "I'm having a 'Back from Iraq' get-together."

"You are?" Jake piped in, reminding Blaine he was still standing there.

There hadn't actually been a party planned, but it appeared there was now. With Jake working in the office this morning and out in the field this afternoon, he was as good of a source for getting the news out to their coworkers as any.

Blaine nodded. "I'll shoot you an e-mail with the details."

"I'll hold you to it." Jake finished fishing the mail from his interoffice folder. After giving Courtney a too-friendly smile, he started for the stairwell that led to the construction and transportation departments on the building's second floor.

"When you said to drop by your house, I thought you meant—" Courtney stopped short, waving the words away with the clink of her bracelets. "Never mind." Her smile returned, slightly diminished but still playful enough to have Blaine eager for a taste of her lips, quickly followed by the rest of her hot body. "Maybe we'll stop by. You still live in the brownstone outside of Kentwood?"

"I do." *And those thoughts of yours were dead on.*

He wouldn't risk speaking the words where anyone could hear, but there was no reason Blaine couldn't convey what he'd intended behind the closed door of his office. "If you'd rather catch up before tonight, I should have some time after lunch. Stop by my office."

"Tempting." Perfectly arched eyebrows rose as her gaze dipped from his face to cruise intimately down his body and back up again. "Seriously, it is," she said in a thready voice when their eyes again met. "But I'll have to pass. I have a proposal going out this afternoon and you know how they have a way of dragging out till the last minute."

"I do." He also knew if his cock jerked that hard in response to her bodily assessment while he was clothed, it was going to do an entire hula when she eyed him up naked. "See you tonight."

Courtney started away from him without responding. Just when she would have rounded the corner to the hallway leading back to her cubicle, she looked back, over her sexily bared shoulder, and flashed a grin that could only be termed dirty as sin. "If you're lucky, you will."

2

"Sounds like someone used the stall with the vibrating toilet seat," Candy observed when Courtney returned to her cubicle.

Breathing heavy with her excitement over what had gone down with Blaine, Courtney sank onto her office chair and laughed out loud.

Though she'd been sitting across the hall from Candy since coming to work for Pinnacle two years ago, Courtney had known little more than the woman's name, that her lively personality made her a superior public relations specialist, and that she had more men at her beck and call than Courtney had met in her entire life.

Witnessing the intense gleam of satisfaction those men left in Candy's eyes on a daily basis had been one of the many reasons Courtney finally said to hell with her upbringing-induced reservations. That gleam was the precise reason she sought out Candy's help in getting in touch with her inner vixen. They still didn't hang out much beyond working hours, but now she knew Candy had a delightfully warped sense of humor and a fierce loyalty to those lucky enough to call her friend.

Courtney kicked a heel against the gray Berber carpet, sending her chair spinning around until she faced Candy's cubicle. Her smile came as quickly and naughtily now as it had when Blaine intuited she should drop by his house tonight for sex. There'd been a second there where she thought she'd read his invitation wrong, that he wasn't as attracted to her new look as she'd been attracted to him from the day they met. The impatient way he eyed her up when he suggested she stop by his office instead of waiting until tonight trumped any misgivings.

He wanted her.

If it weren't for needing to wrap up that proposal and her planned date with another man, she would spend the hour after lunch and then several hours after work tonight showing him exactly how much she wanted him.

There would be another chance. Soon, if the hungry ache he stirred in her pussy had a say. "I'm still getting used to the whole feminine power thing."

A knowing smile curved Candy's lips and edged into her brown eyes. "Who is he?"

"Blaine," she said loudly enough to be heard but not overheard.

"Hate to break it to you, doll, but you could have had him long ago, even without working the feminine power angle."

Candy's assured tone pricked a hole in Courtney's bliss bubble. She knew about Blaine's reputation for getting around, but she thought he was at least as discerning about the women he slept with as she was with the men she did. "He's *that* easy?"

"No. But he has always had a thing for you."

Always? As in, even back when she'd been wearing her conservative clothing and living in fear of speaking her mind beyond from a professional standpoint? "Yeah, right."

Candy placed a hand over her heart, covering almost more of her left breast than her turquoise silk halter top did. "Swear to God. He checks out your ass every opportunity he gets."

"He's been doing this since I started working here?"
"Yep."
Not possible. Not having seen the women on Blaine's arm at various company events. Not one of them had looked average. They were all stunning. All confident. All every bit the sex diva Courtney had become. "Are you trying to boost my confidence?"
"Hell, no. You're doing a rocking job working the assertive, hot-bodied hoochie angle all on your own. Next time you're around Blaine, give him an opening to look at your ass and I guarantee he'll take it without a single bit of encouragement."

The kitchen door swished inward behind him, and Blaine cursed under his breath. Throwing a spur-of-the-moment party, a day after returning home from an extended leave, had been a stupid-ass move. Not only did he have to spend two hours after work shopping for food and drinks, but he was still suffering from jet lag. It was barely after eight and he was exhausted.
With his back to the door, he leaned his elbows against the edge of the sink and stared out the window at the guests milling about his treed-in, half-acre backyard. The short end of an L-shaped, black and gray marble-topped counter separated him from whoever was behind him. Between the partial blockage and his stance, hopefully the person would take a hint and leave him to his alone time.
"Blaine." Courtney's voice came out a mix of surprise and delight.
Just like that he wasn't tired anymore. Just like that he was anxious as hell to entertain.
"Courtney. It's good to see you." He spoke as he turned around, and then realized how big of an understatement the words were.
Standing a foot inside the doorway, she wore the sheer

thigh-high stockings with the sexy black pinstripe she'd had on at the office. The green, off-the-shoulder top and black skirt were gone. Chain-link silver earrings dangled from her ears to nearly brush her bare shoulders, and a hot pink, spaghetti strap sheath dress clung to the swell of her breasts, the material coasting down her trim sides and shapely hips to end an inch before her stockings began. His fingers tingled with the prospect of touching the tanned skin revealed there.

"I've been here a while." The surprise was gone from her voice, the delight now paired with the raw sensuality he felt calling to him this morning.

Blaine traveled his attention back up her body to find her gaze as assessing as his own. He hadn't had time to change out of the blue jeans and casual off-white shirt he'd worn to work, before guests started arriving at his house. The heat sizzling in Courtney's eyes and tipping her hot pink lips up at the corners suggested she approved of his appearance all the same.

She lifted the red plastic glass in her hand. "I didn't realize the kitchen was off limits. My drink got warm while I was visiting, so I was trying to track down some ice."

He smiled over the irony. Ice had been his excuse for retreating to the sanctity of his kitchen. More specifically, refilling the ice bucket from the snack table in the living room for the exact purpose that had brought her here.

Crossing to the counter, he grabbed the steel ice bucket and went to the refrigerator. "It's not off limits," he assured her as he pulled open the freezer-side door. Frosty air rushed out to greet him. With the way his internal temperature shot up at the sight of Courtney in that barely legal dress, the chilly blast was welcome.

"So you weren't trying to escape by hiding out in here?"

He glanced over at her as he filled the ice bucket. He didn't know a lot about her, outside of the fact that she was damned good at her job, but that question had sounded incredibly astute. "Know a thing or two about escape?"

Hesitation passed through her eyes for an instant. Then she gave him a smile that was pure feline. "You know as well as I do some people don't get the concept of no strings."

Blaine's body forgot all about the freezer's calming effect with the sexual intimation. His cock stirred against his zipper. He definitely knew all about strings and he knew right now he wanted to tug down the two thin ones keeping her dress in place.

Shutting the freezer door, he crossed to where she stood. His first thought at seeing her this morning was that she looked just like Candy, minus the hairstyle. Within touching distance, he could see the differences went well beyond their hair. Courtney's legs were longer and her breasts, while still plentiful, smaller. Her face was smaller, as well. Her mouth wider and her eyes more round. The combination of her facial features managed to make her look both sweet and sinful at once.

And had him damned anxious to take advantage of proximity.

Traveling his gaze suggestively along her body, he gave her the opening to do so instead. "Take what you want."

Courtney's throat made a catching sound as she eyed first the ice bucket in the crook of one of his arms and then the growing bulge at the front of his jeans. Her eyes lifted to meet his. With a knowing grin, he silently dared her to reach out and fill up her hands.

She did. With ice.

Disappointment sailed through him as she plunked three small chunks of ice into her glass. With a murmured, "Thanks," she started to turn toward the door.

No way was he letting her walk away that easily. Not when the air between them radiated with sexual heat and energy. Not when her nipples were pushing hard at the front of her dress, making his mouth hungry and it clear she wore no bra.

"Stay." Blaine spoke the word with an edge of demand. Just as he'd been accurate about her naughty thoughts, he had a gut feeling she would be the type who liked to be told what to do when it came to sex. Just as she would want to have her own turn at being the dominant one.

His mind roaming with kinky demands, he backed the few feet to the table, and set the ice bucket on top. He patted the table's black lacquered surface. "Have a seat. You wanted to hear how things went in Iraq."

Indecision warred in her eyes as she glanced from him to the door and back again. For a moment he entertained the idea her new look was all for show, then he recalled she was on a date. The guy was undoubtedly out in the living room, his presence giving her reason to hesitate.

Before he could offer up further encouragement, Courtney's back and forth glances came to a halt. Eagerness took over her expression as she sashayed over on spiked silver heels and set her glass on the table. With a provocative wiggle of her hips, she slid onto the table and balanced her heels on the front edge of a chair. "It had to be scorching hot."

"Sweltering," Blaine agreed with a nod. As was his blood as he appreciated the way her short hem rode up with her position, nearly exposing her panties. *If* she wore any. "Dry heat, but that doesn't make it any less potent."

Her hand shot out, reaching toward him. The thought she was ready to touch was enough to have his breath jerking in and his dick pearling with pre-cum.

Her fingers spread but failed to make contact as her eyes trained on his right arm. "Did you do some of the building work yourself?"

Muscles contracted in his arm reflexively. "I helped out, yeah."

"It shows."

She'd all but purred the words, sounding as strung out with desire as he felt. That being the case, he flexed the biceps in his right arm a second time. Appreciation shimmered in her eyes and her fingers formed into a fist as if she had to contain them.

He let out a rough laugh. "You're allowed to touch."

Her tongue came out, dabbing at her lower lip. "I'm good."

"I bet you are."

Courtney's gaze flicked to his. Humor meshed with arousal, telling him she hadn't missed the way he purposefully misunderstood her. The question was, what would she do about it?

A handful of seconds ticked past as they stared at one another. She looking ready to do him. He waiting for her to follow through on her dirty thoughts for once.

This time she didn't disappointment. This time she reclined back on an elbow far enough to reach the ice bucket and then straightened again with an ice cube wedged between her right thumb and forefinger.

Pupils dilating, she sucked the cube between her bright pink lips—sensuously, slowly—and then traveled it downward. Along the slim column of her neck, past her collarbone. Into the vee of her cleavage exposed above the top edge of her dress. "So in this heat," she asked in a breathy voice, "there wasn't even a little moisture?"

Blaine's body throbbed with her tone. Again with her intent, as she moved the ice cube lower, down her torso to caress it along the inside of a bare thigh above the band of her stocking.

Her question registered then. She was asking if he'd slept with anyone while abroad. Generally, he would never go months without sex. In Iraq, neither his high-risk location nor his priorities had left time or room for pleasure. The bulk of each day had been spent focusing on building the wastewater infrastructure, and the bulk of each night doing his best to shut out the sporadic bursts of distant gunfire and explosions to sleep off the wearing effects of the exhausting work and even more exhausting heat.

That celibacy streak played hell on him now, making his shaft pulse for release. "Not one bit of wetness," he admitted tightly.

"That's hard to believe." Her fingers worked the ice cube farther up her thigh, almost to the point of disappearing beneath the hem of her dress. "You were away a long time."

"I heard there was a lot of moisture here while I was gone."

"Some." The cube pushed higher, and then out of sight. Courtney's breathing picked up. "There could be more."

"Later tonight?" he asked, not bothering to hide his hopefulness.

"Or now."

She didn't bother to hide her hopefulness either. It came through loud and clear and sexy as hell as her upper body inclined toward him. Her free hand finally touched down on his arm, grabbing hold and jerking him against her.

He tipped his head back with the move, caught sight of her flushed face. Then her mouth was there, her lips soft yet hungry against his, urgent, taking. Demanding.

Hell, yes. She was everything he'd imagined and more.

Lashing his tongue with hers, he pulled aside the chair her feet balanced on and moved between her legs. Hot flesh cradled his hips. Her inner thighs squeezed around him.

Blaine's pulse spiked with the carnal move, and he gave his hands over to their urge to roam.

One hand filled with the warmth of her thigh encased in silk while the other moved beneath the hem of her dress and found her fingers flicking the edge of the ice cube against her sex through her panties. He'd wondered if she would have any on, and he was damned glad to learn that she did. It made taking the ice cube from her and pulling the panties aside to slip the cube inside the lips of her pussy that much sweeter.

Courtney's hips surged forward with the frosty contact against her warm folds. She gripped his forearms and whimpered into his mouth. He swallowed the sound with his lips, kissing her harder, deeper, tasting vodka and white-hot female as he worked the ice along the swollen pearl of her clit and into her body until the cube was melted. He filled her sheath with two fingers then, his own sex throbbing with each delectable hug of hers.

Pulling back from her mouth, he nudged aside her short hair and a dangling earring to nuzzle at her neck. The ecstatic moan that tore from her lips had him placing his mouth back on hers fast. Obviously her neck was a serious pleasure zone. And obviously he was more of a gentleman than he'd ever realized to remember they weren't truly alone and would be even less so if she kept up with the moaning. Next time she could make all the noise she wanted.

There would be a next time. Soon, if he had his way.

Tonight they'd already pushed their luck, behaving this way in his kitchen while being essentially surrounded by colleagues. His release would have to wait. Hers was seconds away.

Blaine focused on delivering her to a fast finish, drawing out the rhythm of his fingers as he moved them within her. Playing on the icy hot sensations he could guess were shooting through her body. Stroking her clit to the point of explosion.

Climax tore through her in a rushing wave evident in the tremble of her legs and the clenching of her pussy. Hot cream soaked his fingers.

Courtney's mouth jerked from his. "Oh, God—yes!"

With an inward laugh over her enthusiasm, he clamped his lips back tight to hers and filled her mouth with his tongue, kissing her silent until the last of the orgasm was drained from her body.

Slipping his hand from beneath her skirt, he moved back a step. She looked the picture of sexual fulfillment, reclined on her elbows with her long dark lashes masking her eyes and her puffy lips parted a half inch and panting for air. It was a pose he could happily appreciate for hours. But not one he was willing to share with their coworkers. "Much as I love a vocal lover, your scream should have the kitchen filling up in about five seconds."

"I didn't scream," she said languidly. "I shouted."

"Whatever. I liked it." The hem of her dress had gotten pushed up with his fingering and her panties were still dragged to the side, exposing her glistening pink labia past trimmed brown pubic hair. Definitely his kind of nice. "All of it. Well worth the wait."

She sat up abruptly, destroying his stellar view as her skirt fell back around her thighs. Her eyes opened to reveal hazy blue-green. "How long have you—"

The swishing of the kitchen door cut her off. "Courtney," a male voice said from behind Blaine. "There you are. I thought you got bored and took off."

Courtney's gaze zipped past Blaine, and the passion died from her eyes in a heartbeat. She shot off the edge of the table. "Nope. Just getting some." She stumbled over the words, quickly adding, "Ice, that is. My drink got warm." Reaching back, she flashed Blaine an uneasy smile as she scooped her drink off the table. "Thanks. Really."

"My pleasure. You need more, you know where to get it."

"I'll keep that in mind." Her smile going sensual, she sent a wink to the guy at the door.

Or rather guys, Blaine discovered as he swiveled around to find an unfamiliar, tall blond man accompanied by Jake and Randy Dobson, a mechanical engineer at Pinnacle. In his mid-thirties and garbed in pineapple-patterned swim trunks and a white tank shirt, Randy was the antithesis of the stereotypical think-inside-the-box engineer. He took his premature balding about as serious as anything else.

"Hey, guys." Courtney nodded at their coworkers as she made her way over to her date. "Looking good as always." She took the blond by the arm and her smile grew suggestive. "You look like you should be taking me out dancing."

The idea that she would soon be pressed up against the blond on a dance floor ate at Blaine's gut, but only because he was still hard from being pressed up against her himself. Still, the idea didn't agitate him nearly enough to stop him from checking out her ass as she led the guy out of the kitchen.

The door fell closed, obliterating his view. He looked over at Jake and Randy to find their attention had been directed in the same place as his own. Obviously, they were wifeless tonight, or confident their spouses were nowhere nearby.

Randy met his eyes, a shit-eating grin forming on his mouth. "Was it as good for you as it was for her?"

Blaine bit back a grunt. Lying wasn't his strong suit, but he was still going to try. "I hate to ruin your fun but, like she said, she just came in to get ice. We talked about my work overseas and the heat over there. That's it."

Snorting, Jake crossed to the refrigerator and helped himself to a bottle of beer. "Bullshit."

Randy backed up the field guy's theory. "Yeah, right, man. But, hey, since when do you lie about sex?"

"I'm not lying. We didn't fuck. Christ, she was only in here five minutes. Ten tops."

Jake unscrewed the cap off his beer and pulled back a long drink before saying dryly, "Next you gonna try to convince us Sex on the Beach gives off that realistic of a smell?"

Damn, he'd known his rock-solid state was fairly obvious, but he hadn't considered the smell.

Going to the refrigerator, Blaine used the cool air to calm his body while he transferred bottles of beer from the cases on the floor onto the fridge's lower shelves.

"If you're thinking about getting serious," Jake continued

soberly, "you might want to take some friendly advice and remember what I said. She's after no-strings pleasure for a while, but she already has her sights set on one man for the long run."

"Yeah," Randy piped in, for once sounding serious himself, "and I heard he doesn't work for Pinnacle, so that leaves you SOL, buddy."

"Looks like you stroked somebody the right way." Stabbing a bite of taco salad from a plastic takeout container, Candy nodded past Courtney's shoulder.

Courtney's belly tightened as she set her tuna-salad croissant on her plate on the table and slowly turned in her chair. She half expected Blaine to be standing behind her, ready for a second round of ice play, his devilishly taunting smile making his thoughts clear to every one of the two-dozen-plus employees in Pinnacle's lunchroom.

Or maybe that was half hoping, Courtney realized, given her displeasure at finding not Blaine but Sherry, the front-desk admin, waiting for her.

She noted the woman was smiling then and that in her hands was a nearly foot-long, thin red box with a gilded ribbon wrapped around it.

"For me?" The words came out sounding pathetically hopeful, as was the glee rocketing through her, but Courtney couldn't help it. Despite her revamped attitude toward life and sex, she'd never gotten a gift from an admirer. Not even on Valentine's Day. Not even from her lone boyfriend, a guy she'd dated in college for almost a year before realizing he was more boringly average and reserved than she had been at the time.

Sherry nodded. "I left the front desk long enough to send a fax, and when I came back this box was waiting with your name on it."

Thirty seconds passed where Courtney did little more than

sit and grin, and Candy encouraged, "Open it already. You're starving your coworkers."

A glance around the room backed up Candy's words. Most everyone in the place was waiting to see what she'd gotten.

Courtney quit with the idiotic grinning, took the box from Sherry, and untied the ribbon. Lifting the lid had the strains of "Always On My Mind" filling the lunchroom. The lyrics were loud enough to chase heat into her cheeks, a reaction she generally reserved for those times when her date walked in on her climaxing for another man.

The heat arrowed downward, bringing to life a lusty ache in her core. She hadn't seen Blaine since leaving his kitchen with her panties still damp four nights ago. First, it had been the weekend, and then he'd been working in the field on a road job.

Was this gift from him? Had he really been hot for her long before her transformation, the way Candy had implied and the way his comment on her being worth the wait seemed to suggest?

Since she vowed not to let herself get wrapped up in one man so soon and since Blaine was a known no-strings kind of guy, Courtney forgot about the questions to focus on the gift. She pulled aside a thin red sheet of tissue paper and a dozen rosebud-shaped dark chocolates winked at her.

Candy let out a low whistle. "Nice. Not that cost is the point, but those sell for close to fifty."

Holy cow. Whoever her admirer was, he obviously had money to burn. Courtney did a quick check for a card or anything else that might hint at the sender. Finding nothing, she set the box on the table. "In that case, I'll forget about eating them."

Candy looked stricken. "You will *not*. They're laced with imported liquor and beyond awesome, or so I've been told. Eat one for me, if not for yourself."

Courtney had been raised to save dessert for last, to ensure her body got all the nutrients it needed before being filled with fat. But then, she'd also been raised to believe her body was a temple only her husband deserved the right to worship. Saying to hell with the whole temple concept had left her feeling incredibly good. Saying to hell with saving dessert for last was bound to not only taste incredibly good but would make Candy happy, since her coworker had a cocoa allergy and couldn't eat chocolate.

"All right. For you." Courtney lifted a rosebud from the box, thinking it should be gilded itself for the price. She popped the candy into her mouth. Scrumptious rich dark chocolate exploded over her taste buds. Eliciting an unconscious moan, she bit into the candy's center and liquor filled her mouth.

Strong liquor. Burning strong. Gagging strong.

She sucked in a breath in an effort to cool the burn. The liquor spread, coating the back of her mouth. Leaving her tongue feeling heavy, thick. Cottony.

Attempting to move her tongue had the unchewed portion of the candy sliding back, filling her throat. Stealing the air from her lungs.

Courtney's eyes bulged with the sickening awareness she couldn't breathe. Panic clawed at her from the inside out.

Oh, God! Her first admirer gift was going to kill her!

Slapping a hand at her fiercely pounding chest, she silently begged Candy for help. Her coworker was on the other side of the table and, by the time she realized Courtney was choking, it was too late. Someone else was already there, helping her.

A hard body pressed against her from behind. Strong arms slid around her waist. One fisted hand wrapped around another against her stomach, jerking solidly upward.

Once.

Twice.

Gasps filled the lunchroom as the half-eaten candy flew

from Courtney's mouth and landed on the next table over. Sweet air cruised into her mouth and down to her lungs on a whooshing breath. Tears pricked at her eyes, blurring her vision.

Praise the saints.

Her tongue still felt leaden, coated with the horribly strong liquor. But she could breathe. She was going to live.

Pulling in deep breaths, she wiped the stinging tears from her eyes. Her vision cleared to reveal everyone in the lunch room watching her. Not yet sure she was ready to speak, she gave a small smile and a wave to show them she was all right.

Candy stood at the other side of the table. The usual sass and vitality was gone from her brown eyes, replaced with horrified concern. "Jesus, you scared the crap out of me. Are you okay?"

Courtney cleared her throat. Finding it a little tender but not painfully so, she attempted a response. "Yeah. I—"

"You sure?" It was Blaine's voice asking the question, his warm breath whispering next to her ear.

Delightfully life-confirming shivers skated along her neck. A different kind of awareness gripped her as she looked at the arms still wrapped around her middle, the intimately familiar hands, and realized he was the one who'd potentially saved her life.

So many ways she would love to thank him. With her mouth. With her body. Since they were once again surrounded by coworkers, she just said, "I'm sure. So you can release me."

The press of his body left hers. His arms slid from around her. Ruing the loss, she turned to offer an appreciative smile.

While he was no longer holding her, he was still close. Too close not to savor the way the slate gray T-shirt molded to his chest, the damp material calling out the mouthwateringly work-honed muscles in his upper arms while suggesting he'd been working under the summer sun all morning. Too close not to let her gaze wander down to the tauntingly snug fit of his well-worn jeans. And too close not to appreciate the almost-black stubble dusting his angular jawline and the glistening skin above his upper lip as her attention drifted slowly back up.

Damn, he looked good fresh from the field. Sweaty and unshaven. The overlong bangs of his thick, dark hair hanging at an angle, nearly caressing his right eyebrow. Like she should take him back to his office and see if she couldn't get him sweatier yet.

Behind her, Candy gave a discreet cough.

Courtney's thoughts zipped back to the present, to the fact that she was grinning like a fool again. Well, geez, the guy had probably saved her life, what did people expect if not a little hero worship? Okay, and a little horny drooling.

"Looks like I owe you another thanks," she finally got out. "The liquor was stronger than I thought it would be." Truthfully, the candies were downright nasty, but given their cost, she would withhold her judgment. Beside, maybe others would like them.

Grabbing the box off the table, she held it out to Blaine. "Want one?"

He eyed the chocolates skeptically. "Not if they're going to kill me."

She waved the box around the lunchroom. "Anyone else?"

Apparently deciding she was okay, several people had returned to work. Those who remained declined the offer. Courtney set the box back on the table as she slid onto her chair. She grabbed her water bottle and guzzled a long drink in the hopes of getting the revolting taste of the liquor out of her mouth and making her tongue feel normal in the process.

Blaine moved to stand at the head of the table. He tucked his hands into the back pockets of his jeans and watched her drink through narrowed navy blue eyes. "Sure you're all right?"

Courtney set the bottle down, considering his tone and

stance. He seemed every bit as concerned as Candy. Possibly more so.

Had the chocolates been from him and was he now feeling guilty over her reaction to them? The answer was totally irrelevant, and still she was dying to know. "I'm fine. Aren't you supposed to be working in the field?"

"Keeping tabs on my schedule?"

"I needed a dollar figure for a job and knew you could rattle it off the top of your head much faster than I could look it up. You weren't in your office so I checked the sign-out sheet." Total fabrication, but lying was far better than admitting she wanted to see how he would behave around her after the incident in his kitchen.

The concern left his eyes. "I was on a job site. Things were running smoothly, so I came back to the office to finish up some paperwork. Speaking of which, I should get to it." With a parting nod to her and Candy, Blaine headed for the lunchroom door.

Courtney sighed as she watched him walk away. Given his indifference toward her once she assured him she could breathe normally, their actions Friday night had left him unfazed. She'd been just another woman he'd brought pleasure. Now, he was back to business as usual. While she was left to ogle his ass and wonder if there was still a chance Candy had been accurate about his supposed time-and-again urges to ogle Courtney's own.

3

A knock sounded outside Blaine's open office door, followed by Courtney's "Is now a good time?"

With an absent nod, he looked up from scanning a set of plans. She came inside, pulling out an armless, padded green chair on the opposite side of his desk and sitting down. A half hour had passed since he left her in the lunchroom. Long enough to move past the heart-pounding fear he felt upon realizing she was choking. But not long enough to forget how amazingly good she'd felt cradled against him, once the candy had dislodged from her throat.

In any other venue, he would have given in to his urge to nibble on the sweet spot of her neck. Not at work. Even in his office with his lower half hidden behind his desk, he shouldn't allow himself to be physically turned on by her.

At least he'd made it back to his office before his cock had grown noticeably hard. Closing out the paperwork portion of a project he'd been avoiding had taken his mind off her to the point that his erection had faded away.

Now to keep his mind focused on work while she sat across

from him in that bull's-eye red top. The square cut of the neckline didn't show off her cleavage, like so many of her shirts did these days, but when he'd been standing behind her, he'd had a prime view down the front. Her white cotton bra fit the secretly sensual woman she used to be instead of the outward vamp she'd become.

Blame it on the fact he'd yet to end his celibacy streak, or maybe the way his time in a mostly impoverished area had strengthened his appreciation for the simple things, but the plain style was a huge turnon.

Turning off that line of thinking, Blaine set the plans aside. "Looking for that figure?"

Courtney frowned. "Figure?"

"The reason you knew my schedule."

"No. I ended up tracking it down myself."

Had she? Or had she made up the need for a project fee to avoid admitting she wanted to track him down for another reason like to discuss what had happened in his kitchen Friday night? The openly appreciative way she'd eyed his body in the lunchroom suggested as much.

Resting her crossed arms on the edge of his desk, she sat forward. "I know I sort of said thank you for helping me, but words seem a bit weak considering it's potentially my life we're talking about."

He *had* been afraid. And he *had* been trying to be good. Now his thoughts were centered on the press of her arms around her breasts, creating a generous supply of cleavage where before there had been none.

Pulling his attention back to her face, Blaine risked testing the waters. "Did you have a good time Friday night?"

Wariness shot through Courtney's eyes. Her gaze zipped to his open office door.

For someone who'd recently made a habit of flirting with every guy at Pinnacle, be they single or attached, she was awfully worried about being overheard. "Dancing," he improvised. "I heard you tell your friend you wanted to go out dancing."

Visibly relieved, she looked back at him. "It was a pleasurable experience."

"You're into pleasure?"

Her eyes narrowed a fraction, conveying what he already knew—that he shouldn't have asked the question in this setting. Her voice dropped to a throaty whisper with her response. "I'm not into pain, if that's the alternative."

Since he'd dared to start the conversation, there was no point in backing down. Giving her breasts an open leer, he pointed out, "Then you've never been exposed to the right kind."

"Of pain?" She looked and sounded appalled.

He wouldn't mind one bit changing her stance on the issue. His cock twinged with the idea of pinking her backside, and he amended that "wouldn't mind one bit" to "he'd downright love it." Keeping his tone professional, he said, "Like most anything else, there's good and bad."

Courtney seemed to turn the words over, as if weighing whether to give pleasure-pain a try in the near future. Then all at once, a naughty smile took over her lips and she asked, "Can I take you out to dinner tonight?"

If her smile was a foreshadowing of the night she had in mind, then the answer was a big hell yeah. Before he accepted the offer, Blaine made one thing clear. "I don't date."

"I meant as my way of saying thanks beyond a few lame words. Dating's overrated."

It was what he'd expected her to say, what he'd been counting on. The reply also made it seem Jake and Randy's belief she had a full-time guy lined up for down the road was a crock of shit emerged out of office gossip.

Recalling her Friday night words, about some people not getting the concept of no strings, he nodded his understanding. "Has a way of landing a person in a position where they feel the need to escape."

"Exactly."

"So I'll pick you up at seven, we'll have dinner out, and then go back to my place for dessert?"

"No good. Picking me up will make it feel too much like a date. I'll meet you at Valerio's at seven." Courtney's voice dropped a few notches, and her eyes sizzled with sensual heat. "*Then* we can go back to your place for dessert."

It was sad, really it was. But Courtney couldn't stop from giggling her anticipation of the night ahead as she dropped down on the apartment couch and pulled on a pair of heeled black slingbacks. She'd thought Blaine wasn't interested in sleeping with her for real, after he'd gotten so sedate following her choking session. But he did want to sleep with her for real.

More precisely, he wanted to have her for dessert.

She shivered with excitement just thinking about spreading whipped cream on his meat-flavored banana and then licking it back off.

Perched on the arm of the couch, wearing her typical summertime evening gear of gray cotton shorts and a white, midriff-skimming T-shirt, Gail pointed out, "You're incredibly giddy for someone *not* going on a date."

A few months ago, Courtney would have been dressed much the same and be gearing up for yet another routine night at home, watching movies with Gail. Now she was dressed to get laid and, yeah, giddy as heck about it.

She really didn't think that Gail needed to follow in her sex-diva footsteps, but she wished her friend would at least go on one date this year. Since she'd broached the subject numerous times and Gail seemed less impressed each one, Courtney didn't bother to bring it up. "Did I tell you I got a present from a secret admirer today?"

"No."

"Yep. A fifty-dollar box of chocolates I almost choked to death on."

"You mean over the cost?"

Courtney shook her head gently, careful not to relax the curl she'd spent a good half hour styling into her normally stick-straight hair. "They're filled with some kind of imported liquor. Nasty stuff. I bit into one and ended up gagging and swallowing a big chunk of chocolate. Or I should say not swallowing, since it lodged in my throat."

Gail stiffened. The color rushed from her face. "Oh my God! You could have died, Courtney!"

Oh my God, was right. What a dummy. After her roommate's admission a few weeks back that she was concerned for Courtney's safety, the last thing she should have done was brought up the choking incident.

Purposefully reverting to giddiness, she sent Gail a teasing smile. "There was no chance of dying. Super Blaine had just returned to the office and, as soon as he realized I was in trouble, he swooped in and saved the day. This nondate is my way of saying thank you for performing the Heimlich." She wiggled her eyebrows. "If I'm lucky, I'll get to add a 'thanks for performing the hind lick' to that before the night's over."

As Courtney could have predicted, Gail didn't laugh. She did relax though, and the color returned to her face. "Don't you find it strange Blaine returned to the office right when you got the chocolates and then he was there to save you from choking on one of them?"

"You're getting worried about me again, aren't you?"

"How can I not be? The last day and a half you said he wasn't around the office. And yet there he suddenly is, right when you need him."

"It was coincidence. Pure and simple. He's not even close to the type to take the covert approach to gift giving. I just wish I knew who *is* the type." She'd considered candidates all afternoon. The only guy to show more than a passing interest in her was Craig Dooley, the beefcake who'd let her videotape their sexcapades a few weeks back, and then asked for a copy of the tape. He'd supplied her with his name and address so she could send him that copy. Courtney had sent the tape anonymously ensuring he would have no way of knowing her name, let alone where she worked.

Ironically, she had run into Craig last week at a nightclub. Even flirted with him a bit, but she hadn't left with him, and she also hadn't dished on any personal information.

"Whoever my admirer is, he didn't taint the candy in some way that would make me choke." Or make her tongue feel like ten pounds of cotton. Thank God, that icky sensation had finally passed.

"I hope not."

Courtney sighed at the doubt in her friend's voice. "Seriously, Gail, I love you, but you're starting to sound too much like my mother." Pasting on an innocent smile, she asked the question she'd earlier avoided. "What do you say I set you up with one of the good-looking, single guys from the office?"

The doubt in Gail's voice flowed over into her eyes. "You worked at Pinnacle for two years and never mentioned a good-looking, single guy until after your transformation. That pretty much tells me they aren't the type who went for the natural version of you and so they won't go for me."

"You mean the average version of me. I'm still natural." Courtney eyed her breasts. They weren't huge by any means, but water bras and underwire had a way of creating remarkable illusions. So far no man had complained about the variance in what she put on display and what she really had.

Hopefully, Blaine wouldn't be the first.

Tonight wasn't a date and they probably wouldn't sleep together again after sharing dessert. Still, between having the hots for him from the day they'd met and being aware of all the stunning arm candy that had traipsed through his life the last couple years, she wanted to make as positive and lasting of an impression as possible.

Courtney momentarily forgot about Blaine and the promising night that lay ahead with the realization Gail hadn't said no to her date suggestion. With an encouraging smile, she pushed onward. "For all I know plenty of guys were attracted to me before. I was just too afraid of being rejected to find out. I know you too well to think you'd fear rejection."

Gail considered a few seconds, and then stunned Courtney by nodding. "All right. Next weekend you can set me up. I already agreed to watch Jessica's kids this weekend so she and Matt can have some grown-up time."

"See, even after nine years of marriage, your sister and brother-in-law appreciate the value of a good sex life."

Gail actually laughed at that, shocking Courtney for a second time. Then she stood from the arm of the sofa and turned serious again. "They also appreciate a good security system. I talked to Eddy today about having an electronic system installed here and he said to go ahead."

Courtney frowned, well aware Gail had talked to the super first so that the old guy would get excited about the investment and expect it to happen. In other words, so that Courtney wouldn't veto the idea. "Why are you suddenly so freaked out about our safety?"

"I've run out of comedies to watch while you're out getting your man fix every other night of the week, so I've taken up watching horror movies," Gail joked. When Courtney didn't crack so much as a smile, she soberly added, "I don't know, Court. Maybe it's just how much this part of the city has grown the last few years. Whatever the reason, I'll feel much better once the new system's in place."

"Okay. Go ahead and get one put in." If the system relaxed Gail enough to make her stop jumping to unlikely conclusions that all involved Courtney's safety, it would be a worthwhile investment. "I'll even foot half the bill. But just remember whose idea it was when I have to wake your butt up at three in the morning because I forgot the code and can't get in."

"I'd much rather wake up to let you in than be woken up by someone breaking in."

"Is this weird for you?" Courtney asked Blaine from across the restaurant table once their waiter had presented a bottle of Chianti and left to place the entrée order.

Her serious tone didn't come close to matching the rest of her. In a clingy, scoop-necked top in his favorite shade of blue and black hot pants, her trim body was pure dynamite. Open-toed black heels revealed toenails the same shade of soft pink as her lips. Her mouth always looked extremely kissable. Something about the way she'd styled her hair into soft curls stepped up the sweet and downplayed the sinful appeal of her face, and had him more anxious than ever to taste her lips.

He should have insisted he pick her up at home so that he could have given her a mouth-to-mouth greeting. Her logic for meeting at Valerio's was too sound to refute. Unfortunately, the restaurant was too tasteful to allow for the kind of kiss, and likely groping, that would ensue the moment their lips met. He'd just have to be a big boy and wait an hour or two.

If he were patient enough, he might be rewarded with the kind of kiss that didn't have a thing to do with his mouth.

His pulse stirred with the thought. Not about to let his cock follow suit, Blaine teased, "Eating in a nice restaurant? Surprisingly, I do get out of my cave from time to time."

She laughed. "No. I meant us. Being out on a . . . nondate."

"It's no different than eating together in Pinnacle's lunchroom."

Courtney's eyebrows rose as she glanced from the low-lit crystal chandeliers to the marble wall sconces that sprayed forth trailing greens and small, white heart-shaped flowers to the servers moving about in tuxedo uniforms. Looking back at him, she smiled wryly. "I'd say the ambiance is just a little different. Besides, I didn't mean now so much as what's going to happen later." Anticipation flickered in her eyes. "When we have dessert."

Normally, he didn't rely on euphemisms to get his desires across. Back in his office, with the door wide open, he hadn't felt comfortable talking frankly. Now, he couldn't help but taunt her a little with the idea it really *was* only dessert he had in mind. "I just hope you like it. After what happened at lunch, I made sure to veer away from anything chocolate."

Her mouth fell open a half inch, freeing a low gasp. "You mean we're actually going to—Nothing. Never mind."

Courtney lifted her wineglass to her lips, sipping at the Chianti. Attempting to hide her displeasure was the truth of it, Blaine knew. He considered letting her off easy by leaning across the table and whispering what he planned to do with her once they got back to his place in details so explicit she would be left squirming in her seat, wet with eagerness. Before he could say or do anything, their waiter reappeared.

The dark-haired guy set a loaf of Tuscany bread and a short crock of olive oil on the table. With a clap of his hands and a cheerful, "*Piacere.* Enjoy," he left them again.

Courtney set her wineglass down and eyed the bread appreciatively. "I have a huge soft spot for homemade bread and that smells incredible."

Blaine pulled the wooden breadboard toward him. He sliced and buttered her a generous piece of bread, and then watched as she attacked it with gusto. He'd be the first to admit he could be vain about the women he chose to spend time with. It never bothered him much if so many of them relied on eating tiny portions of food as a way to stay slim. But then, he also never found himself smiling over the sheer bliss one of those women found in something as simple as bread, the way he was doing with Courtney.

Her happiness came out as an elated murmur with her next bite. How much that murmur sounded like the one she made as she climaxed had him quickly slicing and buttering a piece of bread for himself and stuffing it into his mouth.

The bread all but melted in his mouth, the baked-in seasonings enlivening his taste buds. A moan of pure contentment escaped before he could stop it. Not only was the bread delicious, but he hadn't taken the time to indulge in a high-quality meal since returning from Iraq, and the food over there had been basic fare at best.

"Good, huh?" Courtney's voice was edged with amusement.

Setting the bread on a side plate, he looked across the table. While there was humor in her eyes, there was far more desire. The kind of red-hot sensuality that threatened to harden his cock. If he suggested they leave now, to go back to his place to have each other for both the main entrée and dessert, she was likely to say an emphatic yes. But she was enjoying her food, the wine, and she looked too charmingly appealing with her hair curled and those soft pink lips to mess them up quite so soon.

"Excellent." Blaine took a drink of wine as he sought out conversation not likely to have a stimulating effect on his body. "For the record, I don't let my nondates pay for dinner."

"The point of us coming here was so that *I* could buy *you* dinner. But since you probably make a buttload more money than I do, I'll forget the point."

His income wasn't a topic he discussed with his lovers. Since Courtney had access to the billing rates of every Pinnacle employee, he didn't bother to deny the observation. "I did pick up a nice chunk of pocket change working abroad."

"Is that why you went over there? For the money?"

"Money isn't an issue. Like you said, I bring in a decent wage at Pinnacle, and I don't have a wife and kids to support so a good share of my paycheck goes directly to savings."

"Then what would propel a person to thrust themselves into such a dangerous place?"

"The whole country isn't dangerous, just certain parts. Where I went was more of a high-risk zone, though." His gut roiled with the memory of the trip in and out of the rebuild area. He'd seen things so horrific they would be forever embedded in his mind and that he wouldn't share ever, let alone while eating. "Once the convoy arrived at the construction site, we couldn't go outside the designated parameters. Then there are the rodents and insects. Damn camel spiders are bigger than my hand."

Instead of shuddering, the way most of the women he spent time with would do, Courtney smiled brazenly. "Let's not forget about the heat."

"Not possible." Blaine smiled back, thankful for the reminder of a far more pleasant experience. Thoughts of chilling her sex with ice and then warming her up again with the glide of his fingers inside her pussy did rile his testosterone, but it also eased his gut enough to allow him to continue the conversation. "There are days I feel like I'll never get clean again working on the construction sites around here. Over there, it's like a dust bowl. You don't just end up with that shit in places you didn't even know you had. You can feel it in your lungs."

"Yet you volunteered to go over there, not even caring about the money factor." Admiration shone in her eyes. "Where I come from, that's called noble."

"More like intrigue, and might I remind you I didn't care about the money factor—but I still took every dollar they paid me."

The admiration didn't dissipate. If anything, she looked impressed by his honesty. "Which part intrigued you?"

He talked about his family with his lovers as seldom as his finances. Courtney could find out about his background almost as easily as she could learn his salary, so he answered truthfully. "My younger brother's a sergeant with the Army. His unit was called over to Iraq when the war first broke out with an expected year-long tour of duty. They ended up staying an extra three months. Then when he did come home, no more than a month had passed and he was raring to be deployed again. A short while later, he was right back into the heat of things. He's on his third tour now."

"You went over there to figure out why he's always so anxious to get back." The words were a statement not a question, and another testament to her astuteness.

Blaine had appreciated both her work ethic and her ass for over two years. Now he found he was also appreciating the woman beyond her job and looks. "Pretty much. I ended up only getting to see him for about an hour. It was enough to tell that he loves his job. And more than enough to see I wasn't cut out for working twelve- to sixteen-hour days in a hundred-and-twenty-degree temperatures, sleeping on a hard-ass cot, and living in a tent with nine other guys who haven't showered in days." His brother's face filled his mind, and he smiled. "I'd never have guessed it, considering what a whiner he was growing up, but Jamie has my total respect."

Courtney returned his smile. "He sounds great. I don't have any siblings. My parents have always been very focused on the blueberry farm. I guess too much to take time out for more than one kid."

"You're a country girl?"

As if he'd hit on some dirty little secret, her smile wavered. Quietly, she said, "Um. Yeah." She looked away, then quickly back. Relief slid into her eyes with the return of her smile. "Oh, good. Our waiter just came out of the kitchen with our food."

Courtney had never been embarrassed to admit where she came from before tonight.

She was proud of her parents' success in the blueberry industry. Their Newaygo-based farm turned over a healthy enough profit to see her four years of college tuition was paid up front and a steady supply of money was in her bank account, so that she'd been able to focus on her courses instead of working a part-time job to afford groceries and rent. It was their old-fashioned ethics that bothered her. More so, the fact that she'd lived by those same ethics for far too long. Denied herself pleasure because of them.

Tonight, she wasn't about to deny herself a thing. Tonight, she was going to screw the guy standing across the kitchen counter from her, mixing ice cubes into a bowl of boiling water and strawberry gelatin powder, while she kicked back on a barstool and enjoyed a cold beer.

That was, if Blaine wanted to sleep with her.

To think otherwise seemed ridiculous, given what she knew of him. But then, at dinner he'd made it sound like he really did want her at his house solely for the purpose of sharing dessert. The edible kind. The kind that had nothing to do with getting naked, even if the quickly melting ice cubes reminded her of the last time they'd been in his kitchen alone together, and had her sex moist and her nipples erect as a side effect.

"Who would have guessed staring at ice could make a person horny?" Blaine asked.

Courtney looked up from the mixing dish to find him smiling at her knowingly. "What makes you think I'm horny?"

"A vast knowledge of the female mind and body. Your cheeks and lips are rosy, and your breathing's coming faster than usual."

How did he know how fast she normally breathed? Unless he made it a point to pay attention, which would suggest he *had* wanted her for some time.

She took a pull from her beer before asking casually, "Does that knowledge tell you we like to get gifts at work?"

"Like the box of candy you got today?" At her nod, he continued, "My knowledge tells me most women know that kind of gift is just as overrated as dating. Either you eat it and it's gone, which basically makes it a waste of money, or you don't eat it and it goes bad, which definitely makes it a waste of money. If I'm going to give a woman a gift, it's going to be delivered in person and be way better and much longer lasting than chocolate."

"Guess that rules you out as my admirer." Courtney should be glad, considering the guy who gave her the box of candy claimed via lyrics that she was always on his mind. Since she wasn't looking for a serious relationship for the next while, it wouldn't do to sleep with a guy who felt that way about her. Still, part of her had held out hope the candy was from Blaine, if only because it would make certain that he still wanted her.

Now she was at the mercy of his response to give some indication of his feelings. Only, he didn't respond, just focused back on making the pie.

Opening a container of whipped cream, he spooned it into the bowl and whisked the filling mixture for a good minute before adding strawberry slices and starting back in on the whisking. She was ready to say to hell with looking stupid should he answer in the negative, and ask him outright if he planned to sleep with her, when he finally quit stirring.

Blaine looked up at her, his smile as knowing as it had been before. The look in his eyes was different, though. Before, they gleamed with amusement. Now, the irises were dark, almost black with unconcealed want. "I didn't send the candy, but that doesn't mean I don't admire you." His hot gaze moved down her body, stilling on her breasts. "There's a whole lot to be admired about the way I could see down the front of your shirt when you were standing in front of me in the lunchroom today."

Courtney's belly surged with warmth. Her nipples ached beneath his attention. Her pussy joined in, throbbing for his touch. "I thought you just wanted to have dessert?"

"I do."

She groaned with the noncommittal response. "God, call me dense, but I can't read you. Which kind of dessert are we talking about?"

"Both." The single word was edged with rough desire that had her heart slamming.

Blaine grabbed the graham cracker pie crust he'd earlier pulled from the refrigerator, and poured the filling mix into the shell. "There's a reason I waited until we got here to make this. It takes several hours to set. While it's chilling, you're going to heat me up."

4

Though it took all of her self-control, Courtney refrained from climbing off the barstool and across the marble countertop to throw herself at Blaine. She was supposed to be a sex diva. A woman who partook in pleasure often enough that her body shouldn't feel so hot and horny that it was as if she hadn't been laid in months.

She'd had an orgasm at his hands four nights ago. Full-on intercourse with another man just last week. Yet here she sat, trembling with the want to get her hands on his body and his cock buried deep inside her. By the sounds of things, he was giving her the go-ahead to do precisely that.

"You want me to seduce you?" she asked.

"I want you to show me how you like to be fucked."

Her sex fluttered. Juices pooled in her core, making it seem she'd been waiting to hear those words forever. Still, she refrained from moving off the bar stool. "I would have thought you were the type who likes to be in control."

"I enjoy being dominant." Wickedness glinted in his eyes. "Nothing gets my dick quite as hard as pushing a woman up against the wall and taking her from behind. The penetration's deeper that way, to the point she can't help but scream when I pump into her. Can't help but beg for more. Can't help but claw at the wall from the intensity of her climax when I pound my cock inside her dripping pussy and give her that more."

Courtney lifted her beer, taking a quick, cooling drink as her body flushed from head to toe with blistering heat. "Why not do *me* that way?"

"I considered it. But you like being dominant, too, so tonight you get to lead."

Did she like being the one in control?

Since her mind and body makeover, she'd only been with the dominant type—their outright arrogance aroused her so effectively from across the room, it was a given they'd make for a worthy screw. On second thought, that wasn't exactly accurate. Craig, aka Mr. Hot Buns, had started out dominant, but from there he allowed her to take over, with the videotaping and otherwise. He'd been her best lay ever. And now she realized it probably had everything to do with her being the one in charge. Truly working the feminine power Candy had assured, from day one of Courtney's transformation process, was the key to her sexual satisfaction.

Sliding off the bar stool, she gave Blaine her most carnal smile. "You have five seconds to put the pie in the fridge and get your fine behind on the table."

He was at the table in less than five seconds, though standing in front of it instead of sitting on it the way she'd instructed. "You'd make a damned bad sub. I said on it, not in front of it."

"Sure you don't want to do this somewhere we haven't already been?"

"I've come on the table. You haven't." The idea that he may well have climaxed on the table numerous times with other women entered her mind. Placing a hand on the solid wall of his chest, she pushed the thought aside and him backward. "Sit down, Blaine."

He let her shove him back until he was in the same position she'd been in two nights ago—with his legs spread and his thighs beckoning her to move between them. Two nights ago her thighs had been essentially bare. Her sex easily exposed, easily fingered.

She wanted him that same way.

Since pinstriped thigh highs and a short hot-pink dress would never do his incredibly masculine body justice, she would have to settle for baring his lower half completely.

Courtney grinned, all but licking her lips at what a truly decadent shame that would be. "Get back on the floor," she demanded.

Blaine frowned as he pushed off the edge of the table and dropped down onto the kitchen tiling. "What, are we playing some kind of twisted game of Courtney says?"

"Yeah." Her voice laced with desire, she popped the button on his pants. Grabbing hold of the zipper, she yanked it down. "Right now Courtney says you have way too much on."

He'd shaved off the chin stubble and changed into khakis and a short-sleeve taupe dress shirt between the time he'd left work and met her at Valerio's. The loose fit of the khakis wasn't as eye pleasing as the impeccably snug fit of his jeans, but it made removing his pants far easier.

Her blood pumped wildly as she pushed her thumbs into the sides of his khakis. Grabbing hold of both the pants and his underwear, she jerked them down to mid-thigh. Crisp dark hair lined his thighs, but not enough to hide the powerful swell of his quads. Hair much darker and thicker canvassed his groin, but not nearly close to thick enough to hide his generous cock.

His shaft jutted toward her, long and proud. The head deep purple. A silky bead of pre-cum gelled at the tip.

She swept a hand out, trailing a fingertip through the bead, and then brought the digit to her mouth. Flicking her tongue out, she dabbed at his cum. Blaine's groan was raw, deep, raspy. In time with the anxious contracting of her cunt.

Meeting his eyes, she sucked her finger into her mouth, licking at his essence until all she could taste was her own warm, salty skin. Then she purred an honest-to-god cat sound—fitting given how much of her blood and brain cells were being overtaken by her pussy. "Courtney says she likes. She like a whole, whole lot. Now take them off the rest of the way and have a seat."

He removed his pants, underwear, and socks, and then lifted himself back onto the tabletop. The spread of his thighs was pure ecstasy, displaying the snugness of his balls and the exquisite sculpting of his leg muscles.

Reclining on his forearms, he asked, "Is this going to involve ice? As pleasurable as that can be for a woman, I'm thinking it has the makings of shrinkage for a man."

"No ice." No way would she ruin this moment, a fantasy over two years in the fulfilling. "Just you sitting there, letting me use you."

Reverently stroking his strong thighs, she moved between his legs. The tip of his cock nudged against her belly through her shirt, and the tendons of his thighs corded beneath her fingertips. Journeying her fingers upward, she took his erection in hand and slowly stroked.

Blaine's breath whistled in. He cursed just audibly.

Circling her thumb over the weeping eye of his shaft, she sent him a teasing smile. "Anxious?"

"Just a little."

He'd hinted he hadn't slept with anyone while abroad. The tension in his body and voice suggested he hadn't slept with anyone since returning home either. That it was taking all of his strength to hold on to control and let her continue to lead.

It would be fun to push him over the edge. Take his cock

into her mouth and lick and suck him to the point of explosion only to pull back right before he came. Then do it all over, again and again, until finally she allowed him to surrender to release.

It would be fun, if she wasn't every bit as anxious to come as he was.

Each pass of his hard, steely flesh between her fingers had her sex wetter, her nipples more rigid with the want for his mouth. Her lips more eager to draw his own nipples between them and suck.

Her gaze snapped to his chest. My God, how had she failed to take his shirt off?

His eyes narrowed. "What's going on in that head of yours?"

"Are you kidding?" Courtney released his erection to undo the buttons of his shirt. "Like I'm thinking at a time like this." Only when the last button gave away and the sides of the shirt parted to reveal the chiseled definition of his suntanned chest and torso, she was thinking . . . about how she possibly could have gone so long without doing him.

"You are." Blaine's grin kicked up wolfishly. "Incredibly naughty thoughts. Your eyes give you away."

Stepping back from the vee of his thighs, she peeled the black hot pants down her legs and over her heeled slingbacks. His eyes were burning hot darkness and predatory as sin as he watched her cast the pants aside and then return for her shirt.

Her fingers curled in the hem of the scooped-neck top, and she caught the sharp intake of his breath. Like he'd been waiting for this moment as long as she had. "Is that why you've wanted me for so long?"

"How long?" he asked, not bothering to deny her speculation, not bothering to steal his gaze from her fingers.

"Judging by the size of this"—she released her hem to move forward and grab hold of his shaft—"years."

"Tell me your thoughts and I'll tell you if you're right."

"Nah-uh." Not when she was suddenly wondering if he

might be breaking from the norm by hoping for more than no strings with her. And not when she was considering how tempting that idea was herself. "Showing is so much better."

Courtney forgot about wonder to focus on want. She brought her fingers back to the hem of her shirt and whipped the top over her head. Blaine's eyes locked on the plunging neckline of her black silk cami. Her pussy had already felt molten. With the intensity of his gaze, she was ready to go up in flames.

Leaving the cami on, she tugged the panties down her legs and off. His attention shot to her mound and her clit tingled. She resisted the urge to reach down and rub it. Returning to the table, she mounted the side. The heels made climbing on top of him without damaging the tabletop a chore, but one worth accomplishing. Particularly when she was straddling him, the mouth of her pussy brushing along the hard ridge of his sex, wetting his shaft with her arousal.

He lifted a hand, long fingers tracing the cami's neckline where her breasts thrust to their fullest with the aid of strategically placed underwire. His other hand stroked along her side. The rough pads of his fingers caressed along diamond-shaped patches of skin revealed where the front and back half of the cami loosely tied together. "You changed. I liked the white cotton."

Courtney was sinking against his touch from the first sensual stroke, her breath feathering, her eyes falling shut. They opened with his startling admission. She had him pegged as a scanty black lingerie man all the way. "Just full of surprises, aren't you?"

"Not so many. I liked the white cotton. But this"—his fingers moved to a strap, twirling the thin Venice lace, and then pulling it to the side and off her shoulder—"this I love."

The top half of her right breast came free, the areola berry red with passion, and just like that she was sinking into the moment again, her eyes shuttering partway closed. He worked the other strap off her shoulder, and the cami slipped down to her waist, unveiling her tits entirely. If he was disappointed by their size, or anything else about her body, it didn't show.

Searing need filled his eyes as he pulled a taut nipple between his fingers, tugging at it almost to the point of agony.

Even as she cried out in ecstasy, her clit rubbing against his cock with the automatic arching of her back, she remembered him saying that some pain was pleasurable. Instantly, she knew he was right. Knew that she wanted to give real pleasure-pain a try soon and most definitely at his skilled and work-roughened hands.

For now, Courtney leaned forward, planted her palms on the table around his wide shoulders, and turned her mouth on his own nipple. She tongued the small disc erect, and then pulled it between her lips and pressed it hard against the roof of her mouth.

With a low growl, Blaine slipped his hands around to capture her ass. He kneaded the bare skin, found the sensitive opening of her asshole and circled it with two fingertips. One finger lightly entered her, first probing and then penetrating her sphincter muscles.

Her eyes flew wide. Air gasped from her lips, stilling her mouth on his nipple. Clenching her buttocks, she waited for ache. His invasion was gentle, tender, leaving no room for hurt.

"Only good pain." His words were thick, hoarse. Echoing along with the throb of her pulse in her ears.

Slipping inside a half inch farther, he caressed her virgin passage with the wiggle of a fingertip. It felt like so much more. Her belly clamped tight with wickedly tender pressure. Her sex shuddered convulsively as the movement of his finger continued, rubbing, caressing. Building burning wet need deep within her.

His finger traveled another half inch, stroking harder this time, faster. Seconds passed, minutes. The push and play of his fingertip turned to pure aggression, pure gratification. More than she could take without giving up the lead completely and herself over to orgasm.

Shimmering sensation coursed through her, tightening her limbs and rushing cream from her cunt. A shout of rapture broke from her lips as she reared back on his finger and took him deep, milking the digit until her asshole was juicy wet and her climax complete.

Courtney's heart raced so fast she could barely breathe as his finger pulled from her body. She couldn't speak yet. Blaine didn't speak either. Though, when she worked up the energy to sit upright, the restraint in his eyes and the firm press of his lips said plenty about the state of his body and mind.

The state of her own body and mind should be satiated beyond comparison. But now that his finger was gone, she felt empty, needy, desperate to ram onto his stiff cock.

Not wanting to force him into coming the moment she took him inside, she took her time. Used caution she hadn't thought about moments ago, when she'd been on the razor edge of release. "I'm on birth control. Is that enough?"

"Definitely."

With past lovers, it hadn't been enough for her. She'd insisted on condoms. She knew Blaine, trusted him. Wanted nothing but skin separating his body from her own.

Regaining the lead, she slid down his thighs far enough to take his bulging cock in hand. Rising up, she guided his shaft to her opening. She rubbed the creaming tip of his dick along her labia until she feared he might not be able to take any more and wasn't even sure how much more she could take herself. Then, slowly, she settled onto his long, hard length.

Hot air jetted from between his lips on a groan. Courtney sighed as her sex parted and residual tremors from her orgasm reawakened.

Sucking her lower lip between her teeth, she tested the new

position, rubbing her clit against his pubis while her pussy lips hungrily loved his shaft.

The shimmering sensation returned instantly, brighter, more powerful.

She lifted herself up his cock and then back down. Repeated the move twice more, feeling him sink blissfully deeper inside her each time.

"This is how I like it." Her breathing grew faster, her pulse intense. "Your cock's so deep inside me I can feel every little move we make. Every little breath we take. Every little shiver—"

Blaine's hips shifted, pulling down on the table and then surging upward without warning. She grabbed hold of his pecs and sucked in a gasp as he filled her to an extreme she didn't know possible.

Exquisite pressure barreled through her so strong it felt like it could tear her apart. "That was so *not* little!"

"What do you expect from a guy who has wanted you for years?" Arrogance coupled with edgy playfulness in his voice. His fingers returned to stroking the crease of her ass.

Courtney knew in that moment Candy had been right about his longtime want for her. "You're hung up on my butt, aren't you?"

"I told you the other night, I like everything about you." His hands came around to her breasts. He didn't stop at fingering a lone nipple this time, but pulled the mounds fully into his palms and twisted at the sensitized flesh. "From your succulent tits to your beautiful mind."

Against the all-consuming bliss rocketing from her breasts to her pussy, and the daunting idea he really could want more than no strings, she let out a throaty laugh.

The twisting of his fingers halted. His hips stilled. "You think I'm kidding?"

She met his eyes, and found his daring her to deny him. "No. That was just so clichéd. My beautiful mind?"

"You do have a beautiful mind. One minute your head's spinning with technical jargon and the next all you can think about is how my dick's going to feel inside you, the way you were thinking all through dinner tonight."

"You think that's what I was thinking about? Your dick filling me up?"

"Isn't it?" No sooner had the words left his mouth than Blaine's hips were back to their dirty play, shrinking back on the table and then shoving up hard inside her.

The extreme pressure returned, coursing through her body and deep into her cunt on a dizzying wave. Her moan returned along with it. She kept the carnal sound back, locked it behind clamped teeth, struggling to prove his arrogant assumption wrong, if only because she found taunting him so incredibly much fun.

Blaine's lips curved dangerously. Challenge shimmered in his dark eyes.

Courtney knew she was a goner even before he squeezed her breasts together, titled his pelvis, and drove up once more inside her wet sheath.

The angle was different this time, not quite so deep and yet in some ways better. His shaft pressed tight against her clit, tormenting it into a throbbing bundle of nerves as he glided his cock languidly inside her body, as if he had all the control in the world.

Then he picked up the pace.

Taking her butt cheeks firmly in his hands, he thrust into her with quick, solid pumps. Orgasm built in her core as a whirlwind. Perspiration popped out on her forehead and between her breasts. She reclined against him, crushing her achy breasts against his chest, grabbing hold of his forearms, needing that bit of support. Needing it so much more as his neck corded with tendons, his features went taut, and he lost control.

His short fingernails bit into her ass—only good pain, as

promised. His dick pounded into her savagely, pushing her higher. Pushing her over the edge.

She tossed back her head and shouted with the strength of her climax. He didn't shout, but his groan was full bodied and amorous as he filled her quivering pussy with hot cum.

Courtney's arms shuddered and gave out. She let herself fall onto his chest, breathing in his natural masculine scent and the smell of their mixed arousal.

So good. Even better than her fantasy.

Seconds, then a full minute eased past. Blaine's grip on her butt let up. One of his hands moved to the back of her head, pushing into what used to be curls but now was probably stick-straight hair and for all the best reasons.

"Nothing quite like a country girl riding you bareback." Satisfaction filled his words.

Self-consciousness ate at her regardless. She wasn't a country girl. Gave up that old-fashioned way of living months ago. Maybe the words were nothing more than teasing. Just in case they weren't, she lifted her cheek from his chest to look up at him. "I left the country behind long ago."

A contented smile had curved his lips. Now, it receded. "That's too bad."

He sounded sincere. But why would he be? She'd seen many of his lovers—they were all glam and glitz and city. That was the type he went for.

Or was it not anymore?

Despite what he claimed, was he truly ready to leave the no-strings approach to sex and relationships behind and believed a conservative country girl, like the one she used to be, the right woman to do it with?

Given how far from conservative the sex they just shared was, Courtney labeled the idea ridiculous. She pushed it from her mind entirely to focus on the feel of his cock softening inside her. Slowly retracting from her body.

That just wouldn't do. Not when the night was young and the pie wasn't even close to set.

Falling into sex-diva mode, she sat up from his chest and eyed the wall clock hanging over the kitchen door. "Bummer. The pie's not done yet." She swept her gaze from the clock to his face to her mound. Flashing a siren's smile, she slipped a finger between her still moist and blood-reddened pussy lips. "What do you say I let you watch me masturbate to pass the time?"

Nuzzling the crook of Courtney's neck while she lay asleep in his bed and arms, Blaine acknowledged how thoroughly his time abroad had changed him. It hadn't just strengthened his appreciation for the little things. It had broadened his awareness as a lover and of his wants as a man.

No matter how rough he might like his sex at times, he'd always been a courteous lover, ensuring his partners climaxed at least once before he came. He'd been aware, by the sound of their breathing and the pacing of their movements, how close they were to coming undone. Just where to touch to send them soaring into orgasm.

But he hadn't taken the time to wholly appreciate the curves of their bodies. The graceful sweep of their spines. The softness of their skin and the flare of their hips. The scent and silkiness of their hair as it slipped through his fingers.

Each sigh. Each moan.

Tonight, he'd appreciated all of those things. And, tonight, he'd recognized how much he wanted to experience all of them and so much more on a daily basis. Not with a different woman, but the same one.

He'd planned to wait a few more years before taking relationships seriously; time to build his savings so finances would never be a matter of contention. Holding Courtney in his arms, something he'd never done or wanted to do with a lover before experiencing how alone and insignificant he'd felt sleeping on a narrow cot in the middle of a war-torn country, Blaine accepted his plans had changed. The time was now to find a woman who shared his enthusiasm for sex, the glory of having a job you loved and doing it damn well, and valued more in life than the material.

Courtney could well be that woman.

Since she shared his former stance on no strings/no dates, he couldn't find that out by dating her in the traditional sense. But he could continue to sleep with her under the guise that it was all he wanted while getting to better know the woman beneath her sexy clothes and attitude, and seeing why she was so quick to shun the country girl of her past.

As if she knew his thoughts and was scared as hell of him, she shifted in his arms. She came awake on a murmur followed by a whispered, "Shit. I fell asleep."

She didn't sound happy, or like she thought Blaine was awake. Her fingers moved down to take hold of his hand. Slowly, she lifted it away from her body. Without words, she eased from beneath the sheet and off the side of the bed.

The light of a half moon shone in through the blind-drawn windows, allowing him to watch as she moved around his bedroom in search of the clothes she'd put back on to eat pie and then he'd eagerly taken off again a short while later to eat pussy.

She darted down near the foot of the bed, and he asked, "Escaping?"

Courtney straightened on a shriek, black panties in hand and an uneasy look on her face. "I thought you were asleep."

"I can pretend like I am if it helps."

"It doesn't matter." She lifted a leg and jabbed a foot into her underwear. "I just didn't want to wake you."

The second part he was buying. The first part—considering the way she hurried her other foot into her panties and then restarted the clothing hunt—not by a long shot. "It's after two.

Why don't you spend the night?" She paused in her quest to eye him warily, and Blaine tacked on, "I know it won't mean anything."

She continued to stare at him, her suspicion unyielding. Finally, her smile emerged: cordial and, he could guess, fake. "Thanks, but I'd still have to leave before the sun rises to get home and cleaned up in time for work."

Courtney fell back into the hunt, spying the remainder of her clothes within seconds and pulling them on nearly as fast. Fully dressed, she started for the bed. She stopped a foot away from him, opening her mouth and quickly shutting it again.

She looked damned awkward, like she'd always been able to leave her lovers without notice and had no idea how to proceed with this new scenario.

Though he wanted to tell her the best course of action would be to crawl back into bed, Blaine took pity on her, effecting a groggy, "Thanks for dinner. See you in the morning."

"You aren't working in the field?"

In the lunchroom today, she'd made his appearance at the office seem like a great thing. Now, she sounded like she would be happy to never see him again.

In case he'd somehow given her reason to think he was after more than sex, he smiled wolfishly and raked her body with the heat of his gaze. "I figured I'd better stick around the office in case you get another gift from your admirer. It'd be a shame to hear you choked to death before I got a lasting turn at being the dominant one."

Hands settled on Courtney's shoulders. Warm hands. Strong hands. Hands that had gotten to know every inch of her body last night. How she could be certain they were Blaine's hands when she sat facing away from him was a mystery, but she definitely knew. Her sex went moist and her heart took off.

"I need you." His tone was as desperate as his words.

Shaking off his hands, she spun in her chair and stood. A quick scan revealed that, of those coworkers who sat within listening range, only Candy had returned from the lunch hour. Thank God. That he was back for more so soon, and at the office no less, was worrisome enough.

"Right now?" she hissed, wishing she didn't want more so soon herself.

She looked at him then, caught that there wasn't a touch of desire in his sober expression, and realized his need for her had nothing to do with sex.

"I missed a project posting." Blaine's all-business tone confirmed her suspicion. "The proposal's due first thing in the morning. I hate to ask you to put in OT to get it out, but you're the only one I trust to do the job right."

"That's okay. I can do—" Courtney stopped short with the flicker of triumph in his eyes. He never looked that inordinately pleased over her doing a job for him, even a last-minute one. Maybe his need for her was all business, but it also might not be and she wasn't about to risk staying late at the office alone with him. "I take that back. I have a date. I can't work past five tonight and I plan to be too tired to make it in early in the morning. Sorry."

The triumph left his eyes. "Hooking up with your secret admirer?"

She pasted on a lucky-girl grin. "Call me superficial, but nothing gets me hot like a guy who wastes money on pointless gifts."

Across the hallway, Candy let out a derisive snort that suggested she knew what total and utter crap the words were. Yeah, Courtney had gotten an initial thrill out of receiving the box of candies yesterday, but soon after she left the lunchroom the revolting things had ended up in the trash. She'd considered saving the box for a keepsake. Ultimately, her loathsomeness for clutter had her canning that, too. If she was going to get future gifts, she would prefer they be the lasting kind Blaine indicated he might give a woman.

"In that case, enjoy your evening." With a bogus-looking smile, he started to turn away.

She should let him go and end her anxiety, but it wasn't in her nature to leave him empty handed. "Do you want me to call around and see if someone else can help?"

"Don't worry about it. I'll pull something together on my own."

Frowning, Courtney watched him walk down the hallway until he disappeared into the stairwell leading to his second-floor office.

Apparently, she wasn't a sex diva. She was a big damned chicken.

"You two have a fight last night?" Candy asked.

Courtney swiveled to face her. Candy was kicked back in her chair, the lower half of her thighs exposed past the hem of her bright paisley dress and her legs crossed above the ankle strap of her chic magenta sandals. A cup of latte reclined in one manicured hand. It was the pose she always struck while listening to Courtney dish on her latest lay.

Normally, Courtney shared as soon as she got into work. Last night with Blaine hadn't been typical—doing him hadn't alleviated her stress, but increased it—and she hadn't wanted to share quite so soon. "We had a great time."

"Then why lie about having a date?"

She didn't want to admit her fears to the woman she owed for helping her get in touch with her inner vixen. But then, if anyone knew the right words to erase those fears, it would be Candy.

Courtney crossed to her coworker's cubicle. Setting aside a slew of marketing and promotional magazines and a vase of flowers sent by Candy's Saturday-night lover, she sank down on the edge of her desk. "If I stay late," she admitted quietly, "so will Blaine. Then we'll end up working together to review the documents and get everything out the door."

"O-kay. Not seeing a problem here."

"The problem is by the time we finish, everyone else will be gone for the night." It would be the two of them alone with her burning desire to see what it was like when he was the dominant one. She'd gotten a taste last night, when he'd brought her to orgasm by fingering her ass. That taste had her appetite whetted for more and the rest of her wet, period.

"I get it." Candy took a sip of latte. "You don't trust yourself to be alone around him."

"I didn't want to leave his place last night." It wouldn't be so bad if Courtney's reason for wanting to stay had merely been about sex. The problem was she'd gotten to know Blaine on a deeper level, first during dinner and then over pie, and liked him better all the time. For a while, it seemed he liked her better as well, to a point where he had more on his mind than screwing.

"Did he ask you to stay?"

"Not exactly. He said I could stay since it was so late and that I didn't need to worry about him thinking it meant anything. We're both into no strings."

Candy searched her face, looking unconvinced. "You sure about that?"

"I told myself I wouldn't get wrapped up in any one guy so soon and I meant it."

Did she still?

Absolutely, Courtney mentally scolded herself. One stellar night with Blaine didn't change the fact that her sex drive would soon be taking a downward spin, or that once she did get involved in a relationship, the average and boring Courtney of days past would slowly take back over as a matter of course. "Besides, do you really think he'd want more?"

"I can't see it," Candy said without hesitation. Straightening in her chair, she set her latte next to her half-dressed-hunk-adorned mouse pad. "Which is why you shouldn't have anything to fear in working alone together." Naughtiness gleamed in her brown eyes. "Or doing anything else alone together."

"Mmm . . . maybe."

"Hey, it's your call. Personally, I'd say yes." Candy swiveled in her chair, placing her hands on her keyboard and typing a few words, before adding in a low, breathy voice, "Yes, yes, yes. Ohhh, yes, Blaine! Right there, baby. Do it again."

Courtney laughed out loud. "Oh, geez. Shut up before I have to kill you."

"Don't even think about it." Anticipation kindled in her voice. "I'm going over to Ty's for dinner tonight. The way he was talking this morning, I think he has plans to finally fulfill my Sleeping Beauty fantasy. You know the one where I wake up in the pitch blackness, naked and bound, and with a hunk of burning Ty ready to ravish me?"

That explained why Candy hadn't brought up Courtney's night out with Blaine before now. As often as her coworker went out with and slept with other men, her favorite lay and the one who always had her mind occupied well in advance of their date was her condo neighbor. With the promise of her fantasy being fulfilled, Candy's mind was clearly even more occupied than usual. "Have an orgasm for me while you're at it."

"Won't need to," Candy said without looking back. "You'll be living out plenty of your own orgasm-inducing fantasies right here at the office. Or you can borrow mine, and let Blaine tie you up and ravish you. C'mon, you have to admit it sounds really tempting."

"And really good," Courtney allowed, unable to stop her amused smile as she returned to her own cube.

Less than five minutes had passed when she knew she was going to disregard her fears and do Blaine's project. And, potentially, Blaine. "All right. I'll do his job."

"Enjoy the vibrating toilet seat," Candy tossed over her shoulder.

By the time she was halfway to the stairwell leading to the second floor, Courtney did feel like she'd gone a round with a vibrator. The expectation of seeing Blaine had her entire body buzzing with sensual energy. Her mind was obviously overtaken as well, because she managed to walk right into someone's back.

The person turned around. Male hands took hold of her upper arms, the move brushing their owner's body up against her own. "Excited?"

"Incredibly," she responded truthfully.

Her mind cleared enough to realize what she'd said and to recognize Jake standing inches away, smiling in a way that suggested her arousal was evident.

Wonderful. She was *so* ready to have the field guy spreading rumors about her and Blaine around the office. Or, rather, substantiating the rumors that had been circulating since the party Friday night.

Yeah, right.

"So what's the good news?" he asked.

"It's Wednesday." She flashed a playful grin as she stepped back a half foot. "There's no better day than hump day to live out your fantasies." Not the smartest office talk ever, but it fit with her revamped unabashed attitude and, more importantly, didn't involve Blaine.

Jake's gray eyes warmed. "I'm rather fond of fantasies myself." The walkie-talkie phone hooked to the waist of his jeans beeped, and the field supervisor from the construction site he was working on came over the speaker. "Jake, you there?"

After glaring at the phone, Jake sent her an apologetic look. "Sorry, I need to take this."

"Not a prob. Have a great day."

"It's going better already." With a good-bye nod, he moved down the hallway.

Courtney waited until he was out of sight and then continued on to Blaine's office. Her anticipation had died considerably thanks to the impromptu chat. Still, she wasn't about to risk entering his office. Instead she lingered in the doorway, enjoying the view of his strong sexy profile before rapping on the wood of his door.

He looked up from his laptop. "Courtney. What's going on?"

"I'll pull your proposal together. Just make sure you have your part of the work to me before you leave tonight."

"I thought you had a—"

"I cancelled." The triumph she'd detected in his eyes back at her cube returned, and her sex gave an answering flutter. She sighed. So much for her anticipation dying down. "Don't think it was a special favor. The truth is I don't dig pointless gifts any more than wasting money."

He smiled. "Thanks. I'll get you the Understanding of Project by five, though I'm not about to leave you here by yourself."

"I work better without someone breathing down my neck." She also thought much better when he wasn't smiling at her that way, like the moment they were alone she was going to have to fight to keep her clothes on long enough to get her work done.

His smile deepened as his gaze fell to her breasts. "Then I'll be sure to keep my mouth below your neck."

Courtney's nipples beaded achingly tight. She resisted the urge to cross her arms over her chest. First, business. Then, maybe pleasure. "Do you have the solicitation?"

Blaine lifted a few stapled sheets of paper off his desk and brought them over to her. She grabbed the solicitation, but he didn't let go.

He stepped closer. "Did something go wrong last night that I'm not aware of, or why are you trying to blow me off?"

"Last night was . . ." Perfect. Even better than her fantasies of the two of them. In need of an immediate repeat. "I had fun. I just never planned to sleep with someone from work. Things like that have a way of getting messy."

"Only if those involved let it." His hold on the solicitation let up. "I'm not going to lie, I was hoping for another night or two. If you don't want that, I understand. I won't respect you any less than I do right now, which is a hell of a lot."

"I . . ." What she was, was seriously not acting like a sex diva. Since he'd more or less made it clear he was still only after the physical and she was still having a whole lot of fun with him, she didn't have a single reason to act any other way.

A quick glance down one end of the hallway and then the other assured they were alone for the next few seconds at least. Giving Blaine her most seductive smile, she ran her fingers from his chest to his torso. Naturally earned hard-packed muscle coasted beneath her fingertips, and her sex clenched with the memory of how amazing his body both looked and felt naked. There was a definite need to forget her fears and give him another night or two.

First work, Courtney reminded herself sternly and stepped back with a wink. "Give me six hours of alone time to chill out and get this proposal ready for your review, and I'll let you spend the next six heating me up with together time."

5

Seven thirty. Let the games begin.

After verifying that the time on his laptop matched the time on his watch, Blaine shut down the computer and headed for Pinnacle's first floor. Knowing how critical she was of her work and ensuring the proposals that left the engineering firm were flawless, he'd given Courtney a half hour longer than requested.

Now that he'd gotten the nice part over with, he planned to be extra naughty.

The thought of getting his hands back on her body had him taking the steps two by two. Without breaking stride, he shoved open the stairwell door and hurried down the hallway to her cubicle. Outside of her cube, he slowed to a crawl. Her mind was bound to be lost in work, which gave him the perfect opportunity for a surprise necking.

As expected, when he reached the opening to her cube, Courtney was sitting with her nose almost touching the computer screen and her hand on the mouse, scrolling through the proposal pages. Traditionally, Blaine was into long hair on a woman. Her chin-length style suited him in that it made moving the blond-tipped brown strands aside to get at her neck a breeze.

Moving silently behind her chair, he lifted the hair away from her right ear and pressed a damp kiss to the skin beneath. "Time's up."

Her hand jerked, sending the mouse skittering forward while she squealed.

Batting at his mouth with her shoulder, she moved the mouse back into position. "I need five more minutes."

He brought his lips lower, to the spot he knew drove her crazy. The flick of his tongue had her releasing a loud sigh. "You can work as long as you want, but I only promised to leave you alone for six hours. I already gave you an extra half hour."

Courtney had changed her clothes with the end of normal work hours, trading a mint green V-neck top, beige crop pants, and heels for an orange tank top, short white cotton shorts, and bare feet. Along with so many other things, he'd noted last night that her breasts weren't as big as what they appeared to be while she was dressed. She obviously relied on a well-padded bra to create that illusion—a bra that she wasn't wearing now. Only the loose-fitting, built-in bra of the tank top provided support.

Big tits were nice. But so were average-sized ones, particularly when they were this easily accessible.

Blaine released her hair to slip his hand down the front of her tank top. Her right breast filled his hand, soft and supple. The nipple went erect against his palm, and his cock tented the front of his jeans in tandem.

Nudging the hair back away from her ear with his nose, he asked in a hot whisper, "Ready to fuck?"

Her head lolled to the side on a blissful sigh, but her tone was closer to annoyance. "Do you want to win this job?"

"I'd like to. Considering it's a small project and you're meticulous, I bet the proposal was done and ready for review an hour ago."

"Gee, don't I sound anal."

Giving her nipple a pinch, he grinned. "Last night, you liked anal just fine."

She tensed . . . then an instant later let out a boisterous laugh. "You're a lost cause. If I let you seduce me, will you promise to review the proposal before you conk out?"

"You fell asleep, not me." He'd been too keyed up with the depth of his changes brought about by working abroad to even close his eyes. That, and he'd known as soon as she woke, she would be gone.

With the distant way Courtney had acted toward him this morning, it probably wouldn't matter how much he was coming to like her. She would probably never allow more than sex between them. Still, it wouldn't hurt to give finding out for certain more time.

Nah, it was going to feel damned good.

"Besides," he continued, "do you really think I'd fall asleep in your cube with my naked ass hanging out? Talk about confirming the speculation that we're sleeping together." Feathering a fingernail across her nipple, he nodded at the computer monitor. "Print it out. I'll review it while I seduce you."

She shivered as she clicked on the print icon. "Kinky, mixing roadway repaving with sex."

Taking her chin with his free hand, he tipped her head back. "Just wait, sweetie. You'll never think about asphalt the same way again."

Blaine never called his lovers by pet names. He thought she might not notice, or let the endearment pass. But then, her eyes narrowed, suspicion filling them. He did what he'd intended to do when he slanted her head back, covered her mouth with his and slipped his tongue inside.

She melted into the kiss, teasing his tongue back with hot little licks guaranteed to boil his blood. He took possession of both the kiss and her left breast, commanding her mouth with the strength of his tongue and lips while he squeezed and worked her tit into an aching mound of pleasure. Whimpering, she curled her fingers in the short sleeves of his T-shirt and lifted herself partway out of her seat in an effort to rub against his body—impossible with a chair between them, but damn, how he wanted to feel the sweet press of her ass grinding against his cock.

Courtney pulled from his mouth on a groan. "I can't freaking get to you."

"Thought you wanted to get me the proposal to review before you get to me," Blaine teased.

Her fingers left his shirt and she dropped back down in her chair. "I do," she said in a scolding tone he could guess was aimed at herself for losing control as much as it was at him for making her. "It should be printed by now. Move out of my way and I'll go get it."

"Yes, ma'am." He stepped back a few feet. Since her cool voice did nothing to calm his heated body, he focused on taking stock of her cube in a way he'd never before had the time or inclination to do. Where Candy's cubicle reflected her brazen personality, sporting everything from admirer-gifted flowers to a barely clothed man calendar and matching mouse pad, Courtney's cube walls were lined with work paraphernalia, a handful of snapshots likely of family and friends, and about two dozen tiny silver spoons. "Nifty spoons."

Standing, she followed his gaze to the three rows of miniature spoons stuck to the gray cloth of the partition wall with T-pins. "My mother started me collecting them. Everyone needs a hobby."

She sounded defensive, much the way she had when he suggested she was a country girl. Did she think he found the not-quite-so-brazen facets of her personality a turnoff? Or had the astuteness of her Friday night comment, about him trying to escape, been based on more than her experience with no-strings sex, the way she'd implied?

Blaine couldn't ask her the questions, not yet. Maybe not ever. Storing them away for potential later use, he pulled her against him by the front of her tank top and kissed her quickly but thoroughly. Enough to have them both breathing fast when he lifted from her mouth. "Hurry back."

An impish smile curved her lips. She grabbed hold of his erection through his jeans and squeezed. "Maybe. Or maybe I'll keep walking past the printer and right out the front door."

"You'd leave me here with my dick hard and only my hand to take care of it?"

"Watch me." She swiveled on bare feet and started walking, swaying her hips in a way that was obviously purposeful and had his gaze zeroing in on her butt.

All those little skirts and tight pants she wore made her ass look amazing, curvy, ripe. The white cotton shorts put those outfits to shame. The shorts were even smaller than he'd realized: each of her steps had a bare butt cheek peeking out at him and his cock pulsing.

Lucky for his cock it was his turn to be the dominant one.

Yeah, he should be a nice guy and a good construction manager and put reviewing the proposal Courtney had worked overtime on before pleasure. But right now the words weren't bound to make sense, he was so focused on sinking inside her warm, wet body.

Blaine counted to ten and then he went after her.

He found her in the document preparation area. The stack of proposal pages she'd printed lay on the assembly table. Courtney was at the copy machine, pulling something off the glass.

The copy machine he'd been fantasizing about having her on for a week. Hell, long before that.

Blood roared between his ears as he locked sights on her ass in those tiny shorts, all that smooth, bare, suntanned skin peeking out, just waiting for him to grab hold. Breathing hard, he strode across the room. She'd left the door of the copy machine up in the air. Taking advantage, he slipped his arms around her sides and planted his palms against the still-warm glass.

She sucked in a gasp. "Blaine! What are you doing?"

He brought his mouth to her neck, nibbling on her sweet spot while he turned her in his arms. To the sound of her helpless moan, he pulled his lips from her neck. Dragging her breasts against his body, he lifted her up and placed her back onto the glass of the copy machine.

He grinned as he took in her nipples rock hard in a way the built-in bra could never contain. "Fulfilling a fantasy."

With a thigh in each hand, he spread her legs and buried his face against her mound. The layers of her shorts and panties were no match for her arousal. He could smell her excitement lifting through the cotton, musky yet sweet.

There was nothing sweet about the way he planned to have her tonight. The office was empty now—no worries about being caught in the act—and this was all about the sinful.

Blaine pulled aside the crotch of her shorts and sucked at her pussy through her thin yellow underwear. The taste of her seeped through the cotton, urging him to suck harder.

Courtney *ooh*ed and her fingers shot to his shoulders. She wriggled against his mouth. "You've fantasized about copying my butt?"

"Hitting the copy button right when you're about to come," he murmured against her juicy folds. Then he stabbed his tongue forward hard, slicing it down the part of her labia, and pushing her panties inside.

He pulled his head back far enough to appreciate his handwork, the sight of her pussy lips all puffed up and pink around her soggy underwear. "Christ, that's so hot. Your panties up inside your cunt."

"I'm still on the copy button thing." The herky-jerky sound of her breathing and restless shifting of her hips called her a liar. "That's so twisted."

Bringing his mouth back to her sex, he brushed his chin stubble across her panty-filled slit. "Ever feel the amount of heat these things give off? Just think how good that's going to feel on your ass when I'm fucking you."

"Oh, yeah." The words came out half moan, half breathy sigh. "I'd like to feel that."

He'd like to show that to her pronto. And he would, just as soon as she was ready.

Blaine quit with the chin rubbing to bury his tongue back inside her. The sodden panties moved easily, grinding into her sheath, back and forth against her sensitive lips, probably feeling better than any dildo ever had or would again.

Courtney's hands pushed into his hair and her hips started into a reverse canting. Cream leaked from her pussy to tantalize his tongue as she rode it with expert skill, clenching and unclenching her buttocks to bring herself higher and lower in time with the corkscrewing stab of his tongue. She was panting for air, her pussy quivering for release in seconds.

Just before she would have come, he took his mouth from her sex. Her fingers slipped from his hair, and he straightened to find her lips swollen and her eyes shiny, the irises mostly green. Blaine could have laughed out loud with the relief that look brought to him.

She was ready to forget about the proposal. He was over ready, over eager. Over hard.

"What the hell? I was about to come," Courtney grumbled.

He smiled back, knowing she wouldn't be complaining for long.

Not about to waste time by removing his clothes, he yanked down the zipper of his jeans, pushed open the front seam of his underwear, and took his throbbing cock in hand.

Her gaze zipped downward. Her lips parted. Warm anxious breaths panted out.

"Guess you forgive me." Without waiting for a reply, he grabbed hold of her butt and tugged her to the edge of the copy machine. "Open your pussy for me."

Obviously she felt as safe with their coworkers out of the office as he did. There was no hesitation on her part. She just brought a hand to her cunt, tugged the crotch of her underwear from her sex, and used her first two fingers to part the tender lips.

"Farther," he demanded with the shove of his hands against her knees, opening her legs wider. "I want to see everything."

She didn't demand back, didn't say anything, but played the submissive. Spreading her thighs even wider than he'd taken them, she used both hands on her sex. With a cutoff whimper, she splayed her pussy as far as she could open it.

She was creamy inside. So pink and creamy and trembling for him. Blaine couldn't remember ever wanting a woman so badly. His dick twinged with raw need as he took her ass back in his hands and pressed the tip of his cock to her opening. "Ready or not, here I come."

Biting gently on her lower lip, he shoved up into her passage. He groaned with the tightening of her sex around his. Her fingers remained at her pussy, holding her labia open, giving his dick an extra stroking with each of his hard pumps.

The compressing of her sex increased and she went wild in his arms, wriggling as if to escape him again. Not about to let that happen, he pressed his mouth against hers and parted her lips with the force of his own. Her taste was as hot and wild as the rest of her. Though it was supposed to be his dominant show, from the first touch of their tongues, she started plundering his mouth, licking at his teeth, almost savagely nipping at his lips.

An almost savage he loved.

It was the kind of good pain he'd had in mind when he suggested she needed to give pleasure-pain a try. The kind of pain that had him ready to go off in a major way. But he wasn't going anywhere. Not until Courtney did first.

This time as he surged up into her, Blaine hit the copy button. Green light illuminated the space between them. Heat emanated from the glass, warming the underside of his balls and the root of his cock in a totally erotic way.

Courtney didn't miss out on the erotic sensations. With an ecstatic scream, she jammed her fingernails into his upper arms and came hard.

"Oh, God . . . I never . . ." The shock on her face finished what she couldn't. She hadn't seen the orgasm coming. The thrill of the photocopy heat took her by total surprise and she'd loved every second of it, just as she had his anal fingering.

It went to show how completely compatible they were from a sexual standpoint. From other standpoints, he had a good feeling about that, too, and he wasn't about to accept her no-strings take on relationships. Not until he knew for certain how the rest of the package fit with her rocking body and beautiful mind, and then maybe not ever.

Gripping her ass in his hands so hard his knuckles turned white, he pumped into her still spasming pussy until he lost himself inside her.

Contentment he hadn't known until last night washing over him, he braced his weight against the front of the copy machine and settled his forehead against hers. "You're really something."

She closed her eyes on a satiated sigh. "You're really good at making me come."

He laughed. "The feeling's mutual, sweetie."

Her eyes came open and she tensed. Swearing silently, he lifted his forehead from hers and pulled from her body. If he was going to get to know her better without her figuring out what he was doing, he would have to be a hell of lot better about watching what he said.

Blaine stepped back from the copy machine, giving Courtney room to do the same. Juices trickled down her thighs and onto the copier glass as she slid onto the carpet.

She eyed the glass warily, looking nothing like the vamp from seconds ago and everything like the awkward woman from last night. "Whoops. Guess I should have prepared a better dismount."

"Don't worry about it. I'll go wash up in the bathroom and grab some wet paper towel on my way back." Thankful for the chance to give Courtney's anxiety time to pass, he went into the men's room a short way down the hall.

After washing up and righting his clothes, Blaine grabbed the promised paper towel, ran it under the faucet, and headed back for the document preparation area. In the hopes of lifting her unease by getting things back on a physical level, if only temporarily, he teased as he rounded the corner, "If you're through seducing m—" A man's back came into view, and he quickly amended, "my taste buds with talk of the food I'm missing out on by working late, I'll finish reviewing the proposal and we can get out of here."

The guy turned, making his identity known. Blaine eyed him suspiciously. What was Randy doing at the office and why did he look so upset to see him?

Blaine slid a casual smile into place. "Hey, Randy. I didn't realize you were here."

He smirked. "Yeah. Neither did Courtney."

Blaine glanced at her. She stood next to the copy machine, its top down, camouflaging her spill. Hard evidence of what they'd been doing might be out of sight, but between the scent of their screwing hanging in the air, the wet paper towel in his hand, and the way she kept nervously running her hands over imaginary wrinkles in her shorts, it was still blatantly obvious.

He looked back at Randy. "Didn't you have a meeting with a consulting group in Atlanta this morning?"

"Yeah, but I have so damned much work here, I flew back home as soon as it let out."

Courtney quit with the shorts rubbing. An inviting smile curved her lips. "Think of it this way." Crossing the few feet to Randy, she brushed the back of his hand with her fingertips. "The more time you spend at work, the more we get to take pleasure in your company."

A hint of levity emerged in Randy's eyes as he returned her smile. "There *is* that."

Blaine had always liked the guy, even if his jokes had a tendency to be immature, but something about that smile ate at his gut. "Are you planning to work much longer? We'll be done soon, so I'm wondering about locking the doors."

The hardness returned to Randy's gaze. "I was on my way out when I heard Courtney."

Heard her doing what? And did that something have to do with Randy's atypical attitude?

With a parting nod to Courtney, Randy moved out of sight. The front door thudded shut a few seconds later.

Back to looking anxious, Courtney yanked the paper towel from Blaine's hand and lifted up the copy machine door. "That was close."

"Yeah, you were."

She scrubbed at the smeared secretions. "What do you mean?"

Blaine knew he should let his apprehension go, but he couldn't block his irritation over her behavior any more than he could block Randy's smile. "Ever hear of sexual harassment?"

She laughed. "Like you'd have a case."

"I wouldn't. Plenty of other guys would. That little hand rub and do-me smile you gave Randy is all it takes to give someone the wrong impression."

She swiveled around on a gasp, nerves replaced with anger. "I did not give him a do-me smile, and he certainly doesn't think that I want him. He's married, for God's sake."

Sure he was, but happily so?

Randy's wife hadn't been at the party Friday night. In the five years he'd known him, Blaine couldn't recall Randy showing up for an event—company sponsored or otherwise—without the woman. Was their marriage on the rocks and Courtney's forward behavior making things worse by leading Randy to believe she was after more than a little friendly flirting? "Then why'd he act so upset to see me here with you?"

"He's stressed about work. That's why I rubbed his hand, to soothe his nerves."

"I've known him for years and his outlet for stress has always been joking. He didn't look one bit amused tonight." Nor had he Friday night, when he'd backed up Jake's theory that Courtney had a full-time lover waiting in the wings so Blaine should leave her alone.

She mulled the idea over, then concluded the totally ludicrous, "You're jealous."

Or maybe not so ludicrous, considering the way her flirting with other men had started to stick in his mind and burn his gut. Even so, that wasn't why he was making an issue about things. "What I am is concerned. About your safety and your future with Pinnacle."

Courtney exited her bedroom, and Gail sent her vibrant red and pink floral halter top and matching shorts a critical look from the living room couch. "You're wearing *that* to see Blaine?"

Courtney looked down at her outfit. It happened to be one of her favorites, something her parents had picked up for her during their thirtieth anniversary trip to Hawaii two years ago. That trip was one of the few interesting things they'd ever done. They played it safe, lived by their boring, average, old-fashioned rules.

Of course, if Courtney had continued to play it safe, the way she'd done the first twenty-five-and-a-half years of her life, she wouldn't have argued with Blaine. By the same token, she also would never have slept with him.

"I'm not seeing Blaine tonight." As she'd told him before leaving the office, she wasn't really mad over his accusations—after all he'd been looking out for her welfare. It was the giddy adrenaline rush she'd gotten with the idea he could be jealous over her that had her refusing his offer to go back to his place last night and staying in with Gail tonight.

"Then what man are you going out with?"

Wanting her mind off Blaine and on to a relaxing, stress-free evening, Courtney disappeared into the kitchen. She emerged a half minute later with her hands behind her back. "I have a date, just not with a man."

Gail's eyes went wide. "Do *not* tell me you're going out with a woman. Not that I have a problem with homosexuals, but you love men and that would be a hugely extreme step."

"I'm not going out with a woman. I'm staying home with one." She produced a bottle of Mojita mix and two glasses from behind her back. "We haven't had a Movie and Mojita night in months."

"*You* haven't had an M & M night in months. *I've* had plenty."

Shrugging, Courtney slid onto the couch. "Same difference.

The point is, tonight I'm staying home and having a great night in with you." She offered the glasses to Gail.

Instead of taking them so that Courtney could pour the mix in, the way they'd done numerous times before, Gail stood from the couch. "Did you ever consider *I* might have a date?"

Guilt washed over Courtney at the anger in her friend's voice. Maybe she had been placing Gail a little low on the priority list as of late, but that only made her determined to see tonight was extra fun. "On a Thursday"—Courtney sent Gail's routine shorts and T-shirt a teasingly snarky look—"and wearing *that*?"

"It was a last-minute thing," Gail said sternly, not batting a white-blond eyelash in the way of amusement. "Besides, I'm perfectly comfortable with my *average* self."

The doorbell rang before Courtney could remind her she'd pointed out the same thing just the other night. Gail's grin was pure Cheshire cat. "There he is now."

Feeling like a total heel, Courtney watched her go to the door, half expecting her to leave without a good-bye. Gail opened the door but didn't move through it, just stood there talking to someone Courtney could neither see nor hear from her position on the couch.

A couple minutes passed and the chatting came to an end. Gail closed the door, leaving whomever she'd been speaking with on the outside of the apartment and herself on the inside.

"Is your date invisible?" Courtney bit back the words the instant they left her mouth. Clearly, Gail wasn't in the mood for jokes.

"Hardy har. I don't really have a date, but you do have a package." Rejoining her on the couch, Gail dropped a small, inch-thick rush mail envelope into her lap.

Courtney picked the package up. The blank sender area had an eerie sense of déjà vu trickling along her spine. The last time she'd gotten an anonymous package, she nearly choked to death on the gift within. This one was probably nothing more than junk mail. Just to be safe, she gave the envelope an appreciative smile—all for Gail's sake—and then dropped it onto the end table at the foot of the couch.

She picked up the remote to page through movie rental channels. "Comedy or drama?"

"You aren't going to open it?"

"Sure. Later." When she was with Blaine, just in case she needed to put his Heimlich skills to use again. And, truthfully, she would like to see his reaction to her getting a gift from another man—if it even was a gift—to see if he might not be jealous after all. Over the box of chocolates, he hadn't seemed so, but time, talk, and sex had happened since then. "Right now, it's M & M time."

"Oh, c'mon!" Gail razzed, some of her anger giving way to curiosity. "I know you're dying to see what's inside. Go ahead and look."

"All right." If it would help to further ease Gail's irritation toward her, Courtney was prepared to do most anything—well, other than give up her sex life.

Setting aside the remote, she pulled back the envelope's flap far enough to look inside. That damned déjà vu reared its head again, this time settling heavy in her belly, much like the leaden way the liquor from the candies had settled on her tongue. "It's a spoon."

Gail frowned. "A spoon? Is it like a sampler promo piece?"

Not wanting to open it any farther, though not certain why, Courtney jiggled the package to get a better view. "It looks like the type I collect." She remembered the conversation she'd had with Blaine last night, about the spoon collection lining her office wall, and her unease lessened. The spoon had to be from him. It wasn't delivered in person, but it was a lasting gift.

What did that mean to him?

He'd called her sweetie twice last night, sounded incredibly sincere both times. It was still so hard to believe he could want more. But what if he did? And how could she find out for certain without jeopardizing the great thing they had going?

Gail, ever the voice of logic, intruded on her thoughts. "Why don't you take it out so you can tell for sure?"

"If it'll make you happy." Her thoughts far removed from the spoon, Courtney upended the envelope over her palm. The spoon fell onto her hand and then slipped down onto her lap. The flesh color was so opposed to the sterling silver she'd expected, her gaze zipped to the object lying suggestively between her thighs.

"Oh. My. God," Gail uttered as Courtney thought the same of the miniature penis-shaped spoon. Convex on one side, pink pea-sized testicles hung on either side of the fluted handle.

"You gave one of your fly-by lovers the apartment address?" Gail's voice was half accusation, half tremulous question.

Courtney couldn't stop her own apprehensive shiver. She wanted to fling the spoon across the room, then rush over and close the curtains, shutting out any potential prying eyes. But she knew doing so would raise her roommate's anxiety. "Of course not! You know I always leave when the guy's sleeping or otherwise engaged. My admirer must be from Pinnacle. If you have an employee ID, home addresses are easy to look up. Then there's the fact that I listed collector spoons on my Secret Santa list this past year and have a set of them hanging in my cubicle at work." All very valid points, which made her feel better. Made her appreciate the tasteless humor in the gift.

She pasted on an amused smile. "It's sort of funny. Original." Not Blaine's style. However, it was something Randy might appreciate. Randy, who had been at the office tonight. Randy, whom she'd smiled at and caressed the back of his hand, talked about taking pleasure with.

Courtney's unease resurged. Had Blaine been right about her casual touches being construed as more?

"It's disturbing." With a sidelong look at the spoon, Gail

pulled her feet up on the couch and hugged her knees to her chest. "I'm so glad the guy's coming to install the security system in the morning. At least that way I can feel a little better about leaving you alone this weekend."

"I'll be fine. If for some unlikely reason I get nervous, I'll have Blaine spend the night." Confident enough time had passed to not have it look like she was distressed by the penis spoon, she lifted it from her lap and set it on top of the envelope on the end table.

"You're still convinced he's not the one sending you stuff?"

Just as convinced as she was that he wouldn't be staying over while Gail was away. Two days alone together would be a good time to find out what he was after, but it was also liable to bring them closer. Even if he did want more and she did like the idea of him jealous, Courtney wasn't ready to forget her vow to enjoy herself and her vigorous sex drive, and return to her boring ways. She also wasn't ready to do what Candy was bound to suggest, and move on while things were still going good.

She'd sleep with Blaine again, find a way to decipher his desires toward her. After the weekend. And not at her house. "Neither the candy nor the spoon is his style. He told me as much."

Gail snorted. "Well, that's comforting. I know I trust a stalker to tell the truth."

"I'm not being stalked. I just have someone hot for my bod." If that guy was Randy, she couldn't come close to returning his interest, even if he wasn't married. But if that guy *was* Randy, she would know he was simply misguided and, more importantly, totally harmless.

Feeling almost as satisfied as she had last night, when Blaine photocopied her ass and that massive orgasm took her by surprise, she grabbed the remote and stabbed the TV on. "So what's it going to be, comedy or drama?"

6

Blaine had waited two days to confront Courtney, see how pissed she was at him for suggesting she led men on. His thought had been to give her breathing space, but in doing so he'd also given himself time to sit home alone at night. Yeah, he could've called up one of the guys, headed out to some bar, and shot the shit. Only, the bar scene had grown old long ago and he talked enough shit while working on construction sites.

Today it was too hot to work in the field, the mild weather he'd appreciated last week a thing of the past. Barely after eight A.M. and the temps were already in the high eighties, with the humidity making it feel closer to a hundred.

It was a day to be damned glad he lived in a modernized country and had the ability to work inside Pinnacle's air-conditioned office. A day he planned to start out by making amends with Courtney, so he could spend at least part of the night with her in his arms.

Forgoing his morning coffee, he stopped at his office long enough to set his laptop bag down and then headed for her first-floor cubicle. The cube was empty, but her computer was logged in, the monitor displaying a graphic design program.

"Looking for someone, stud muffin?" Candy asked with her usual feistiness.

Blaine turned to find her swiveled around in her chair, wearing an expression in complete contrast with her tone and cheery canary yellow sleeveless dress. She looked worried in a way he'd seen her only one other time—when Courtney had been choking in the lunchroom.

Her worry now and then could be unrelated. His gut tightened regardless, and he guessed, "Courtney got another gift."

Brown eyes narrowed, she searched his face. "What makes you so sure?"

The answer was as good as a yes. And a clear sign Candy thought he was responsible for sending Courtney an obviously disturbing present. "I didn't send the damned thing, whatever it is. But it's not hard to tell something's wrong when you're missing your 'you know you want to fuck me' look."

A hint of a smile played at Candy's lips. "I've never wanted to fuck you."

Yeah, and he'd never wanted to talk this frankly at the office, when anyone could overhear them. Concern for Courtney was making him stupid. "The feeling's mutual. What's going on with Courtney?"

Her smile vanished. Candy stood and crossed the hallway to Courtney's cube. Sliding onto the end of the wraparound desk, she said softly, "She got a package last night at her apartment. Then when she came into work this morning, there was a letter waiting in her interoffice folder. Admirer Man wants to rendezvous and live out their fantasies."

"She went to meet him?" Blaine snapped.

Candy grimaced. "Do you think you could say that a little louder? I'm not sure they heard you in Nairobi." Her scowl let up. "I get that you're worried but like I'd really let her go alone to meet with a guy who could be the prince of toads as easily as a serial killer. Not to mention, she's a helluva lot smarter than that."

With a nod of acknowledgment, he asked more quietly, "So where is she?"

"In the bathroom. She was pretty unnerved by the letter and needed a few minutes to regroup." The unease returned to Candy's face. "At first, I was all for this admirer thing, thought it was good for her ego. But it's seriously starting to worry me."

Her ego? From what he'd seen the past week, Courtney's self-esteem was plenty strong. Or maybe it wasn't, considering how she got huffy when he mentioned both her country girl roots and her spoon collection.

Before he could question Candy on it, Courtney appeared at the entrance to the cube. She didn't look shaken so much as peeved to find them talking about her.

She sent an accusing look Blaine's way. "Having a nice chat?"

Ignoring her irritation and his plans to make amends, he held out a hand. "Let me see the letter."

She pushed past him to pull out her chair and sit facing the computer. "It's harmless, so you can both get back to work."

"You didn't seem to think it was harmless ten minutes ago when you were shivering and swearing," Candy put in from where she remained perched on the end of the desk.

Courtney sent her a "thanks for nothing" look. " 'Oh, God' hardly qualifies as swearing." Her expression softened as she spun around in her chair. "Really, guys, I've had time to think it over and I realize it's nothing. A guy with a crush. I'll just ignore him and he'll go away."

Blaine stepped forward, hand still extended, and repeated himself, this time with an edge of demand. "Let me see the letter."

"It has nothing to do with you."

"I'm your superior. You received it on company grounds. It *has* something to do with me."

Courtney gave him a tight-lipped smile more effective than calling him an asshole. "Way to abuse the pecking order."

Leaning to the side, she stuffed her hand into the wastebasket under her desk and lifted out a crumpled sheet of paper. "Here."

He took the paper and uncrinkled it. The letter was typed on Pinnacle letterhead and someone—Courtney, presumably—had taken something sharp to it, leaving a dozen little holes behind.

Now was hardly the time for teasing. By the same note, he could guess she was tense as hell past the façade of calm. Meeting her gaze, he smiled. "I have a tendency to mutilate things that don't scare me, too."

She closed her eyes, opening them an instant later on a loud sigh. "I didn't deface it because I was scared. I just didn't want someone finding it and gossip starting up that I'm being pursued by a coworker."

Blaine brought his focus back to the letter. Considering it was on the firm's letterhead, the odds were favorable it was from someone who worked with them. After mentally sorting through the best candidates and placing Randy at the top of the list, he started to read.

"Speaking of gossip"—back to sassy, Candy's voice registered on the fringes of his awareness—"guess what I heard this morning? Apparently someone found a photocopy of a butt and some other very interesting body parts in the copy-machine tray yesterday. Tom's on the rampage to find out who's responsible."

"Oh, God," Courtney gasped. Then quickly tacked on a composed, "And that didn't qualify as swearing, either."

Another time, Blaine would have been torn between taunting her over the explicit scan neither of them had remembered to pick up following Randy's intrusion and hoping like hell the office manager wasn't able to pin down the guilty parties. Now, as he finished translating the letter past the holes and wrinkles, he was too concerned about Courtney's safety to care.

Frowning, he handed the letter back to her. "This doesn't

sound like a guy with a crush." It sounded like a man fixated on getting Courtney in his bed and then making her his, permanently. Blaine had potentially similar aspirations, but he wasn't sneaking around behind her back to make them known, or liable to take desperate means should she refute him.

Candy nodded. "That's what I said. The penis spoon was one thing but this—"

"Penis spoon?" Blaine interjected, for now letting himself off the hook with the reality he *was* sneaking around behind Courtney's back, trying to discover the depth of her no-strings feelings toward sex.

"Creepo sent her a penis-shaped collector spoon to her house last night."

Between the spoon and the letter, trepidation worked at his gut. He leveled his gaze back on Courtney, who reclined in her chair, fingers bridged loosely over her belly, looking as serene as if they spoke about the weather. "He knows where you live, and that doesn't disturb you?"

Her calm lessened with the narrowing of her eyebrows. "You two sound just like Gail."

"Who's Gail?" he asked.

"Her stuffy roommate," Candy supplied.

"Gail's not stuffy," Courtney said defensively. "She's just . . . average."

Blaine frowned at the way she made the word "average" sound caustic. Was she affronted by her roommate's run-of-the-mill behavior since she herself had transformed into a vamp who operated somewhat outside the norm? And how did her roommate feel about Courtney's retooled image?

They'd assumed the letter and the gifts had come from a man, but what was to say it wasn't a woman's handiwork? Courtney was liable to have Pinnacle letterhead at home, where her roommate could easily access it. "Gail's worried about you?"

"To put it mildly. She's scared to death some guy's going to take one night of sex for more than it is and come after me." Courtney dragged her lower lip between her teeth.

Blaine's thoughts strayed as he eyed her mouth. She often did that same thing when aroused. The action and the resulting stab of desire in his groin made certain he knew exactly how a guy could want more than a single night.

"Scared enough to try to get you to stop sleeping around?" he asked, forcing his mind back on what mattered and clearly doing a shitty job of it, by Courtney's glare.

"Nicely put, Casanova," Candy said dryly.

"Sorry. You know what I meant." Courtney's sedate look returned, and he tossed out his speculation. "Do you think Gail could be sending the gifts?"

Gripping the arms of the chair, she jerked up from her relaxed position. A silent death threat shot from her eyes. "Of course not! She's one of my best friends."

"You sure about that?" he pressed.

"Yes," Courtney bit out. "I'm sure about that." She kicked a heeled foot against the carpet, whirling her chair back around to face the computer. Placing her hands on the keyboard, she voiced a dismissive, "I need to get a job out."

"I think Blaine should spend the weekend with you," Candy suggested.

"*What?*" Courtney spun back around, panic making her blue-green eyes appear rounder than ever. "I don't need him to protect me. Gail's having a security system installed this morning."

Blaine considered the idea. Staying with Courtney this weekend could work twofold, by allowing him to see she remained safe and giving him the chance to get to know her better.

Aware he was liable to get farther with a sexual offer, he slid his gaze back to her mouth and smiled wickedly. "Sure you don't want me 'keeping you company'?"

Her throat worked, making the sexy little catching sound that guaranteed she wanted the kind of hands-on company he had in mind even if her eyes did still betray her nervousness over the idea. Then she opened her mouth and denied him. "Not this weekend."

"Okay, you'll stay with me," Candy said.

Courtney smiled gratefully. "No, I won't. I know you already have plans to go flying and do the devil only knows what else with Ty. I'm not about to intrude on things. Thank you both, really, but this isn't the huge deal you're making it out to be. I will be absolutely fine by myself."

Courtney was *not* fine.

Of all the freaking times for the lights to go out, it would have to be tonight—when Gail was out of town and the so-called high-tech security system that had been installed this morning disarmed the moment the power failed.

She should have allowed Blaine to stay over, her fears of getting too close and forgetting her vow be damned. Since she hadn't, she would have to be a big girl.

Sleeping with the sheets pulled over her head couldn't hurt anything either.

The breeze coming in through the bedroom screens was moist with humidity, but it was still better than the total suffocation by heat effect she felt beneath the sheet. Taking off her T-shirt and shorts was bound to help. But she felt a bit safer with them on, knowing she could slip out of the apartment, if the need arose, and not have to worry about nudity in the process.

With a grunt of disappointment over her cowardice, Courtney tossed the sheet back. The odds some guy would break in tonight were next to nil, particularly when she had enough candles burning in her bedroom to make it look like daylight inside and to step up the room's temperature by a good five degrees.

Disregarding her rapid heartbeat and the stickiness of her skin, she rolled onto her belly. She snuggled her arms into her pillow and closed her eyes, visualizing horses jumping over a fence, a device that had worked like magic to get her asleep fast as a kid.

Tonight, it wasn't working fast. Tonight, no matter how hard she tried, she couldn't completely escape the feeling someone was standing nearby, watching her.

Still, she counted on. One hundred horses. Two hundred horses. Number three hundred and seven was mid-vault when a grating noise came from the living room.

Her eyes snapped open. Nerves jumped to life, tensing her body and chasing a shiver down her spine. "Go away," she murmured into her pillow.

God, could she sound any meeker? Act any more pathetic?

The sound was probably nothing more than her imagination. Willing her body to relax, she reclosed her eyes. The unfamiliar noise came again, louder.

I'd much rather wake up to let you in, then be woken up by someone breaking in.

They were Gail's words from earlier in the week. At the time, Courtney had all but laughed them off. Thought her roommate was being paranoid. Now they rallied through her head, making her more anxious by the second and, at the same time, emerging Blaine's accusation that Gail could be trying to frighten her into stopping sleeping around. She'd thought the idea preposterous, had been ready to deck him over it. But then, the more she'd thought about it this afternoon and evening, the more she recognized how Gail's growing fears coincided with the number of guys Courtney slept with. Her friend had also been insistent that Courtney get a better look inside the envelope containing the penis spoon, like she already knew what lurked inside.

Still, it was probably ridiculous.

Only one way to find out . . .

With the hasty beat of her heart and a lone candle as her guide, she slipped from bed and padded barefoot through the bedroom door and down the hallway. One step into the living room confirmed her speculation that the grating sound had been her imagination at work. The apartment was deadly silent.

Make that silent as a tomb.

Better yet, she would forget the comparisons altogether because no matter what she thought of it had her nerves on end.

Courtney turned back for her bedroom. Two steps into the short trek, the front doorknob jiggled. She jerked to a halt. The air lodged in her throat, stifling her breathing almost as effectively as the nasty rosebud candy had.

Chocolates that were given by the psycho man attempting to break into her home.

Her heart stampeded against her ribs. She sucked in a deep gulp of air. Holy hell, what was she going to do if the flimsy lock didn't hold?

Every move she'd learned in the college self-defense course had suddenly gone AWOL from her memory. The pepper spray was in her purse, which she'd left on the table less than a foot from the front door. Totally useless. Pushing the screen out of one of her bedroom wind—

The lock *snicked* open, the tiny noise deafening.

Blood rushed between her ears, sounding like a freight train about to barrel her down.

Think, damnit!

She whipped her gaze around the living room, able to see very little clearly with the light of one lone candle and the faint glow coming down the hallway from her bedroom. Her eyes landed on Gail's pink free weights resting against the wall, and she nearly wept with relief. They weren't a guaranteed lifesaver, but they gave her hope.

After blowing out the candle in the hopes she could escape through the front door without the intruder noticing, she grabbed a five-pound weight in each hand and shrank against the wall.

The front door opened with a foreboding creak. Rustling sounded as someone moved inside. No, not someone. Her admirer. Her stalker.

Or maybe Gail.

Crap, she didn't want to make her whereabouts known, but she also didn't want to hurt her friend. For now, Courtney stayed where she was, with beads of sweat popping out all over her body and her fingernails digging into her palms with the force of her grip on the weights.

The intruder moved into the living room near silently. The candlelight bleeding from the bedroom was just bright enough that, when the person was almost to her, she could see the silhouette didn't belong to a woman.

Pinching her lips tight to quiet her overloud breathing, she lifted a dumbbell and prepared to wield it like her life was counting on it . . . because it was, probably. A second passed that seemed eternal. Then he was standing directly in front of her.

His arm came up. A whimper escaped her as a flashlight beamed to life. The guy turned, aiming the brilliant light directly at her face, exposing her. Blinding her.

Praying for mercy, she jerked her hand back, took aim—

"Courtney?" The light left her face to shine on the intruder's own.

"Blaine!" The weights thudded to the floor. "I almost dumbbelled you!"

"Sorry. I thought you might be asleep and didn't want to wake you."

"Like I'm going to sleep when my security system's shot and there's a guy out there waiting to make me his!"

Frowning, he stepped forward and attempted to take her into his arms. She sidestepped him to retreat to the well-lit sanctity of her bedroom.

She wanted to crawl back beneath the sheets and not emerge until daybreak, screw roasting to death. She settled on scooting against the headboard with her knees drawn up against her chest. "What are you doing breaking into my apartment!"

Blaine entered the bedroom. "I knew your security system would go down with the power outage and wanted to see how good your regular lock was—I picked it in less than a minute. Besides, I thought you weren't shaken by this guy?"

Courtney ran her hands over her forearms, shivering despite the oppressive humidity. "So did I." Considering those were her first words to him that weren't shouted, she'd done a damned good job of fooling herself.

Leaving the flashlight on top of her dresser near the door, he came to the edge of the bed and sank down on the mattress. Sympathy filled his eyes. "You have a right to be scared."

Did she also have a right to ask for his company after she'd already refused it? "Yeah, I guess, though it's probably for nothing." Uncurling from the sitting-up fetal position, she pasted on her best attempt at a seductive smile, given the situation, and raked her gaze along his body. "Your staying with me would probably be for nothing, too, but if you still want to, I promise to make it worth your while."

His sympathy gave way to a guilty look. "I won't sleep with a woman who's pissed at me."

"You scared me, but I'm not angry about it."

"I meant for what I said the other night, about your flirting giving men the wrong impression."

Her smile faded with her surprise. "I told you I wasn't mad."

"Yeah, and took off the second the proposal was bound and sealed."

Only because refusing the offer to go back to his place had been the safest route to her peace of mind. After the last heart-pounding minutes, her peace of mind could only focus on the here and now, and it begged for his touch. "How about if you hold me, the way you wanted to do out in the living room, and we call it even?"

Blaine didn't comment on the fact that the stakes weren't exactly equal. He just moved farther up the bed, lay down on his side, and took her into his arms.

Courtney sighed with the solidness of his front against her back. Already she felt safer and like she could nod off were she to close her eyes. She left her eyes open, savoring his strength and nearness enough to dismiss how like a furnace his body felt.

After a full minute of silence, where her heart got itself beating normally again, she asked, "Do you think Randy could be my admirer?"

His head moved, brushing his lips against the back of her neck in the process. "This morning I thought there was a good chance, but now I would say not likely." Warm breath tickled her nape. "He stopped by my office before leaving work to explain his odd behavior on Wednesday night. Apparently, he and his wife had some tension brewing for a while. It finally released as a hellish fight and he'd planned to crash at the office while the air cleared some, but then he came upon us and figured he didn't dare risk it."

She fought off the urge to wriggle with the continual caress of his breath in order to focus on the conversation. But that was hard to do when each of those breaths was doing a serious number on one of her most highly charged pleasure zones. "They've worked things out?"

"Yeah." The breath came again, followed by Blaine's rough palm moving beneath her T-shirt to rub along her belly. "The way he was smiling when he mentioned her name, I'd say you don't have to worry about any unwanted affection on his part."

His hand was moving in a completely nonsexual fashion, but it was just so hot. The room. The bed. His breath. Her.

Hot and arousing.

She couldn't deny the urge to wriggle a second longer.

Her heart back to beating fast, Courtney squirmed against him, letting free the moan that had been building from the second she came into his arms and he'd started talking. His knee-length, black canvas shorts did little to hide how quickly his cock responded to the carnal sound, going hard against the crease of her ass. Her memory of how shockingly good his finger felt pushing into her asshole surfaced, and her pussy went damp with anticipation.

For now, the physical danger was past. The danger that he could want more than sex was still very real. Since she'd asked him to stay the weekend, there were only two alternatives—spend the entire time screwing or sleeping. No time to talk meant no time to get closer.

Hoping the reassurance wasn't just an excuse to make her feel better for wanting him so badly, she reared back and pumped her hips. His erection ground against her butt and her sex throbbed hungrily. "You ready for me to make staying here tonight worth your while?"

"I was ready the second I left my house." The words growled out as a last fluttering of breath against her neck. Blaine had her turned in his arms in the next instant.

His mouth fused with hers, tongue rushing out to greet hers with urgent licks. She forgot her earlier fear, her worry over the weekend ahead, and thoughts of being taken from behind as the raw need to be taken any way at all, so long as it was soon, hurtled through her.

She kissed him back with reckless desire, pushed her hands between their bodies and yanked his sleeveless T-shirt up to get her palms on the hot skin of his hard-packed stomach.

Freeing her of her shorts and underwear, he lifted his mouth from hers to zero back in on her neck. Erotic sensation zinged downward with each of his feathering kisses, leaving her nipples rigid and her pussy liquid and sizzling in a way the sultry night could never replicate. His lips parted, his tongue teasing her flesh. She cried out with the shockwave tremors ignited in her core, then gasped in pure ecstasy when two big fingers pushed between her thighs to ride into her wet body.

Courtney closed her eyes and tipped back her head, giving his mouth easier access to slowly drive her out of her mind with pleasure while his fingers did the same. She was nearly there, shoving her tingling clit wantonly against his flicking thumb, sucking his pumping fingers deeper into her body with each clamp of her slick cunt, seconds away from screaming with the intensity of her climax.

Then she opened her eyes and saw the man staring back at her past the curtains billowing in with the breeze, and there was no seconds away about it. She screamed.

Blaine lifted from her neck, cockily teasing, "Gotta love that. Already screaming and we're not even to the good part." Either he caught on to the fear in her voice then, or it was evident in her expression, because the amusement drained from his face. He pulled his fingers from her body. "What's the matter, sweetie?"

Though it went incredibly against her vow to enjoy life as a no-strings sex diva for a year or so, she'd liked that endearment leaving his lips before. Now, she clung to it, clung to him as she lifted a shaking hand and pointed toward the window. "He's out there. Watching us."

7

Every ounce of desire drained from Blaine's body with Courtney's words and the stark terror in her face. He rolled off the bed and moved to the window she'd indicated. Between the dozen-plus candles and the light of the moon, he could see a decent-sized tree out the window, but nothing that remotely resembled a man. "I don't see anyone."

The softness of her breasts pressed against his back as her arms wrapped around his middle. "He's gone now," she said shakily. "But he was there."

No matter how good her arms felt, she was holding him out of fear, he reminded himself, not because she was ready to take things beyond sex. "Did you recognize him?"

"I couldn't see his face clearly. I could just make out the outline of his body."

He gave her hand a reassuring squeeze and then unhooked her arms from his waist to close the windows and curtains. When he turned around she was on the bed again, with her back to the headboard and her knees drawn up tight to her chest, the same way she'd been less than fifteen minutes before.

Truthfully, Blaine had wanted to scare her a bit with his uninvited entry, show her how easily it was for him or anyone else to get inside. Make her lose that unaffected air she'd held on to at the office today. He didn't want her like this, though, looking jumpy enough to chuck a free weight in the direction of the next unfamiliar noise.

Probably what Courtney had seen was nothing more than the tree appearing to look like a man when her mind was clouded with passion. To settle her nerves, and on the slim chance there really had been a guy watching them, he wasn't going to make her take his word for it.

Blaine started for the bedroom door, adjusting his softening cock as he went.

"Where are you going?" Her panicked voice came from behind him.

"I'm not leaving. I just want to see if he's still around."

"No! He could be dangerous."

Reaching the doorway, he grabbed the flashlight off the dresser and looked back at her. "Worried you won't get to wake up to my smiling face in the morning?" he asked jokingly, in an effort to ease some of her tension, and yet wanting to know the answer damned badly.

First surprise and then hesitation entered her eyes. She released her knees and crossed her arms over her stomach, looking awkward and uncertain about how to respond—the way she had a habit of doing around him. "You shouldn't be risking your life to see that mine is safe."

He also shouldn't be appreciating the way her bared sex peeked between her legs, when there could be a stalker hanging around her window, waiting for an opportune moment to come inside and make her his.

The severity of the thought, and the odds Blaine would be around if or when that moment came, had him focusing back on her face. "I spent over two and a half months in one of the more dangerous parts of Iraq and came back without a scratch. Besides, my brother taught me some techniques for taking down the enemy." A glance at the bedroom door determined it lockless. "Go in the bathroom and lock the door. Don't come out until I give the all clear."

Courtney stood from the bed to pull on her shorts, but then remained in place. "Maybe I overreacted and just imagined some guy out there. I don't normally spazz out like that, but with the power being out, Gail gone, and then that letter today . . . it was a little too much, I guess."

"Maybe it *was* your imagination. Or maybe he's out there waiting for me to leave so he can drag you off somewhere and have his way with you." Not words he wanted to speak, but the phrase "better safe than sorry" had never more applicable.

"All right. Just please be careful."

"Don't worry. You'll be waking up to my smiling face tomorrow morning." And most every day after that, going by how disturbed he was at the thought of some other guy laying a hand on her, and how concerned she looked for his well being now. Far more so than guilt for letting him put his safety on the line, or even their working relationship, should warrant.

Setting aside thoughts of a future with Courtney, Blaine saw her safely locked inside the bathroom, with a fat three-wick candle to illuminate the small space, and then turned the flashlight's beam on high and left the apartment.

A search of the area outside her bedroom found neither a man nor signs of there ever having been one in the flowerbed that lined the length of the windows. A thorough check of the hall and sunken-in doorways of the first and second floors and the stairwells connecting them revealed the building to be dark and quiet. He walked the fenced-in stretch of grass surrounding the multi-building complex for good measure. A few teenaged boys took advantage of the moonlight, playing a game of hoops in the courtyard, and a handful of other people were visiting on their porches. No one looked suspicious and definitely not like a Pinnacle employee.

Nearly certain it had been her imagination at play, Blaine returned to Courtney's apartment. The door was locked, the way he'd left it. Any lingering remnants of doubt vanished as he picked the lock a second time and opened the door to find silence within.

After relocking the door, he moved through the living room and down the hall to the bathroom. "Hey, it's me. I didn't see anyone out there."

She opened the door, looking both relieved to see him and nothing like the woman he'd left behind a short while ago.

She'd changed out of her shorts and T-shirt to a pale blue bathrobe. Tied loosely at the front, the exposed line of her cleavage had his mind and body right back to the highly aroused state they'd been in before she thought she saw someone.

Courtney lifted a wet washcloth from the sink basin. She brought it underneath the right edge of her robe, cleansing that side of her neck and the swell of her breast. Droplets of water remained in the washcloth's wake, glistening in the light of the candle resting on the sink basin. "Hopefully he figured out I'm already taken and won't be back."

Thoughts of running his tongue over her shimmering skin fled from Blaine's mind. He jerked his gaze to her face. Was she talking about him, or had Jake and Randy been right about her having some other guy lined up for in the long run? "You are?"

Her hand stilled in its journey to her left breast. "For tonight."

Relief sighed from between his lips. It was only him in the picture. "Make that for the weekend. I'm not leaving you here alone so long as the power's out. I heard on the radio on the drive over that all the AC units running in the city were too much for the system, and power probably won't be restored until Sunday."

She started back in on washing her right side. "Then I'll go to my parents' first thing in the morning. They only live an hour north."

"We can stop at my house on the way to get a change of clothes."

Courtney's hand stilled again, and she narrowed her eyes. "I said *I'll* go."

"I'm not letting you get behind the wheel as stressed as you are. Your parents would kill me if I let you do that and something ended up happening."

"Along with a whole bunch of other people," she admitted with an accepting frown. She smiled then, an openly naughty smile that had him eager to get back in her arms. "All right, you can go . . . if you make my agreeing worth the while."

Not about to give her time to change her mind, Blaine closed the distance between them and jerked the sash of her robe loose. Spinning her around, he pushed her up against the wall opposite the sink. The wall that was one huge mirror, probably done in an attempt to make the room appear bigger, though all he could see right now was the fun to be had with it. Her hands came out, stopping her descent a couple inches away from hitting the glass. She held herself there, with the sides of the robe parted and her bare tits and pussy on stunning display in the reflected flickering candlelight.

The look in her eyes was one he'd seen hundreds of times before. The slightly lash-lowered look that suggested her mind was spinning with dirty thoughts. Now there wasn't a doubt in his head—she was wishing for naughtiness and he was ready to deliver it.

Stepping to the side far enough that she could see his reflection past her own, he yanked his shorts and underwear off. Courtney's gaze slid to his mirror-image erection. He took his cock in hand, petting the solid flesh, feeling it throb a little harder with each pass of his tightly coiled fingers and the anticipation kindling higher in her eyes.

The scent of arousal lifted into the moist air. Making a show of sniffing it in, he commanded, "Step back a few inches and play with your cunt."

Breathing heavily, she did as he ordered, stepped back and traveled her fingers down her belly, between her legs, and into her pubic hair. Her eyes strayed from his handling of his dick to her own reflection. Hazy hot need brought her eyelids to half mast as she parted her labia with one hand and penetrated her opening with two fingers of the other.

With each pump of her fingers inside her body, mewling sighs slipped from between her lips. The sound of her pussy's hungry slurping soon accompanied them, filling up the small space and making him increase the stroking of his shaft.

Juices leaked out around her fingers, catching the candlelight as they trickled along the insides of her thighs. She released her labia to run her fingers through the silky trail. Meeting his gaze, she brought them to a rosy erect nipple. She coated the nipple with her cream, making the tip shiny red, and then pinched it between her fingers. "Ahhh . . . yeah. Good pain."

Pre-cum rushed out the tip of Blaine's dick. Balls gone snug, he yanked aside the robe to give her bare ass a gentle whack. "Such a tease. So hot. So mine."

Caution entered her eyes for a split second. Then it was only desire filling them as he grabbed her left hip in one hand and guided his cock to her perfectly rounded backside with the other. He teased her asshole with the weeping head, inching it inside the moist entrance just far enough to have her gasping and increasing the pump of her fingers inside her sex. Sucking in a gasp of his own, he pulled her fingers free of her body and filled her pussy up from behind.

Any way he took Courtney was an extraordinarily pleasurable experience he planned to repeat many times. But, like he told her that first night at his house, fucking a woman from behind while she was pressed up against the wall was as good as it got.

Only, this time it was even better.

The intensity of the rear-entry angle was still there. The helplessly sexy breathless wails still leaving her throat as he pumped into her wet passage. The mirror was a new and welcome addition, replicating their every move, showcasing the repeated push of his cock inside her pussy and the cream that gushed from her in eager response, giving an added edge of ecstasy that had him coming nearly as fast as she did, and twice as loudly.

"Blaine's not the type of man your father and I would have picked for you." Beverly Baxter stopped washing dishes to give Courtney an assessing look.

Courtney kept on drying the plate in her hand. She'd known it was only a matter of time before this conversation happened. The question was how effectively could she pull off a lie to her mother? It wasn't something she'd ever had a need to try.

Focusing on the dishes she'd dried and stacked on the two-story farmhouse's kitchen counter, she shrugged. "He's just a friend."

"We can see now how wrong of a choice we would have made."

"Really, Mom, he's *just* a friend."

"The kind of friend you give benefits?"

Courtney's gaze flew to her mother's. "Mom!" With her mother's incisive look, she let out a nervous laugh. "Where did you hear that?"

"Katie Hill hired on for the summer. If that girl's mother knew what a filthy mouth she has . . ." Shaking her head so the short, graying brown curls bounced, Beverly put her hands back in the dishwater. "Katie's still in her teens. You're not."

That made it okay, in her parents' eyes, for Courtney to sleep with her guy friends? Seriously doubtful. "I like him," she allowed. "I just don't know that I'm ready for anything serious. Besides, Blaine doesn't do relationships." Except she was beginning to think more and more that he did want to do one. The way he laid verbal claim to her last night seemed about more than sex. Like he really did want her to be his.

"He seemed to be 'doing' one fine with you at dinner," Beverly pointed out as she scrubbed at a bread pan.

Heat raced into Courtney's cheeks. She fought the urge to look away. Was her mother talking about the way Blaine had treated her from a conversational standpoint, or the way he'd slipped his foot between her thighs to tease her pussy? She'd thought the tablecloth had hid the toeing, or she would never have allowed it to continue.

Or, heck, maybe she would have.

Maybe the reason she'd given in so easily to his decision to join her on this trip to her parents', where she would be forced to act almost completely removed from Sex Diva Courtney, was because she wanted the exact same thing he did, and it was clouding her judgment. "I meant the committed kind."

"Any man who volunteers to do chores with your father is in it for the long haul."

"He didn't know what he was getting himself into," Courtney argued in vain, because she'd heard her father tell Blaine what the nightly work entailed—workers saw to the blueberry crop, but the animals still needed tending. Blaine couldn't have looked more thrilled about pulling up his figurative sleeves and getting to it.

Lifting aside the white and blue curtains, Beverly nodded at the window over the sink. "Look at them out there. It's hard to tell which one's having a better time."

The way Courtney's belly tightened said she was going to

regret the move even before she leaned over and looked out the window. Her father sat perched on a fence railing, grinning from one big ear to the other while he instructed Blaine on the evening feeding routine for the handful of riding horses and beef cattle.

Crap. They were bonding. And her sex-diva days were as good as gone.

As appealing as she found Blaine on a normal day at the office, in his jeans and a casual shirt, he looked so much sexier with hay sticking to his clothes and his dark, breeze-ruffled hair. His plain white T-shirt was smudged with the dust kicking up in the air from the recent lack of rain, the cotton molded to the mouthwatering muscles of his biceps, chest, and torso with perspiration from heavy lifting.

He looked like an extremely well-put-together farmhand.

Obviously, despite her best attempts, Courtney hadn't left the country girl of her past behind. Looking at him out there, acting so happy to be indulging in something so simple and uncultured, she'd never appreciated or wanted a guy so badly in her life.

"Your father's going to want to keep him around after this."

Yeah, and it appeared Boring Courtney was going to be making a comeback, too, because her father wasn't the only one.

Blaine aimed the beam of his flashlight Courtney's way. A contented smile stayed on her lips as they walked between seemingly endless rows of short, fat blueberry bushes en route to what she'd called "something great he needed to see outside of the house." Considering she'd waited until her parents were in bed to show it to him, he could guess that "something" involved their naked, intertwined bodies.

He wasn't about to turn down an offer of sex. At the same time, just sharing a stroll in the moonlit countryside, when the day's humidity was mostly past and there weren't a million city lights to ruin the overhead view, was damned nice.

Even better was the way Courtney's personality changed the moment they stepped foot on the farm.

She'd still attacked her mother's homemade bread with gusto and happy little moans and sighs. Still maintained the intelligence he consistently witnessed at the office. And she still sent him naughty glances when her parents weren't looking. But she was also softer here, more natural like the Courtney of a few months ago, the one who didn't feel the need to make the entire male population lust after her by wearing a tiny skirt and cleavage-baring top.

The laid-back version of Courtney that walked beside him now made him believe her no-strings stance on relationships was as insubstantial as her vow she'd left the country behind. This version made him think he had incredibly good odds of getting her to agree there was more going on between them than sex.

Smiling with the thought, Blaine noted, "You're really in your element here."

She glanced over at him. For a few silent seconds, she did that awkward hesitation thing and he expected a defensive reply on her part. In the end, she hung on to her smile, admitting, "I'd be lying if I said I missed the killer heels."

"Then why wear them?"

Coming to a stop, she shone the beam from her flashlight down at her legs, bared from the cuffs of her jean shorts to her ankle socks and work boots. "They make my legs look great."

He gave her long legs a lingering look, appreciating the muscle tone that suggested she wasn't one to remain idle for long. He let out a low whistle. "I've got news for you, sweetie. They look great without the spikes."

Either Courtney had grown used to the endearment slipping out of his mouth, or she chose to ignore it. Whatever the case, her unpainted lips curved higher in an irresistibly sensual smile. She let out a throaty laugh. "First a plain white bra and now leather work boots do it for you, huh?"

"I like the boots." Letting his own voice go low and rough, he stepped toward her. The moon appeared brighter out here than it had last night, when he'd been searching outside her apartment for uninvited guests. He was close enough he could read her features without the aid of the flashlight. See how anxious she was for his touch.

Blaine was just as anxious to get her back in his arms, clothed or otherwise. Thursday night had been damned quiet and lonely without her around. Still, he hadn't realized how much he'd truly missed her as a person until he was with her again last night, finally getting to sleep with her in his arms and wake up to find she was still there, warm as hell in the muggy morning heat and yet so completely appreciated.

Ready for some skin-to-skin appreciation, he flicked off the light and bent to glide a hand along her silky smooth inner thigh. "I like your bare legs even more."

"Know what I like?"

Courtney was on him before he had a chance to consider a response, flinging her body up against his and knocking him on his ass in the middle of the blueberry patch. The flashlight slipped from his hand as he came up on his elbows. Hers joined it, the light still on and illuminating the three-foot-wide strip of grass that had been their walking path.

Playfulness glinted in her eyes as she crawled over him, stopping with her thighs pressed intimately around his. "My bare legs wrapped around your bare body."

She pushed at his chest, trying to get him off his elbows and back to lying down in the path the rest of the way. Eager to see if her relaxed behavior would come through from a physical standpoint, he let her have her way, lying back and crossing his arms casually beneath his head. "Lots of stars out tonight."

She scooted down to his mid-thigh and popped the button of his shorts. "Lotta material between us."

The zipper hissed down. She pushed her hand into his underwear and grabbed hold of his shaft. Blaine's cock went from mostly flaccid to incredibly hard in less than fifteen seconds and five strokes. With her face averted from the moonlight, he couldn't make out much, but Courtney's elated smile would be hard to miss.

"Ah, there he is." She bent toward his groin.

His stomach tightened in preparation for feeling her lips wrap around his shaft—the one place her mouth had yet to journey. Instead she pushed her hands against the ground and bounded to her feet. She moved artlessly, with no thought to teasing or building up his want, no thought to playing the vamp. Just hastily unhooking her shorts and pulling them and her panties down her legs and past her work boots.

From his horizontal position, he did the same with his shorts and underwear. She came back over him with an approving murmur, resettling her upper thighs against his, bringing the mouth of her damp sex tight to the head of his own. Her breathing kicked up as she grabbed hold of his biceps and started to slide onto his erection.

Blaine caught her sides in his hands, stilling her descent. He recognized her candid behavior, but did she? Did she get how much easier going she seemed this way? How much he approved?

"What, I don't get a finger-fuck or ice cube show this time?" he teased, hoping to snap her into realization.

Courtney shook her head. "I don't have the patience after you spent all dinner toeing me." She contracted her feminine muscles around the inch of cock she'd managed to get inside before he stopped her progression. "Gotta get this fella in me right now."

Grinning over the slang talk, he raised his eyebrows. "Gotta? Fella?"

The constricting of her sex let up with the stiffening of her body. "There's a reason I don't come back here as much as I used to." Defensiveness rang in her voice. "This place has a way of bringing out the redneck of my youth."

"Judging by the rock-hard dick of my present, I don't have a single problem with that." Since he knew she needed more than verbal convincing, he let her sides go.

She slipped down his shaft in time with the upward shifting of his hips, and all the tension drained from her body on a sigh. "Oh, yeah. Better already."

"Here comes your better." Holding her close, Blaine flipped their positions so that she was lying on her back in the grass.

Moonlight lit up her face once more, revealing every little shift in her expression, every little excited flick of her tongue over her lips; the fevered way she snapped her eyes closed and parted her lips on a ragged cry as he took her ankles in his hands and brought them up on his shoulders.

Her breath panted out, her fingers digging into the grass as he planted his knees in the ground and sank deeper inside her, pushed his cock to the depths of her pussy, where she was burning hot and liquid with her want for him.

Trusting her to keep her legs in place, he released her ankles. He slipped his palms beneath her butt, spreading her soft cheeks and tilting her pelvis, taking her deeper yet, harder. Faster. Claiming her. Telling her with actions what she wasn't quite ready to hear with words. Holding on to his own blistering climax until she cried out with the strength of hers.

And then he let go, filling her with his cum as hers flooded around his cock with such force it had him revaluating his theory that taking a woman up against the wall was as good as it got. With Courtney, every way he took her was simply the best.

Her ankles slipped off his shoulders and her legs came to rest on his extended arms. The erratic sound of her breathing and the fact that she had yet to open her eyes suggested she didn't quite have the strength to lift her legs away. He wasn't feeling any too strong himself after that mutual orgasm, but he managed to free his hands from under her butt, leaving her legs to slide intimately down around his hips.

"Told you there was something great to see out here," she said lazily, blissfully.

Trapped as she was beneath him, Blaine could respond any way he wanted, in words or actions, and she would be powerless to escape. With her eyes closed and her expression unguarded, what he wanted was to kiss her. An easy, tender kiss like they'd never before shared.

Placing his palms on the grass to brace his weight, he bent his head to hers and brushed her lips softly. Once. Twice. Nibbled gently at the corners. Her mouth opened a fraction on a contented sigh, and he slipped his tongue inside, just tasting, just savoring. Just loving until his body again warmed with arousal.

He lifted his head as stimulation arrowed to his groin. They were past the point where he wanted her to think everything between them was about sex, and so it wouldn't do to have her again so soon.

It would do to hold her. To lie joined together under the stars, with the illusion they were as isolated from the bulk of humanity as he'd been while working abroad. The difference was then he'd been anxious for the trip to end. With Courtney, he never wanted their time together to end.

Before the silence could get to her and make her uneasy, Blaine sat back, disconnecting their bodies but leaving enough of his weight on her thighs to keep her in place. Her eyes remained closed, her face serene. His gut told him her calm was about to evaporate. "Do you seriously avoid seeing your parents for fear of how it might affect you? They're simple folk, sure, but they also have their priorities straight. That's not something to be taken for granted."

"What are your parents like?" Her eyes opened, but the serenity didn't leave, at least not completely the way he'd anticipated.

She also hadn't responded to his question.

Hell, maybe she didn't know the answer. Maybe it was going to take a leap of faith and one damned big shove on his part to get her to see things clearly. "Average. In their sixties and still working forty-plus hours a week in the hopes of saving enough money to eventually retire. That's one of the reasons I'd planned to not take relationships seriously for a few more years. I wanted to have a nice chunk of change in savings, whether for a run of bad luck or to roll over into a retirement fund, before I settled down and had to rely on my paycheck taking care of more than just me."

Hesitation entered her eyes. But then, so did curiosity. "You've changed your mind about—"

"Courtney?" a familiar male voice called from somewhere to their far right. "That you, honey?"

Curiosity turned to dread as Courtney hissed out, "Dad!" Her hands flew to Blaine's chest and pushed hard.

He didn't budge, just smiled down at her wide-eyed panicked look. "Afraid he's going to catch us and demand that I make you an honest woman by marrying you?"

"Yes! Now get off me."

He came to his feet slowly, only giving up his hold on her body because she might never get over it if her dad caught her in the buff.

She scurried to her knees and crawled the few feet to her shorts and underwear. Jerking them on without standing, she glared. "Don't just stand there. Hide!"

Laughing, he tugged on his clothes. "Right."

"I'm not joking." She came to her feet to give his arm a shove. "Jump over the bushes and flatten yourself to the ground. Dad will never see you."

He frowned, but again didn't budge. It seemed she needed a lesson in reality as much as she did in being comfortable with her average heritage. "You're almost twenty-seven. Don't you think that's old enough for your parents to accept you have a sex life?"

"No," Courtney snapped, her glare back in place. "You might get that they prefer life without a lot of fuss, but you have no idea how old-fashioned they are." The glare conceded to suspicion. "How do you know how old I am?"

"From Pinnacle's newsletter, and I think I do know how conservative they are. What I don't think is that they expect you to be a carbon copy of them."

"Courtney?" her dad called again, close enough they could see his dark form moving up the end of their blueberry row.

"Right here," she yelled back. "I'm . . . taking advantage of the cooler air and moonlight by picking berries." She sent Blaine a distressed sidelong look. "You're not going to hide, are you?"

He shook his head. "Sorry, sweetie. You've proven to me what a big girl you are plenty of times. It's time you prove it to your parents, as well."

"I should never have let you toe me at dinner tonight," she bit through her teeth as she grabbed their discarded flashlights from the ground and handed him the unlit one. "You would think since I had that would be proof enough."

Before Blaine could respond, Rick Baxter's relieved face and nearly bald head came into view. "Came downstairs to take my medicine and saw a light out here. Thought the neighbor kids were up to their tomfoolery again." Rick flicked the beam of his flashlight on Courtney's hands and then turned it on

Blaine's. Sending the light back on Courtney, he frowned. "Where's your picking buckets?"

She looked at Blaine accusingly. "I asked him to bring them."

Blaine almost smiled at the bite in her tone. She hadn't been able to get rid of him so she planned to make him look the bad guy, probably in the hopes her dad wouldn't want his help with chores tomorrow. Not a chance Blaine was sitting them out—he liked her parents and he loved the fresh country air and good honest work.

Playing the scapegoat, he gave Rick a rueful look. "I didn't see any sitting around, so I figured my shirt would do."

Rick tskked. "Good way to crush the berries."

"I'll run up and get a couple buckets from the shed," Courtney offered too brightly.

"Keep an eye out for roots," her dad said. "Snagged my foot on one a couple weeks ago and damn near broke my ankle."

Blaine watched her take off at a run with the beam of her flashlight guiding the way. The moonlight accentuated the curve of her ass, calling out each delectable bounce as she traveled back to the shed. Probably not something he should be checking out with her dad standing right next to him, but like he'd told Courtney, they were adults. Besides, he didn't have any intention of letting her image be tarnished in her parents' minds.

"You don't think I buy that berry-picking excuse?" Rick asked astutely, making it easy to see where Courtney picked up that particular trait.

Smiling, Blaine looked back at him. "Nope."

"So you plan on marrying her, then?"

"Yes, sir, I do."

8

Courtney sighed in relief when Blaine pulled into her apartment complex, and she spotted Gail's black Taurus. This weekend with Blaine had been great, as both an eye opener and a retreat from the harsh reality that she still had a stalker to deal with at home. But now she was ready to get away from Blaine, consider what he hadn't said the other night in the blueberry patch. Why it was he no longer planned to avoid relationships. And if she was really ready to give up her sex-diva ways and settle into a life of boring normalcy.

Or maybe a future with him wouldn't be boring, considering how eager he seemed to be to let her dad in on her little secret that she was screwing his makeshift weekend farmhand with no care to what might happen between them tomorrow.

Only, if she didn't care, why had she gotten so upset with Blaine over his behavior and then so easily let it slide the moment her dad returned inside the house?

Too many questions. All of which required getting away from him.

Blaine pulled his truck into a parking spot next to her car.

Before he could cut the engine, she pointed out her friend's vehicle. "Gail's home, so you don't need to stick around."

"I can still stay. Keep guard over your bedroom windows."

A shiver pushed through Courtney with the reminder of her potential Friday-night peeper. Allowing Blaine to stay over again would be beneficial to her peace of mind, but, no, she had to stay firm on this. "Thanks, but I couldn't let you do that. You already gave up too much of your time for me."

"It was all my pleasure." A suggestive grin tugged at his lips with the wiggling of his eyebrows.

She wanted to melt into that grin. Wanted to lean across the truck's center console and kiss that too-sexy look right off his face. She curbed the urge by opening the truck door, dropping down onto the cement, and grabbing her overnight bag from behind the seat. He got out of the truck and came around to take the bag from her. Figuring she wouldn't get far by suggesting she could find her own way inside, she fell into step beside him on the sidewalk.

When they'd cleared the main building entrance and her door was in sight, giving her an easy out if needed, Courtney broached the subject she'd been avoiding the last eighteen hours. The topic that had to be the reason for the joyous looks both her father and mother had spent this morning giving her. "You never told me what you and Dad talked about while I went to get the blueberry buckets last night."

Blaine shrugged. "Man stuff."

Coming to a stop in front of her door, she narrowed her eyes. "Sports, beer, and porn? You, I buy that of. Dad, not the porn part at least."

Humor warmed his navy blue eyes with his laughter. Within seconds the amusement vanished, replaced with a sobriety that had her on instant edge.

Setting her bag down against the wall near the door, he admitted, "He said what you thought he would."

The breath caught in her throat, making her feel like another revolting liquor-filled chocolate was stuck in her esophagus. This scenario wasn't revolting, but it also couldn't be serious.

Could it?

"He asked if you plan to marry me?" she managed to get out in a semi-calm voice. Blaine nodded, and she swallowed down a hard gulp. "What did you say?"

"Yes."

"You did *not*!" He nodded again, and she focused every ounce of panic into her fist as she punched his shoulder.

While his biceps were scrumptious to look at it and touch, the hard muscle hurt like hell ramming into her knuckles. Retracting her stinging hand, she glared. "You idiot. Now what am I supposed to do when he finds out you were kidding? God, you said you knew how old-fashioned my parents are. Obviously, you don't."

"What makes you so sure I was kidding?"

The apartment door opened in time with the mad crashing of her heart against her chest. Gail stepped out into the hallway, a welcoming smile on her face. "I'm so glad to—" She stopped short, the smile disappearing as she looked from Courtney to Blaine then back at Courtney. "I'm interrupting something."

"Nah," Blaine responded, his voice steady, his relaxed expression making it seem he was oblivious to Courtney's anxiety. "I was about to take off. I'm sure you need a while to do your girl-talk thing." He looked over at Courtney and did the unthinkable at a time when her world was already in a crazy spin, by grabbing hold of her and kissing her.

She did something even worse, by taking his little lip brush and making it into so much more with the flick of her tongue into his mouth. His hands came around to caress along her spine. So good, so strong, so steady. Savoring his familiar taste and the heady heat suffusing her, she moved against him, sank into his hard body, and ground her pelvis against his.

"So you were leaving?" Gail asked impatiently.

With a last panty-wetting stroke of his tongue, Blaine lifted his hands from Courtney's back. His mouth left hers, and he moved back a couple feet. "Not so sure I want to anymore, but, yeah, I am." He gave Courtney a huge grin. "See you tomorrow."

Courtney watched him walk down the hallway and disappear out the main entry door. She wanted to run after him, both to drop him to the ground so she could get him naked and ease the burning wet hunger that kiss surfaced in her sex and to demand an answer as to whether he was teasing about marrying her.

"I take it you two had a good weekend?" Gail asked dryly.

Courtney grabbed her overnight bag from the floor and moved inside the apartment. "We went to my parents' place," she admitted in a not quite steady voice.

Behind her, Gail's breath dragged in audibly. "You did *not*!"

"Actually, we did."

"Why?"

Considering how much to tell Gail, Courtney took her bag into her bedroom and dropped it on the foot of the bed. She returned to the living room where her friend stood with her hands on her hips. "We lost power Friday night. It was too hot to stand it here, so I told him I was going to my parents', and he invited himself along."

Skepticism filled Gail's green eyes. "And you—Miss 'I'm not looking for anything normal or serious, I'm just having fun'—let him go?"

"Yep." She sucked in a breath. "And he just said he wants to marry me."

"*What?*"

"Maybe he didn't." Maybe he'd posed the question simply to get a rise out of her. Though, honestly, that hadn't seemed the case. It seemed he really did want to take that monstrously huge step away from a no-strings affair.

Needing a drink of something strong, Courtney started for the kitchen. "Blaine told my dad he was going to marry me after Dad more or less caught us having sex. So I told him he was an idiot to kid that way, and he asked what made me so sure he was kidding."

Gail followed fast on her heels. "What does your inner slut have to say about this?"

Courtney jerked to a halt midway into the kitchen. She turned around to consider the look on her friend's face. Amused? Or maybe snarky? "I'm not a slut," she bit out.

Gail put her hands in the air, palm side out. "Chill, Court. I was just teasing."

"Were you? Or does it disturb you that I enjoy sex without strings?"

"It doesn't bother me if it makes you happy. It just concerns me that you could get hurt. Though, that's probably not even a consideration anymore, since you're marrying Blaine."

There was definite relief in Gail's eyes as she spoke those words. Was it possible that Blaine had been right about her friend being the one to send Courtney the gifts?

Forgetting the drink, she returned to the living room. She sank down onto the familiar comfort of the couch and reached for the remote on the end table. "I'm not marrying him. I don't even think I'm going to see him again outside of work. I miss the bar scene, the excitement of getting naked with a different guy every few nights."

"Oh." Displeasure rang in Gail's voice. "Whatever does it for you, I guess." She went to the small table next to the door and picked up a thick yellow envelope. "This came for you over the weekend." Crossing to the couch, she tossed it on the cushion next to Courtney. "I'm going to run to the store for groceries. The power stayed out long enough to wage a major assault on the refrigerator."

Courtney's belly turned as she took in the package lying a

few inches from her hip. The sender area was blank, which made the odds favorable it was another gift from her admirer. Or Gail. It was almost too convenient how her roommate remembered the envelope right after Courtney spoke words that displeased her.

If Gail was the one to blame, Courtney wanted to find out fast so that she could focus her stress entirely on her dealings with Blaine. The contents of the package weren't liable to reveal any more of the sender's identity than its outside. Accompanying her friend on the drive to the store, however, would give her time to ask questions that Gail wouldn't be able to walk away from.

Forcing a smile, Courtney stood. "Let me grab my purse and I'll go with you."

"No," Gail retorted. Returning Courtney's smile, she added calmly, "You just got home. Stay. Unpack. Relax for once."

Relax by opening the package when she was alone, stressed, and primed to freak out? She would let Gail go by herself, but Courtney wasn't opening the gift. "Okay." She reached into her purse and pulled out a couple twenties from her billfold. "Get something good for dinner. After eating Mom's amazing cooking the last couple days, my body expects the best."

Gail left and Courtney went into her bedroom to unpack. Only, thanks to the package in the other room, she was too tense to concentrate on something as mundane as putting her stuff away. Knowing it was probably a pointless move in the early afternoon, when the sun was shining bright and people were milling about everywhere, she returned to the living room and turned on the electronic lock system.

Then she tried to go back to her bedroom to gather clothes for the wash. But the thick yellow envelope on the couch entered her line of sight, halting her in her tracks, beckoning her to come over, to open it.

To scare the shit out of herself.

She was being pathetic again, Courtney acknowledged, particularly given that she was locked inside her apartment. Whatever was in the package couldn't be that bad.

Summoning her courage, she went to the couch and sat down, poked at the package. It didn't make any noise. Of course, a decapitated cat folded up into a mailing envelope wouldn't make any sound, now would it?

Yeah, okay, so the chances were next to nil that some guy, or Gail, would send her a murdered cat as a token of affection, or otherwise. It was probably just another harmless spoon surrounded by a lot of thick padding.

Her nerves semi-eased, she lifted the package onto her lap and pulled at the glued flap. The flap lifted. She caught sight of the envelope's contents, and froze as she realized she'd been wrong about the contents not revealing the sender's identity; as she accepted how naïve she'd been, believing she would recognize a psycho man if she saw one. If she'd slept with one.

Oh. My. God.

Ohmygod.

Mr. Hot Buns, Craig Dooley, was her stalker. No way.

But yes, way, it was all right there in living color, just as Gail had predicted it would be when she scolded Courtney for making the videotape in the first place.

Heart pounding and feeling like total crap for nearly accusing her friend of trying to scare her away from sex, Courtney pulled the black VHS tape out of the package. The tape had no label, but it had to be a copy of the one she'd sent to Craig. Feeling paper on the tape's backside, she turned it over to find a note attached and quickly scanned it.

DITCH THE JERK. WE HAVE MOVIES TO MAKE, AND I PROMISE THE SECOND TIME AROUND WILL BE EVEN BETTER THAN THE FIRST.

Tension mounted as a tight knot formed in her stomach. She swallowed back the bile attempting to rise in her throat. There was no typed "or else" associated with the order to ditch Blaine, but the implication was there and strong. The truth of her feelings for Blaine was there, too, as she accepted how desolate she would feel if something happened to him.

Blaine grabbed his ringing walkie-talkie phone from the cup holder built into the truck's center console. Courtney's name came up on caller ID, and he hit the TALK button. "Hell—"

"I need you." The words quavered through the line.

His grip on the phone increased with the quickening of his pulse. Forgetting about reaching his house, which loomed less than a mile ahead, he turned right into the next driveway and backed out again. "I'm on my way."

"Another package came to the apartment over the weekend," she said unnecessarily, because the fear in her voice went well beyond the anxiety she'd shown over his mention of marriage and told him exactly what was wrong. "It's a note."

"He sent you a note before and you didn't sound this worried."

"It's not the note." She hesitated, taking an audibly long, deep breath before adding, "He sent something else with it."

"What?"

"I'll tell you when you get here. Just hurry."

The line went dead, and Blaine tossed the phone to the driver's seat. At least, that was the intent. The concern eating at his gut must have been channeled into the throw, because the phone crashed against the passenger door and ricocheted onto the floor panel, landing with a crunch.

Fuck the phone. It was a work model he could swap for a new one tomorrow if needed. Courtney wasn't replaceable.

Pressing the gas pedal down as far as he dared, he sped back to her apartment. He threw the truck into park next to her car, yanked the keys from the ignition, and hurried inside the building. Relief slid through him when he reached her door and found the security system engaged.

"Courtney," he yelled through the door. "It's Blaine."

The system made a beeping noise. She opened the door a few seconds later to reveal her eyes weighted with fear. Hugging her arms around herself, she stepped back to let him inside.

He wanted to hold her close and reassure her they would catch the bastard behind her unwelcome gifts. But she wore the same hands-off look she had Friday night, right after she almost attacked him with a free weight. "You okay?"

"I'm not worried about me," she said in a low voice.

Then who was she worried about? He surveyed the apartment, finding it oddly quiet. "Where's Gail?"

"Grocery shopping. Nothing in the refrigerator survived the power outage." Disgust crossed her face. "She remembered about the package and gave it to me right before she left."

Blaine felt his own disgust as understanding sank in. Damnit, he'd known her so-called friend was up to no good. Not about to make Courtney feel any worse by playing the "I told you so" game, he murmured, "Mmm . . ."

Scowling, she uncrossed her arms and moved to the couch. "Gail's not the one sending me gifts, so quit with the freaking ridicule." She lifted a padded yellow envelope off the cushion, and her irritation turned to unease. "I know who *is* sending them."

A rush of hopeful anxiety pushed through him. As much as the motive was there, he would prefer Gail not be the bad person here. He would prefer even more to get whomever *was* the bad person out of Courtney's life, so they could focus on their future. "How?"

She pulled a videotape out of the envelope and waved it at him. "This."

He frowned at the tape. "What is it?"

"A videotape."

"No shit. What's on it?" The need for answers had his voice coming out unintentionally harsh.

Her eyes narrowed, but then let up with her unsteady, "I am."

"And?" he prompted more calmly.

"A guy." She looked away before adding, "Doing stuff."

"Doing—Oh." Blaine looked at the tape in her hand again, torn between aversion to think it held footage of her and some other guy fucking, and happiness to know she was embarrassed to tell him about it. The vamp she'd acted around him so much as a week ago would never have looked away. "You said there was a note?"

Gratitude he hadn't asked more about the tape filled her gaze as she turned over the videotape to reveal a piece of paper taped to its backside. "He wants me to stop seeing you. Or non-dating you. Or whatever it is we're doing."

She tossed him the tape, and he read the note. Short, simple, and potentially dangerous. Looking back at Courtney, he gave her a reassuring smile. "He's shit out of luck, because I'm not going anywhere." He realized how authoritative that sounded, and tacked on, "Unless you want to be with this guy."

"God, no. He was a one-night deal. I ran into him at a club a couple weeks ago again, but it was nothing more than casual flirting." She pulled her lower lip between her teeth, sucking on it a few seconds as she considered what she'd said. Guilt entered her eyes and she freed her lip. "To me it was casual flirting, but maybe you were right about the guys on the receiving end taking it as more. Maybe I accidentally led him on and now you get to pay the price."

There was a very good chance she'd done precisely that. Pointing fingers wasn't going to help and no one would be paying any price.

Feeling like acid had overtaken his stomach, Blaine glanced at the videotape. "I need to watch this."

"*What?*" Courtney's eyes went wide. She hugged her arms back around her. "No. It should never have been made. I'm just going to trash it."

"You're not trashing it. There's an alleged threat against me in this note. If that threat happens to be real, then you're at risk as well. If I see the tape," he reasoned, both for her benefit and to ease his own loathing of the idea, "I might be able to get a better sense if this guy is really a concern."

"And if he is, then what? I don't even know where he lives. I threw away his address right after I sent him the stupid tape against Gail's order not to do so."

"You know his name, right?"

"Yeah."

"If we find something to make the police suspect he's a threat, then his name and a mugshot off this tape is all you'll need to file a restraining order." She ran her hands over her upper arms, looking almost convinced and incredibly miserable. It was enough to eradicate the turmoil of his stomach, to accept that the guy on the videotape meant nothing to her and that Blaine must mean a whole lot, for her to continue to be so uncomfortable.

With a reassuring smile, he risked her hands-off look by going to her and holding her as close as her crossed arms would allow. "We both know I wasn't exactly a saint in the past either. But the past is the past, and my feelings for you aren't going to change because I watch a sex tape you made with some random guy before we became involved."

Courtney tried to find a smile past her nausea—that Blaine admitted to having feelings for her had her coming darned close to one. But in the end, the thought of sitting beside him while he watched her screw some other guy was too much to allow her to even force a smile.

Accepting that, just as action had gotten her into this unwanted scenario, only action would get her out of it, she nodded. "All right. We can watch it in my room. I don't want Gail coming home and seeing it."

Taking the videotape from him, she trudged down the hallway to her bedroom. The irony of the situation wasn't lost on her as she slid the tape into the dual DVD/VHS unit on the stand beneath her television. If the movie was of anyone else and she was alone in her bedroom with Blaine, she wouldn't be feeling anxiety, but wet with anticipation. As it was, she couldn't bring herself to look at him as she hit the PLAY button and stepped back a handful of feet to stand awkwardly beside the bed.

In the version of the tape she'd sent to Craig, the movie started out slowly, with them teasing each other with subtle caresses and dirty words while they slowly undressed. In the version playing on her television, the movie cut right to the heart of the matter, with her climbing onto the bed wearing nothing but a tiny red thong and a supremely naughty smile.

She climbed over Craig's lower legs, taking his naked thighs in hand as she demanded, "Spread your legs. I want every inch of you on tape."

He parted his thighs, exposing his stiff cock and snug balls. With a murmur of approval, she moved up his body, shimmying her hips and dragging her pussy along his hard thigh.

Licking her lips, she took his meaty shaft between her fingers and stroked. "I'm going to fuck you like you've never been fucked before, and you're just going to lay there and take it."

"Dominance suits you." Blaine's voice broke through the fog of denial Courtney had built around her in the hopes of convincing herself he wasn't really in the room.

She groaned. "Please don't talk. It's bad enough as it is."

"It's not so bad. I mean so far it's been pretty run of the mill—" He stopped short as the Courtney on screen dipped down to take the head of Craig's dick between her lips. Her tongue swiped at the weeping hole at the tip, and she let out an eager moan.

"Hey, how come he got a blow job on the first date? I've never gotten one," Blaine said in a voice that suggested he would be pouting if she had the balls to look over at him.

But she didn't have balls; she was a total chicken shit. Only, at the moment she did have balls, in her mouth on the television screen. Wincing, she closed her eyes and wished for the freaking tape to end. "That is so *not* funny, and we don't date."

The tape played on for long excruciating hours. Technically, it was more like minutes, but it felt like she stood stiff as stone for hours, with her eyes closed, and listened to the sound of herself moaning and sighing and coming for a man she didn't know a thing about.

Finally, Blaine said, "You can turn it off. The guy never even shows his face."

Courtney's eyes snapped open with what had to be an inaccurate observation on his part. "Of course he does. I made sure the angle of the camera was focused on his face when he was going down on—" Heat rushed up her neck and into her cheeks with the realization of what she'd almost said. Daring to glance at Blaine and, thankfully, finding him neither aroused-looking nor appalled, she waved the words away. "Never mind. The point is his face should be in the movie."

But, as she forced herself to watch another excruciating five minutes of the film, Craig's face never came into view. The camera remained focused on her alone. "Something isn't right."

Blaine went to the TV. Crouching down, he hit the DVD/VCR's "Pause" button, and then knocked a finger against the television screen. "See this pattern."

All she could see was that he'd stopped the movie so that her naked ass was front and center on the screen, and that the portion of Craig's condom-covered dick not currently inside her body was visible between the vee of her thighs. She forced herself to forget about the images and draw closer to the TV, to focus on what Blaine was pointing out: a faint mesh pattern covering everything on the screen. "What is it?"

"I'd guess the screen of an open window." He looked back at her, sympathy filling his eyes. "This wasn't a solo shoot. Someone else taped you."

The nausea she'd only begun to move past returned full force, cramping her belly with the reality of how long someone had been following her, stalking her.

Blaine turned off the television and came to his feet. "You do realize this puts Gail back in the suspect ring?"

"It's not her!" Courtney's tension sounded in her voice. "Yes, I'll admit that she might like the idea of me not sleeping around, but she would *not* follow me to a hotel and videotape me doing some guy. For one thing, I was using *her* camera that night." Argh! She wanted to scream. To find Gail's free weights and use them to de-nut whomever the idiot was stalking her.

She settled on balling her hands into fists and growling. "Why is this happening to me? If anyone should be going through this, it's Candy. She's slept with and flirted with way more guys than I've ever even met."

"She does flirt, but she doesn't touch a guy unless she wants him. She's never laid a hand on me, or anyone else at the office that I'm aware of."

"Oh." Apparently, that supremely important tidbit of info had been left out of her vixen training.

Blaine flicked his attention to the bed. "Get on the bed."

She glared at him. So much for believing he wasn't aroused. "I don't want sex."

"Me either." Going to the bed, he lay down fully clothed and opened his arms.

All the pent up breath whooshed out of her with the understanding it was comfort he offered. She was starting to make a habit out of finding comfort with him, something that had to go severely against her working the whole feminine power thing. But, hell, she'd already blown the whole sex-diva thing to smithereens, so why not?

Courtney climbed onto the bed and into his arms. As always, his warm, hard body pressing against hers felt so strong, so steady. Like exactly what she needed at this moment.

She gave a contented sigh, and tipped back her head to nip a kiss at the corner of his mouth. "Thanks for coming back."

Smiling down at her, he brushed her lips feather light. "We'll say you owe me a future blow job and call it even."

Though she would have sworn she didn't have it in her, a laugh bubbled out. "Deal."

"Or you could marry me. Something like that has to be a deterrent to a stalker."

Her momentary humor died as the breath left her. Back to the marriage talk, and this time there was no denying his seriousness. There was also no denying that she was tempted, damned tempted to say yes and spend the rest of her life in a certain dullsville. "We said no strings. We haven't even gone out on a date. Not only is my sex drive going to start petering out any day now, but I'm going to get really boring really fast the second I settle down."

"Like your parents?"

"Yes!" Blaine gave her a disappointed look, and she amended, "No." Only, that "no" was a lie, and they both knew it. "Okay, yes, but that doesn't mean I don't love them or dislike spending time with them."

"Life's what you make it, sweetie. It's the simple, average, boring things that make it worthwhile. Spend a couple months in a third-world country and you'll figure that one out pretty quickly. And, for the record, most women don't even reach their peak sex drive until their late thirties. After that, if you know what works for you and you have a guy eager to deliver, you have nothing to worry about in the orgasm department."

He kissed her again, this time not feather light, but a hard, commanding kiss that demanded she part her lips and let him inside.

She did so gladly, let his tongue move into her mouth and stroke hers to needy, anxious life. Let his hands move over her body, down her back to cup her ass through her shorts. Let him rock his growing erection against her mound until she was clinging to his T-shirt, rocking right back, writhing against him in an attempt to extinguish the fierce ache in her pussy.

Blaine lifted his mouth away. His hands and the contact of his body left hers as well, and he eyed her soberly. "You have that guy eager to deliver, Courtney." His mouth curved in a wickedly sexy grin. "You don't have to say yes today, but that means you still owe me the blow job."

The yes she wasn't quite ready for. The blow job she couldn't get started on fast enough.

Placing a hand on his chest, she shoved him onto his back, and moved down his body. "Lift up your butt," she ordered after undoing his jean shorts.

"Yes, ma'am."

He lifted up his hips, and she tugged the shorts and underwear down his legs, freeing those awesomely developed thighs. She stroked the long, lean muscles, and then his blood-reddened balls. After turning her tongue on the sensitive sac, she licked her way up thc bulging vein at the underside of his cock.

Silky fluid rushed out to greet her tongue as she flicked it across the tip of his shaft. She dabbed at the pre-cum, savoring his unique salty taste, and then wrapped her lips around his solid sex and worked them down its length.

Blaine groaned. His hands came into her hair, tugging at the strands, tipping her face upward as she sucked him deep. Raw ecstasy gleamed in his dark eyes. "If you're really worried about boring me, all you have to do is this once a week for the rest of our lives, and I'll be one damned happy man."

Courtney finished off her beer and set the empty bottle on the semidarkened nightclub's table. Blaine had stayed at her apartment the last four nights, seeing to her safety while alternately making her laugh and delivering her to pleasure. Tonight, she asked that he stay at his house so she could spend girl time with Gail. After getting Courtney's promise she would activate the electronic lock system the moment she got home from work, he'd agreed.

The system wasn't going to protect her in the noisy downtown Grand Rapids club. But she could hardly stay home after mentioning how long it had been since they went out dancing to Gail, and her friend shocked her by suggesting they do so tonight.

The last hour, tossing back beers and the occasional shot in between sweating their asses off and giggling like schoolgirls on the crowded dance floor, had been a blast. Whatever happened between her and Blaine, beginning tonight Thursdays were reserved for either going out with Gail, or staying in for an M & M night.

Standing from her stool, Courtney smoothed the short red silk dress along her thighs and asked loudly, "Ready to dance?"

Gail shook her head and shouted back, "I'm ready to go."

"After an hour?" What the heck happened to her having a good time?

Gail came around the table. Her once styled white-blond hair hung limp around her shoulders from their time on the dance floor and her green eyes lacked all trace of the mirth evident only five minutes ago. "I had fun. But I'm tired and starting to feel drunk."

"That's why we took a cab here. So we could get drunk and act stupid." That Courtney had barely thought about her safety the last hour was an added bonus she didn't want to end.

"I'm just not into it anymore, Court. Sorry."

Well, damn. Courtney really did *not* want to leave either her happy little buzz or this exuberant setting behind. Gail would never relax if she stayed here alone, though. Yeah, Courtney had been to plenty of clubs the last few months on her own, but in each case she'd led Gail to believe she was either meeting up with Candy or another friend from the office.

Tonight, she was out of luck.

Courtney forced a smile. "That's okay. I'm feeling pretty drunk, too. Let's go."

With a thankful nod, Gail started for the door. Courtney worked her way through the boisterous crowd behind her, unable to stop her jealousy of those around them, laughing and dancing and having a great time. She'd had a great time a lot lately, thanks to Blaine. Still, she wanted to know she could have fun without him. Not because she had plans to say no to his proposal, but because with each passing day she was more certain she would say yes.

They were almost to the entrance when a hand wrapped around Courtney's arm and a male voice shouted, "Hey, beautiful. Leaving so soon?"

With the blaring music, the speaker's identity wasn't clear and her stomach tightened with the idea it could be Craig. He might not be her stalker, but she still didn't want to see him.

Courtney turned around slowly, breathing a sigh of relief when she spotted Jake Markham and a handful of guys she didn't recognize. She gave his fingers, which still rested on her arm, a friendly rub. "Jake. Hi. It's great to see you!" She remembered then that she wasn't supposed to be touching him. Probably acting positively thrilled to see him wasn't a wise thing either.

She smiled elatedly anyway with the realization her excuse to not leave the feel-good atmosphere of the club had arrived. "My roommate wants to go home," she yelled loud enough Gail was certain to hear.

Gail appeared beside her. "Your roommate *is* going home," she snapped before tugging Courtney aside. "What about Blaine?"

Courtney frowned. "What about him?"

"You think he'd approve of you staying here, playing with these guys?"

Playing? Was that supposed to be some kind of symbol for sleeping with them? Like Gail thought she'd turned into such a slut that she would screw some other guy—make that guys—her first night away from Blaine.

Maybe if she didn't have liquor cruising through her system, Courtney could have looked past the accusation. Right now, it pissed her off to no end. "I told you the other night I'm not marrying him. I've kept on sleeping with him for the sake of my safety."

Gail narrowed her eyes. "He cares about you and you pay him back by stringing him along? God, I really *don't* know you anymore."

No, it appeared that she really didn't to believe Courtney's lie.

Frustration seething through her, Courtney faked a seductive smile. "I care about staying here and hooking up with Jake. Don't wait up. Or expect me home at all tonight."

Not waiting for Gail's response, Courtney returned to the spot where her roommate had pulled her away from Jake and his friends. Disappointment hit her when she found the spot had been overtaken by another group of guys. She waded through the crowd to the edge of the dance floor, where she could see a portion of the club clearly.

Grinning, Jake waved at her from a table a couple dozen feet away. She grinned back and started over. Leaning down, she placed a hand on his shoulder and spoke into his ear to avoid shouting. "Looks like I have no one to party with. Mind if I join you?"

He pulled out the chair beside him. "You bet."

Jake was just finishing introducing her to his friends when a female server arrived with a round of drinks in huge steins. The clear amber color of the drinks made them look like beer but they smelled like something far more potent.

Courtney leaned over to speak into Jake's ear again as he took a drink. "What is that?"

He set the stein down. "A Bellringer. They're known for curing whatever ails you."

With the way Gail's accusation continued to eat at her, the drink sounded like exactly what she needed to get this night back on the fun side. She smiled. "In that case, I'll take two."

Humor shone in Jake's gray eyes, but he cautioned, "If you've been drinking something else, I wouldn't mix."

"Hey, I'm fine. Feeling really good as a matter of fact." Deciding to test the waters before jumping in headfirst, she reached for his drink. "You don't mind if I try it, right?" He shook his head, and she used both hands to lift the heavy stein and take a long, thirst-quenching drink.

There was definitely liquor in the drink—she could feel it scorching down the back of her throat—but there was also a surprisingly light lime twist. She took another drink, enjoying the continued slow burn. "This is really good."

Jake's grin returned. He slid his gaze the length of her. "You look really good."

Laughing, though she wasn't all that sure why—maybe just

because it felt nice—she took another long drink. Heat balled delightfully in her belly and warmed her cheeks as she set the stein down. "Wanna dance?"

"Definitely."

Excitement shot through Courtney as she grabbed his hand and pulled him toward the dance floor. It was so rare to find a guy who actually liked to dance. Maybe Blaine did. She hadn't yet gotten around to asking him. Making a mental note to ask him tomorrow, she glanced back at Jake. He nodded toward the dance floor and mouthed something incomprehensible. She turned back around in time to deduce he was trying to warn her about the blond-ponytailed server weaving her way through the crowed with a tray of drinks balanced on her palm.

As it was, Courtney saw the woman a heartbeat before she slammed into her. The blonde's eyes went wide. Glasses and bottles wobbled on the tray. All righted themselves but a lone martini glass, which tipped over the tray's edge and splattered its contents onto the front of Courtney's dress.

The server bent for the martini glass. Glaring at Courtney, she stood and mouthed, "Pay attention, drunk bitch."

Typically, Courtney would feel bad about the situation and apologize. Right now, all she could see was the blonde's doe-in-the-headlight look replaying in her mind and feel the sticky liquor seeping through the thin silk of her dress to her skin.

The whole scenario was just plain funny. And sort of foggy.

With a raucous laugh, she tugged harder on Jake's hand until they were out on the dance floor, surrounded by dozens of moving bodies. The crowed pressed in around them, forcing them against each other and into the blaring rhythm of rock music.

Courtney's happiness at running into him tonight grew with each passing second and the discovery he was a great dancer. Flashing white lights started up on the dance floor with the next song, lighting up his eyes and playing off the angles of his face, making his cheeks appear leaner, sexier somehow.

His wife was a lucky lady.

Not only did he move well and look great, but his body felt good rubbing against hers. Not as good as Blaine's, of course, but considering there was two of Jake wavering before her eyes, it was like his potency was doubled.

He bent his head, and his lips brushed the skin beneath her ear. "Your roommate expect you home anytime soon?"

Shivering with the swipe of his mouth against her sweet spot, she brought her own mouth to his ear. "Nope. I'm all yours."

Tomorrow, she would face reality, figure out what to do about Gail, and if she was really ready to be Mrs. Blaine Daly. Tonight, she was going to have some innocent fun with a friend and dance the night away.

9

"Morning, stud muffin," Candy said when Blaine stepped into the hallway between her and Courtney's cubicles.

As had been the case when he came upon her last Friday morning, she was seated in her office chair, striking in a miniscule white and gold sundress and matching heeled sandals, but with the expected feistiness missing from her tone and expression. And too, like last Friday, Courtney was missing from her cube.

His gut clenched as he turned back toward Candy. "Where's Courtney?"

Worry edged into her eyes. "I was hoping with you." She stood from her chair to join him at the cube's entryway, divulging in a hushed voice, "She didn't come to work."

"She didn't call in?"

"No. I checked with the front desk. No one's answering at the apartment either, and her cell goes straight to voicemail."

"Shit." The clenching of Blaine's gut spread outward. He brought his fisted fingers to his sides to keep from taking his rising concern out on the cube's thin partition wall.

Candy stuck her blond head out into the hallway, glancing in both directions before again meeting his gaze. Fear pulled her brightly painted red lips into a frown and vibrated in her voice as she asked, "You think Creepo took her?"

"Christ, don't even talk that way. I'm sure she's fine. She had a girl's night in with her roommate last night. They probably drank too much and overslept as a side effect." It was barely after nine, which only made her an hour late. Unless she had a meeting or a proposal going out this morning, she probably wouldn't even think coming in late would be noticed.

"I can't see Courtney doing that," Candy disagreed. "She takes her work too seriously."

"Fuck. I know." Blaine pulled in a deep breath. He let it out slowly in an attempt to decrease the furious beat of his heart, because he knew too well that if Courtney was going to be even twenty minutes late, she would call in. "I'll check out her place. Just . . . stay here and let me know if she shows up."

Candy smiled encouragingly, but it didn't come close to combating the anxiety in her eyes. "I'm sure she'll show any minute. When she does, I'll kick her ass for worrying us."

Hoping she was right, but with the roiling in his gut suggesting otherwise, he returned to his office to grab his keys and then headed for the main entrance.

Blaine stopped at the front desk, ready to grill Sherry on the whereabouts of every Pinnacle employee. Since that first note had come on company letterhead it still stood to reason a coworker was behind Courtney's gifts. The admin held up her first finger, letting him know she wasn't going to help him right away. Nearly a full minute passed, while he struggled to keep his temper and concern inside, before she smiled up at him. "Morning, Blaine. What do you need?"

"Anyone call in sick today, or just not bother to show up?"

Sherry inclined her red head at the clipboard resting on the raised front of her desk. "Check the sign-out sheet. I haven't had a chance to look at it yet this morning."

He grabbed the clipboard and scanned the paper attached. No one he'd seen show even a slight interest in Courtney was out today, but then the sign-out sheet only covered the in-office personnel. That left several dozen field guys, and no good way of checking up on them outside of dropping by the construction sites.

With a "thanks" to Sherry and a burning in his gut over the reality of how long conducting a staff inventory could take, Blaine hurried out to his truck and exited the parking lot en route to Courtney's apartment.

He was almost to the apartment when the walkie-talkie part of his phone chirped. One of the field supervisors came over the speaker. "Blaine, you there?"

Hell, he didn't feel like talking business right now. But then, he could make this call work in his favor, by finding out who was working the site today. Grabbing the phone from the center console cup holder, he pushed the TALK button. "I'm here. Over."

"Have you heard from Markham? He didn't show up at the site this morning. Thought maybe he had his days confused and came into the office. Over."

Blaine's attention jerked from the road to the phone. His heart slammed against his ribs as he stared at the cell.

Jake? *He* was Courtney's stalker?

Nah, he couldn't be. The field guy had barely been married a year . . . and gave Courtney inappropriate looks every chance he got. He'd seen Courtney touch Jake several times the last couple weeks alone. She flirted with him openly. Then there was the fact that Jake had been the one to suggest Blaine stay away from Courtney, because she already had a guy lined up for the long run. Randy had agreed, but Jake could easily have planted the information in his head.

Christ, it was Jake.

Or maybe not. He couldn't crucify the guy without proof.

The urge was damned strong to chuck his phone against the passenger door a second time. Since he'd just gotten this one Monday, in replacement of his old one, Blaine disregarded the urge and answered the guy on the other end of the line. "I didn't see him, but I wasn't in the office very long. Let me check with Sherry and get back to you. Over."

"Morning, beautiful."

Courtney opened her eyes at the familiar male voice, and brilliant daylight slammed into her pupils. She winced as ache speared through her head. Sitting up, she scrubbed the heel of her hands at her eyes.

"My head feels like—" The identity of the voice's owner sank in, stopping her short and sending her pulse into a mad dash.

She jerked her hands away from her eyes. Jake stood feet away, his naked upper half outlined by the sunshine pouring in through the windows a short distance behind him and his gaze fixed in the vicinity of her breasts.

Her bare breasts, Courtney realized with a downward glance.

Resisting the urge to squeak, she grabbed the sheets pooled around her waist and dragged them up and around her chest.

What the heck had she done last night?

She couldn't remember. Not beyond Gail acting like she believed her a faithless slut, and then joining Jake and his friends for drinks. Really strong drinks that had her laughing over something she would normally feel badly about. Drinks that had her on the dance floor, rubbing up against some other woman's husband. Drinks that had her acting precisely like a faithless slut who didn't care one iota about Blaine.

Oh, crap.

Giving her spinning mind a chance to slow, she glanced

around what looked to be a one-room cabin. A rustic bedframe fashioned of birch logs held the mattress beneath her. Matching log chairs and a round, birchwood table occupied one corner of the room; a doorless pantry filled with food and a small refrigerator nearby. A well-worn couch sat facing a fireplace with a low-burning fire a handful of feet from the bed.

Another time, the homey setting would have appealed to the country roots she hadn't quite managed to move past. Now, she wanted out of there fast.

Wherever *there* was. "Where are we?"

Grinning, Jake sank down on the edge of the bed. "My home away from home." His attention fell to her lap. "I helped you out of your dress since it was sticky from the martini, but I didn't take off your panties. You tried to get me to, but I want you alert and eager once I have you naked. I've waited too long for everything not to be perfect."

In other words, they hadn't had sex. Yet.

"Waited too long for what?" she asked, hoping she was mistaken about his implication.

"To live out our desires."

A sick feeling curled in Courtney's stomach that she couldn't disregard as a hangover no matter how much she wanted. Jake was the one who'd been sending her gifts. The one whose mind she was always on. And last night she'd done about everything in her power to prove she wanted him just as badly.

She wasn't afraid for her life the way she thought she would be if she ever came up against her gift giver. But she also wasn't comfortable sitting a foot away, with him leering and her nude, aside from a tiny pair of panties and a thin sheet. "It probably seemed differently last night, but I don't have any desires that include you."

He gave a dry laugh. "Yeah, right. You've been touching me and sending fuck-me eyes my way at least once a day for months now. Last night just made it clear you're ready for me to quit with the secret admirer routine and make a move."

"But you're married."

The smile fell from his lips. "Not for much longer. Doreen turned into a frigid bitch less than a month after we said 'I do.' " His eyes warmed again, and he reached out a hand to stroke her leg though the sheet. "She doesn't know the first thing about passion. Not like you do."

Courtney fought the desire to recoil. He really was a nice guy and, normally, she wouldn't feel disgusted by such an innocent touch. Right now, with that whole "naked and a foot away from a half-dressed man who wanted to fuck her" scenario happening, she was a little icked out.

Reminding herself that it was her own fault, that Jake was primarily an accidental bystander swept along first in her sex-diva game and then her drunken stupidity show, she gave him a sympathetic smile. "I like you. But not the way you think. I'm sorry if I made you believe otherwise. I led you on when all I was trying to do was have a little fun and see that those around me had more fun, too."

He stiffened visibly as his smile again left. "Is this about Blaine?"

"No."

"Good, because the guy's a jerk. He might pretend like he'll be there in the long run, but his reputation tells the truth. He'll never be happy with one woman."

A couple weeks ago, Courtney had thought the same thing. She hadn't even wanted to try to hold Blaine for longer than a few nights of sex. Now, she knew better. Now, she hoped like hell her behavior and coming home with Jake last night hadn't managed to get back to the office and destroy her chances of a future with Blaine. "The thing is, Jake, that you have no idea who Blaine really is. Just like you don't know me."

Cold fury entered his eyes. Fury that had him balling his fists at his sides, and her biting her tongue with the realization she might be wise to fear for her life, after all.

Wherever Jake had taken Courtney, it was probable he used his company truck. Blaine still had no concrete proof that Jake *had* taken Courtney, but both of them were missing and, thanks to the GPS tracking units installed in all of Pinnacle's fleet vehicles, he had a good chance of locating them.

Fifteen minutes later, with the aid of a support operator from the GPS dealer, who made him jump through a dozen fucking hoops before accepting he was who he said and in need of verifying one of his subordinate's whereabouts, Blaine had a fix on their location.

Setting the tracking unit in his own truck to the coordinates, he followed them out of the city toward the Lake Michigan shoreline. A hundred different gut-roiling scenarios on what Jake could be doing to Courtney had crossed his mind by the time he pulled down what looked like a deserted dirt drive surrounded by thick woods.

A half mile in, the drive ended and a cabin emerged with smoke puffing out its chimney despite the humid morning. A small measure of relief sailed through Blaine at the sight of the white Pinnacle Engineering truck in front of the building.

He turned off his truck a few hundred feet from the cabin, where trees still camouflaged the drive. Sucking in deep breaths in an attempt to slow his heart rate, he got out of the truck and edged the perimeter of the trees until they ended thirty feet from the cabin.

He never thought he'd find a use for the commando-style workout his brother made him endure at least once every time Jamie was back in the States. It came in useful now, as Blaine dropped to the ground and low-crawled along the grass to the cabin's front wall.

Sweat beading on his forehead, he came to his knees and rose up to peer inside a window. His heart stilled for an instant, then knocked hard against his ribs with the sight of Jake sitting shirtless at a kitchen table. Courtney sat across from him, wearing Jake's missing shirt and, from the looks of things, nothing else.

Disgust and betrayal slammed Blaine in the gut.

She didn't appear like she was being held against her will. She appeared like she was back to playing the role of vamp, nearly naked and fresh from the fucking.

Only, hell, he had no way of knowing that. She wasn't exactly smiling; she just didn't look scared. But she also hadn't looked scared last week when she'd gotten the suggestive letter, and time showed him she'd been plenty afraid.

There was only one to find out for certain what was going on inside that cabin. Since his mind wasn't functioning well enough to think of a better option, he took the caveman approach and crashed into the front door, sending it slamming back against the wall and bringing both Courtney's and Jake's stunned gazes zipping to his face.

The shock left Jake's expression, and he let out a derisive snort. "Just a regular white knight, eh, Daly?"

Blaine ignored the comment to look at Courtney, to see the happiness shining in her blue-green eyes.

Elation filled him with the reality she wouldn't be smiling at him that way if she was pleased to be here alone with Jake. Revulsion to think Jake might have hurt her took over then, sending Blaine across the room in a heartbeat. Grabbing the field guy's arm, he wrenched it behind his back and jerked him to his feet.

Wrapping his other arm around Jake's neck, he vowed in a deadly voice, "If you touched her, I'll kill you."

Courtney shot to her feet, the happiness drained from her face. "No! It's okay, Blaine. *We're* okay."

He glared at the shirt all but hanging off one of her shoulders and barely covering her crotch. Maybe she wasn't so pleased to see him. "That why you're wearing his clothes?"

She narrowed her gaze. "It's not like that. We were getting ready to drive back to Grand Rapids, and the only other thing I have to wear is sticky and smells like liquor."

"Why?" he demanded, applying more pressure against Jake's throat.

"It doesn't matter. He didn't touch me or hurt me or anything." Guilt settled over her face and into her voice. "It was a misunderstanding. I led him on with my touching and flirting, a lot like you said I would."

Jake nodded his head as much as Blaine's hold on him would allow, and squeaked out something unintelligible.

"You're sure?" Blaine pressed.

"I'm sure." Courtney pulled her lower lip between her teeth. "Please don't hurt him."

Fuck, he *did* want to hurt Jake, even if the guy hadn't harmed Courtney. But he couldn't do it. Couldn't even hold on to his anger when she was sucking at her lip that way. The familiarity of the move was a balm to his frayed nerves and ego. Still, he asked, "Not even a little bit?"

"Blaine!"

"Fine." He freed Jake, giving him a lethal look before shoving him toward the door. This might be his cabin, but right now he wasn't welcome in it. "Get the hell out of here."

Choking out a cough, Jake halted at the door. He rubbed his throat as he scowled at first Blaine and then Courtney. "I thought she wanted to come here. I thought she wanted—Shit, never mind. I don't know what the hell women want. I probably never will."

Courtney saw the fury return to Jake's eyes before he left the cabin. Earlier, it had scared her. Now, she got that he was pissed at the female population as a whole, and that her actions last night and then this morning telling him he didn't know a thing about her hadn't helped matters.

Blaine gave her an assessing look. "You're really okay with him walking away, after all that he put you through?"

Pissed, Jake might be, but considering he'd neither taken advantage of her eager drunken state nor turned his anger on her, he was no threat to anyone's safety. "Most everything that's happened has been my fault."

"You forced him into videotaping you screwing some other guy?"

"That was pure coincidence, and something he did before he got the wrong idea I was interested in him. He happened to be at the same hotel club I was that night." The same one they'd been at last night, but the less Blaine knew the better. "When he left, he saw me getting it on through the open window of one of the first-floor hotel rooms." She smiled at him knowingly. "Like you wouldn't have stopped to watch the show."

"I wouldn't have videotaped it," he said without a trace of humor. "That doesn't explain the rest of the stuff. The phallic spoon. Hovering outside your bedroom windows. The notes."

"He thought I'd get a kick out of the spoon, which I actually did, once I got over my initial panic. And he wasn't outside my window that night; he has a sound alibi. As for that last note, he never meant it to be threatening. He just didn't think you were the type to make a commitment and was trying to convince me to stop seeing you so I didn't end up getting hurt. Throwing in the videotape was his way of showing me he knew I liked sex beyond the basic vanilla and was ready to take part in whatever I wanted."

"Hell, you make him sound like a saint." A hint of a smile curved his lips, but she couldn't tell if it was amused or sarcastic.

"He's not, obviously. Heck, he was ready to cheat on his wife for me—they're separated but married all the same. He never meant to come across as a stalker though. Like I said, this whole thing was mostly my fault. Working with Jake after this is going to be seriously strange, but he doesn't deserve to suffer for my inappropriate behavior."

Blaine's gaze weighed heavily on her face, seeming to search for some unknown answer. She held her breath as the seconds ticked past and his stare continued. Finally, the hard look let up.

This time when his lips curved it was into a full-fledged, sexy-as-sin smile. "So does this mean no more Sex-diva Courtney at the office?"

Tension sagged out of her with the teasing in his voice. Eagerly, she returned his smile. "At least not to the extent she was coming out the last few months. I like the clothes, but the killer shoes and too-friendly touches and looks have to go."

Sensual heat entered his eyes, darkening them to midnight as he slid his gaze down her body, to where the tails of Jake's shirt ended just south of her crotch. "I don't know. I kind of have a thing for your too-friendly touches."

Unlike with Jake, Courtney didn't fight with revulsion at the thought of Blaine touching her. Her pussy went liquid with the desire for him to get his hands on her ASAP.

He reached out a hand, and she shivered with expectation. He never made contact, just opened his hand and offered it to her. "Ready to go home? To *our* house."

She hadn't set out to fall permanently into the arms of one guy so soon—vowed to do precisely the opposite—but his invitation sounded incredible. Before she could take him up on it, she needed to get a hold of Gail and Candy and let them know she was okay. Let Gail know that she was forgiven for her harsh words last night and apologize for lying to her in return. "I really need t—"

"You don't have to be a vamp twenty-four/seven for the rest of your life to be interesting, Courtney." His hand fell to his side. He closed the distance between them, pulling her into his arms and brushing her mouth with a hungry kiss. "I love the natural you that came out at your parents' place just as much as the siren who likes to taunt me by rubbing ice cubes against her pussy. By the way, your parents are expecting us for dinner on Sunday to celebrate our engagement."

Between the intensity of his kiss, words of love, and more marriage talk, her mind was back to spinning. Still, she managed to feign a frown. "That's low, Blaine, using my parents' happiness as a crutch."

Grinning, he moved his hands beneath the back of her shirt and squeezed her butt. "Hey, whatever it takes, sweetie. I'm willing to stop at the first office store we pass and enlist the aid of their copy machine, too."

Carnal warmth surged through her, spiking her nipples, with the reminder of the copy machine heating up her aroused body and sending her soaring into orgasm. Boring times couldn't possibly be ahead so long as they kept living their fantasies.

Taking advantage of his sleeveless shirt, Courtney slid her hands up his arms to stroke his biceps. "Okay."

Disbelief flickered in Blaine's eyes. "You're going to let me do you on a copy machine with a store full of people watching?"

"I meant 'Okay, I'll marry you.' " She lifted her arms around his neck and rubbed against his deliciously hard body. "But only if you promise to make it worth my while. What do you say we install a copy machine in the basement, right next to the brand spanking new ice machine?" She grinned naughtily. "Feel free to take that spanking out of context."

"You're serious?"

"Maybe," she said, purposefully misunderstanding him. "The copy machine could come in handy when it comes to last-minute proposals, and I rather enjoyed it when you slapped my ass in the bathroom the other night. Gotta love that good pain."

Blaine gave her butt a swat again now, and her cheeks tingled with the delightfully stinging sensation. "About marrying me," he growled.

"I'm serious. I love you." Courtney pushed the hem of his shirt up to his chest and bent to run her tongue across his ridged abdomen. Her sex clenched with the contracting of his muscles. "Particularly when you're doing chores with my dad and your shirt's all covered in dirt and sweat and matted to this big, beautiful body."

Humor gleamed in his eyes. "So much for leaving the country girl behind."

"So much for no strings."

"No kidding. I have a whole roll of string at home just waiting for the right moment to tie you up."

Courtney quit her licking to eye him in wonder. "Plain white bras, work boots, and, now, bondage do it for you. You never cease to surprise me."

"Good. Then you'll never have to worry about being bored."

Hard Candy

1

"Only you could make a floor-length skirt and long-sleeve blouse look sexy."

Heat rushed through Candy Masterson at the sound of her condo neighbor's deep voice coming from the hallway behind her. She stiffened with her hand on her doorknob. In his routine sweatshirts, which hugged his broad shoulders, and faded jeans, which molded to his hard thighs and divinely scrumptious ass, Ty Louis was the arch nemesis of her good intentions, aka. her pussy's favorite plaything.

He was also full of shit.

She looked drab in the maroon and black full body garb, with her hair pulled up in an austere clip and sensible, low-heeled dress shoes in place of the glitzy stilettos she adored. Nothing at all like the fun-loving sex siren she'd been nearly the whole of her adult life, and precisely like the staid but sophisticated woman she'd set out to become.

The staid but sophisticated *celibate* woman.

Not about to turn around and torment her deprived hormones by taking in the sensual offer bound to be sizzling in his hazel eyes, she opened her door and went inside. "I'm not sleeping with you, Ty."

He followed her in, closing the door behind him and making the four-room unit seem incredibly tiny and arid. "Since when does a compliment count as an invitation for sex?"

"Since you moved in next door three years ago."

"You were the one who claimed to need a cup of sugar and then proceeded to jump me. Not that I was complaining. In fact, just thinking about it now . . ." He trailed off, probably in the hopes she would recall that night and be instantly turned on.

Candy did and was, but she wasn't about to tell him so.

"I get that you're still a little shell-shocked about what happened with your coworker," he continued, "but that was months ago. Besides, I'm no lunatic."

"Says you." She hung her keys on the brass holder on the wall outside of the open kitchen, then started to turn back. His hands came around her waist mid-swivel, pulling her against an obvious erection and sending her internal heat soaring.

"On second thought, I am crazy . . . for this rocking hot body you decided to up and deny me from touching." Warm breath tickled her earlobe with the brush of his unshaven upper lip. "It's not right, Candy. Not right at all."

Snorting, she lifted his hands away and crossed to her bedroom.

Ty hadn't attempted to get into her pants in weeks, and she thought he'd finally accepted their time as lovers had reached its end. Apparently, he hadn't. A normal woman would be annoyed with him over it, but Candy was pissed at herself. Because, damnit, going months without getting laid was a whole lot harder than she imagined and she wanted him bad.

"I have a date tonight, Ty. With a *nice* guy. Accept that I'm off the fuck-friend market and move on."

"All right."

She whirled around two steps into her bedroom—once tropical-themed to go with her laid-back, easy-living attitude, now decorated in the same sedate shades of blue, gray, and taupe as the rest of the place. "You're not going to give up that easily. I know you better than—" The words ended on a whooshing breath as he tackled her on the bed, with her back to the mattress and her hands trapped between their bodies.

Spreading her legs with the shove of a knee, he rocked a steely thigh against her mound. "Yeah, you do. Just like I know you." A cocky grin flashed across his face before his mouth came over her open one and he slipped his tongue between her lips.

Push his ass off you! Knee him in the balls, if that's what it takes!

The voice of Candy's good intentions screamed the words in her mind. Just not loudly enough to counteract the pussy-wetting anticipation that came with Ty tugging up her long-ass skirt and pushing his fingers beneath the miniscule crotch of her thong.

His fingers moved lower, to twine in the string of black lace lining the crack of her butt. Giving the string a tug, that had the front of the thong riding arousingly between her pussy lips, he lifted his mouth from hers. "I knew you couldn't handle going good girl all the way."

"Arrogant prick." Arrogant *accurate* prick.

As if he heard her silent confession, his lips slanted in a smugly sexy grin.

His mouth returned to hers then, his tongue pushing back inside, devouring with licks and sucks while his fingers journeyed back to her hairless mound. One finger teased along her damp folds, nudging the thong deeper into her slit. Delicious friction vibrated in her sex with the chafe of the lace, quickening her breathing and welling juices in her core.

Her hands were free to roam now. She used them to take his head in her hands as she took possession of the kiss.

For a few scorching seconds he let her lead, let her nibble and lap and be too damned conscious of his stiff cock rubbing along her bare thigh, bucking with its fervent hope to escape his jeans. Then he jerked her focus back to the inferno building between her own thighs by tugging the thong from her slit.

Swallowing down her gasp, Ty pulled the damp lace to the side. He parted her swollen lips with his thumb and rocked the pad against her clit. Erotic sensation burst from the bundle of nerves, puckering her nipples as elated whimpers crashed from her mouth into his.

This time Candy ended the kiss . . . to follow the voice of her good intentions and push his ass off her.

Then she said to hell with that annoying voice, shoved him onto his back, and came down over the top of him. "Five minutes." She yanked her skirt up to her waist as she straddled him.

"That's when your date is?"

"That's how long you have to fuck me." Curling her fingers in the hem of his black sweatshirt, she pulled it up past his chest, taking in his small hard nipples while her own throbbed for his touch. "This is the last time, Ty. I swear to God, I'm through with casual sex and you're not about to change my mind."

"You can't stop me from trying."

Oh, but she could.

This time Candy might be giving in, might be running her tongue and lips over his leanly muscled torso and working the jeans off his fine-ass body so quickly it was as if she couldn't get him naked fast enough. But next time she wouldn't relent to her hormones. Next time she would remember that more was stopping her from giving her sex drive free rein than the fear some man she barely knew would take her forward behavior as meaning she wanted to be his permanently, the way that had happened to her coworker.

This time she would indulge in one final screw with a guy who knew exactly how to push her buttons.

Ty's hand slid into the pocket of space created between their pelvises. His fingers moved back beneath the crotch of her thong, and he pushed her button, all right. Pushed and stroked and tugged at her clit until she was wriggling against his stomach and ready to come before she even got his cock inside her.

That just wouldn't do. Not for a final screw.

Going up on her knees, Candy knocked his hand away and pulled the thong down her legs and off. With her skirt balled in one hand, she pushed her other hand into the slit at the front of his boxers and took out his erection.

Her mouth watered at the sight of his thick member, deep red with the tip oozing silky fluid.

Mmm mmm mmm . . . Suck-u-lent.

"Go ahead and suck it," he encouraged in a rough voice. "You know you want to."

Damn, he knew her too well. Only, he didn't, not as a person. He just knew how she liked to fuck. Knew she was a sucker for the feel of his cock sliding between her lips, the taste of his cum filling her mouth.

Yeah, she loved giving him head. Wanted to do so right now. But she'd already given in to him too much and she also had that date with another man in a half hour.

A man who looked nowhere as good as Ty, Candy acknowledged as she traveled her gaze up his body, past his solid abdomen and lightly hair-lined chest to the days' worth of golden brown stubble dusting his upper lip and jaw line. Shaggy curls a shade darker covered his head and groin. Most guys couldn't pull off curls like his. Ty was just rough enough around the edges that the look worked in his favor, softened up his tendency for conceit and the sharp angles of his cheeks and nose. Made him look damned edible.

Too bad she'd already determined she wouldn't be eating him. Just one final, fast, run-of-the-mill screw and he would be her pussy's favorite plaything no longer.

Increasing her grip on his shaft, she guided the weeping tip to her sex and rubbed it along her slit. "All I want is your dick in me long enough to get us both off, and then you out of my condo."

"Abstinence is making you cranky," Ty observed as she inched onto him.

"It's not the abstinence." Though abstinence did have her sucking in a euphoric breath when he thrust his hips upward and filled her the rest of the way, stretching parts that hadn't been stretched in far too long.

Gripping her sides, he eased their bodies into a steady rhythm. "Lack of good food?"

His shaft slipped farther inside her, and her heart raced as exquisite pressure her vibrator hadn't come close to duplicating built. Candy also hadn't come close to duplicating the carb-rich, energy-fortifying, totally tantalizing dinners he used to make for her in preparation of their long, steamy nights. But there was a time and place for speaking the truth, and this was neither.

Reclining back, she grabbed hold of his thighs, placing her pelvis at the perfect angle for optimal pleasure and giving her a gripping point to pick up the pace. "I can cook for myself."

"No one giving you a massage after a long hard day at the office?" He kept up with the guessing game as he jerked her shirt from the waist of her skirt.

His hands pushed beneath the shirt and then the cups of her black bra. His fingers stroked across the tips of her nipples, massaging the erect, achy points in the same fashion he'd massaged all of her too many times to count.

She closed her eyes on a sigh of pure pleasure. "All right. I'll give you that one."

"I'll give you one you won't forget." Wicked intent clung to Ty's words as he pulled from her body and rolled them over so that she was on bottom again.

Her eyes snapped open in time to see him moving down the bed. Scooping her butt into his hands, he used his head to nudge her skirt back out of the way and her thighs apart. His smoldering gaze fell on her crotch, and she opened her legs wider, giving him one last look at how juicy wet and swollen he made her pussy.

"Still the same ol' hussy." Amusement entered his eyes before he bent his head and licked at her center.

Candy's heart raced and her hips thrust toward his mouth with that first lick. She curbed the urge to cry out and confirm his speculation. But, damn, how she loved that he didn't have a problem putting his mouth where his dick had been, tasting his pre-cum mingled with her own.

She was sincerely going to miss doing him. Already had been missing it and his friendship in general.

That was just too bad.

The two of them were no good at separating physical gratification and friendship, and Ty took sex the way she used to, as a fun, cheap, and great-feeling source of entertainment. What she needed now was a guy who took the time to get to know the woman behind the big boobs and blond hair before slipping his hand into her pants. A guy ready to make a commitment. A guy like the one due at her condo in less than a half hour.

"You're down to two minutes," she warned as he drew his tongue down the length of her labia and around her clit, spiking her pulse and curling her toes in the process.

He lifted his head to frown at her. "You can't rush a good mouth job."

"Yes, *you* can."

"Not tonight. I'm sucking your pussy the right way or not at all."

"Not at all."

"Candy, baby, that there's the stuff of regrets."

Hell, yeah, it was. Already ruing the loss, she fisted her hands in his sweatshirt shoulders and tugged. "Get up here and make me forget about it."

He surprised her, not bothering to delay any longer, but rising up over her. His tongue slid inside her mouth in time with the push of his cock into her body, and she sucked in a wheezing breath. Keeping his hold on her ass, he hoisted her hips off the bed and pounded into her slick sheath as he kissed her until her lips felt raw and puffy, and she had to fight for air.

The breath panted from Ty's mouth when he lifted from hers. The motion of his hips stilled, and he released her butt to strip off her shirt and bra. His mouth was on her breasts instantly, warm and damp, licking first one and then the other.

Sucking the pebbled flesh of a nipple between his teeth, he bit down hard enough to have her moaning. He toyed with the hard bud, eliciting another throaty moan before his teeth let up, and he gathered her breasts in his hands.

He eyed the ample mounds reverently. "You don't want this to end, do you, boys?"

Candy almost laughed at the heartfelt way he addressed her tits. Since laughter would give him hopes for a repeat session, she kept her mouth shut and lifted her hips, drawing his cock deep inside her body and clenching it tight. He followed her move in seconds, resurging the thrusting of his shaft as he palmed one of her breasts and resumed the none-too-gentle nipping of his teeth around the nipple of the other.

God, yes! It drove her absolutely bonkers with lust when he played rough.

She wanted to taunt him into playing even harder, until he

was biting a lot more than her nipples. Until he was using his hands to swat her ass, pushing her down on the mattress and taking her from behind like some uncageable, feral animal.

But they only had a minute left and, while things got hot fast with rough play, it wasn't fast enough.

Gripping the sheets, she lifted her legs, wrapping them high up on his back and drawing his shaft intensely deep. He moved his mouth to her other nipple, first lapping at the crown and then biting that one, too.

Candy's eyes watered and she blinked.

Oooh, yeah. Such good pain. Such awesome pleasure.

Climax barreled a little farther to the surface with each of his stinging bites, the driving of his dick inside her, the pummel of his balls and the tickle of his pubic hair against her ass cheeks.

The pumping of their bodies increased. Sweat beaded up on those places where their skin touched and the scent of their stimulation filled the bedroom, making it seem like old times, like she hadn't transformed herself and most everything around her into the serenely mundane. Like she was a wild woman all over again.

Ty's mouth wrenched from her nipple, breaking the façade of sex-filled days past. Then he looked up at her, like the wild animal she'd wanted him to be—eyes dark, unfocused and predatory, lips firm and slightly parted in a primal showing of clenched teeth, and thick tendons corded in his neck and shoulders. And just like that orgasm exploded over her.

Tremors shook through her, arching her up on the bed beneath him and bringing her back down, leaving her weak and momentarily helpless. Unable to stop her mews of absolute ecstasy as he fisted her tits and pumped his magnificent cock into her until his seed flowed freely and hotly, filling her to the point of overflowing.

With a low growl, Ty collapsed on her. She committed the

feel of his weight and the hard press of his body to memory; cherished them in the present, even if they did make it that much harder to breathe when she was already winded.

A half minute of silence passed, broken only by their heavy breathing, before he murmured something about crushing her and rolled to the opposite side of the bed.

Candy remained inert, savoring the residual pulsing of her sex and the warmth of his cum inside her and trickling along the crease of her butt. She sent her breasts a satiated smile. "As final five-minute fucks go, I give it two nipples up."

He came up on an elbow with his mouth curved in a lascivious grin. "You can't go without this."

"Nothing wrong with your ego, eh?"

"I'm talking about sex, not my body." He reached out a hand, tracing circles around the still throbbing, dark pink crown of her nipple. "We're sensual people, Candy. We thrive on pleasure. Need it to feel complete."

Ah, enlightenment. And here she thought her recent moodiness had to do with turning the big 2-9 and starting on the road to her final year of fibroid freedom.

Shutting out her health concerns, Candy rolled her eyes at his absurd observation and climbed off the bed. "You might need sex to feel complete, but my vibrator takes care of things just fine. I'm getting in the shower."

"Don't be in your bed when you get back, right?" he asked dryly, all hint of playfulness gone.

She nodded in agreement, but otherwise didn't bother responding before crossing the bedroom to the adjoining bathroom and moving inside. If there was one thing she could count on with Ty, it was that once he got what he wanted, he would let her have the same.

Now, if she could get her body to want the same thing as her mind.

One little nipple stroke from Ty and her body was right

back to ignoring her mind's better judgment, going wet between the thighs and making her want him all over again.

Candy had thrown him a curveball.

Ty thought if he left her alone for a few weeks, she would realize what a mistake she was making by closeting her tiny clothes and fuck-me heels, and becoming a born-again virgin. He thought she'd get that she was ruining both of their fun by ending their weekly Sunday dinner and massage date, which consistently led to a long, hard night of loving. He thought she'd see by now how unhappy the slow-moving schmucks she'd been dating lately made her.

He'd taken care of that born-again virgin thing, made them both happy for a little while, but it appeared otherwise his efforts hadn't been worth a shit.

It was a good thing he knew how to throw a curveball of his own.

The shower water started up behind the closed bathroom door. Ty waited a couple minutes, kicked back on the bed and breathing in the fresh apple scent of Candy's shampoo and lotion that she couldn't take the sexy out of no matter how hard she tried.

Between the scent of her seducing his senses and the thought of her in the shower rubbing that puffy purple mesh ball thing she loved so much over her nude body, he was semihard as he climbed from the bed and moved to the bathroom door.

He cracked the door far enough to see steam rising about the closed shower curtain, and then went inside. Going soundlessly to the tub, he pulled the curtain aside a half inch. Candy stood facing away from him, one slender foot hiked up on the tub's corner ledge and her succulent ass wagging at him as she washed her lower leg with the soaped-up purple ball and the water pelting down from the showerhead.

She straightened a bit, trailing the ball up her inner thigh.

His cock went hard the rest of the way as he recalled all the places he'd used that ball, and ones similar to it, on her over the course of the last few years and numerous showers. Each of those times, when he'd stroked the soft mesh edges over her aroused flesh, she'd tipped her head back and sighed in ecstasy.

This time, as he stepped into the shower and slid his body up against hers, cradling his shaft against the wet crack of her butt as he bent for the puffy ball, she screamed.

The ball dropped to the tub floor. Candy spun around and stepped back a foot, leaving the spray of the hot water as a shield between them. "*What* are you doing?"

"You said not to be in your bed. I'm not."

Her soft brown eyes took on a look between disbelief and annoyance. "I have a date," she bit out.

"Yep, with a nice guy. Rumor has it they like their women extra clean." Grinning, he lifted the container of liquid soap off the tub's inner ledge and lathered up his hands. "Ty the human sponge at your service, ma'am."

"Ty, please . . ." she warned, but there was invitation in her eyes that didn't match her tone. There was hope.

There was the tightening of her nipples as he grabbed the puffy ball from the tub floor and turned his focus on her breasts. "You don't have to beg." He brought his attention lower, to her bare mound, where her feminine lips peeked at him. "It's my pleasure."

The rock-solid response to eyeing her nude pussy lips brushed against his thigh as he went down on his knees. Letting the showerhead's spray pelt the back of his head and shoulders, he brought the purple ball to the juncture of her legs and started into a slow, circling massage.

Candy's fingers moved into his hair. "You can't keep pushing your way into my pants."

Sure, he could.

To prove his point, and because he loved teasing her almost

as much as he loved pleasing her, Ty spread her labia and roughed the ball's mesh edges against her clit.

Her grip on his hair increased. Breath wheezed from between her lips. He bit back a laugh over her eagerness to alternately keep him in place and get rid of him. "I'm not pushing my way into your pants."

"You're not?"

"No. I couldn't do this if you were wearing pants." Taking the puffy ball in his left hand, he slid the first finger of his right hand inside her passage and found her wet in a way that had nothing to do with the shower water.

She gasped and then moaned. "You seriously have *got* to go."

"Sure thing. Just as soon as you're clean." With his blood and dick pulsing in tandem, he pulled his finger from her body to lather it up with the suds accrued on the ball.

Slipping the digit back inside her along with its middle-finger friend, he cupped them to the shape of her cervix and tapped a slow, sweet melody against her inner walls. Candy's legs spread apart an inch and she gave a sigh of surrender.

Christ, how he wanted to surrender to his own desires by satisfying her building want.

He couldn't satisfy her want this time around. He could take his fill of her hazy-eyed expression as he fingered her to the edge of climax.

Tilting back his head, Ty risked the spray of the hot water in his face as he moved his fingers, pulling them partway from her body and then twisting them back up inside. Her channel hugged him in, sucking his fingers deeper with his next pump.

He increased the rhythm, and her legs spread apart another inch. On an indrawn breath, she melted into him, bringing her pelvis nearly flush to his face.

He peppered kisses along her flat belly, slipped his tongue into her navel. Her hips bucked forward and her heavy breasts taunted him with their jostling. She picked up the pace until she was fiercely gripping his hair and riding his fingers as eagerly as if it were his dick inside her cunt. Long, dark blond lashes fanned her face with the closing of her eyelids. Breath exhaled from between her glistening lips so hot he considered forgetting his intention in coming in here.

The feel of her pussy tightening around his fingers brought some of the blood back into his brain, enough to remember he had a purpose other than making her feel good.

Ty pulled his fingers from her sex and curled them around her own fingers, prying her hands free of his hair.

Candy opened her eyes on a whimper. "Why'd you stop?"

Smiling, he turned her around, bringing her butt inches from his face. "Can't forget this side." He glided his soapy finger along the crease of her lush ass, and she whimpered again and bucked back toward him.

Damn, he also couldn't resist that fine of an invitation.

He swatted her backside, just once, just hard enough to have her crying out with rapture and to surface a pretty pink shade that was gone almost as soon as he bent his head and brushed his lips across the tender flesh. Another of those sexy, breathy sighs escaped her with the sweep of his mouth. His erection bobbed with the needy sound, and he forced himself to stand before his hand took on a mind of its own and returned to paddling her ass.

Lifting the unfettered dirty-blond waves of her hair, he brought his mouth to her neck. He nibbled on the moist skin as he breathed in her fresh apple scent, so much stronger now than back on her bed. So much better.

Ty was about to admonish her for punishing her hair by putting it up into those damned clips when her hand snaked back between their bodies and cupped his balls.

"Go ahead and take me in the ass," Candy taunted as her fingers caressed his sac. "You know you want to."

He groaned with the bold words, spoken as the feisty Candy of three months ago and a parody of the words he'd said to her back on the bed. She'd vetoed his suggestion that she suck him. Much as he ached to take his cock in hand and feed it into her tight behind, he had no choice but to veto her idea, as well.

She was asking for him to do her, and that meant it was time to go.

Disconnecting his balls from her fingers, he stepped back to the end of the bathtub and opened the shower curtain a few inches. He hooked a leg over the edge of the tub. "Later, baby."

"You're leaving?" She whipped around, shock and stimulation doing a mixed number on her face. The water streaming down from the showerhead cascaded in hard droplets against her big breasts and swollen nipples, doing its own number on Ty.

Forgetting about his throbbing dick, he stepped the other leg out of the tub. "Just doing what you said you want me to do. Besides, I wouldn't want to make you late for a date." With a parting air kiss, he pulled the shower curtain back into place. "Have fun with the stiff."

2

Candy couldn't stop smiling. Not at her date's witty repartee, but rather at how accurate Ty had been in calling Steven a stiff. From his tailored white dress shirt and crisp navy slacks to the fact that not one bit of his conversation this evening had been witty, Steven was a total stiff.

He was also a nice guy.

The kind of guy who appreciated her for her brain as much as her body. The kind of guy who wouldn't tease her to the edge of orgasm and then walk away. The kind of guy she needed to focus on, she reminded herself as she opened the passenger side door of his silver Lexus.

A crisp autumn wind filtered into the car, sending the portion of hair she'd left down into a wild dance around her face. Steven's immaculate chestnut brown hair didn't budge as he hurried around the front of the Lexus to extend his hand to her. This was their fourth date and, with each passing one, the urge grew to run her fingers through his hair to see if he might not be sporting a rug. Since that move wouldn't be staid or sophisticated, Candy took his hand and let him help her out of the car and into her condo's light-brightened parking lot.

"I had fun," he said as he placed a hand at the small of her back and guided her up the sidewalk to the three-story building's central entrance.

"It was nice." Not fun exactly but, from a long-run standpoint, not bad either.

The food at the Grecian restaurant had been excellent and hearing about the flamboyant set Steven routinely worked with as a tax attorney for the wealthy had been interesting. Not as interesting as hearing Ty recount the shocking things couples did in the backseat of his hourly rental adventure plane. And not nearly as interesting as remembering all the kinky things the two of them had done in every inch of the six-seat Cessna. Still, though, interesting, and unlikely to do naughty things to her panties, unlike thoughts of the last time she'd gone flying with Ty.

Candy flushed her neighbor from her mind as she stepped onto the elevator with Steven at her side. The car rose to the top floor. They stepped out, and his hand returned to her back to guide her to her door.

He was such a gentleman. Totally opposite from most any other man she'd ever known. Or maybe not quite so opposite, given the anxious way his blue eyes trained on her mouth and he leaned toward her when they reached her door.

Well, what do you know? She was going to get some tongue action, and from a guy she could possibly have a future with, no less.

She encouraged with a smile. He took her head in his hands and brought his lips toward hers. Her pulse sped up with his firm hold, the lust that shimmered in his eyes, the idea he could be domineering in a way she'd never have guessed but thrilled at the potential.

Then he brushed her lips with a hasty kiss and quickly straightened. His hands fell at his sides. "Can I see you this weekend?"

Candy sighed. Obviously, he was different than the fast-moving, horndog men of her past to an extreme.

She didn't want him doing her until she knew they had a chance at something lasting, but shouldn't they be past surface kisses? Shouldn't the twenty-some hours they'd spent getting to know each other so far warrant at least a minor lip lock where she had the chance to respond before he lifted his mouth away?

The respectful way Steven smiled at her, showing off a killer set of pearly whites, suggested she wasn't going to get any farther tonight. Really, though, that was good—it just meant she had more to look forward to with date number five.

Going with the whole building anticipation thing, she nodded. "I'd like that."

"Dinner on Sunday?"

"I can't make Sun—" She stopped short, glancing at the door across the hall with the realization the words she'd spoken a hundred times before no longer applied.

Sundays used to be reserved for Ty. First, he'd make her dinner, and then he'd make *her* his after-dinner snack. Now, Ty would be spending his Sundays cooking for and pleasuring some other women and Candy had no reason not to take Steven up on his offer.

"Sure." Her voice lacked enthusiasm, so she added cheerfully, "That sounds great!"

"Excellent." He leaned forward again, brushing her mouth with another fleeting kiss. "I'll pick you up at a quarter to eleven. Mom likes everyone there an hour early so there's plenty of time to visit."

Candy's attention jerked from juvenile thoughts of sticking

her tongue out at Ty's door. What did Steven's mother have to do with date number five? "Mom?"

"I always spend Sundays with my folks. I know they're going to love you as much as I do."

Her heart skipped a beat with the word that sounded a whole lot like love. Only it didn't just sound that way, he really had said it. He couldn't mean it though.

Yeah, she wanted a guy to want her beyond her looks and exuberance in the sack, but Steven couldn't know he felt that way about her by their fourth date and no tongue action, let alone sex.

Could he?

"Great." She gave him a brittle smile while her belly turned circles. "I can hardly wait."

Candy sat on the edge of Courtney Baxter's desk, where she'd downed her morning latte while recounting her date with Steven to her across-the-cubicle coworker at Pinnacle Engineering. "I just don't get how he can he love me, he barely even knows me."

"Look at Jake." Fingering the thin strap of her breast-hugging lavender chenille tank top, Courtney reclined in her seat. A waist-length smoke gray suit jacket with lavender flecks hung from the back of her chair and matched her mid-thigh-length skirt. Strappy gray heels complimented the look.

The heels were shorter than those Candy favored, but she still felt no small bit of jealousy over her friend's chic, flirty style. Even Courtney's chin-length, blond-tipped brown hair screamed glamour girl. But then, Courtney could afford to look how she pleased since she had a man who wanted both her brains and her body for the long run.

If Courtney's words were accurate, all Candy had was the equivalent of a lunatic. "You think Steven's a stalker?"

"Jake was misguided, not a stalker." Courtney lowered her voice as she discussed the coworker she'd accidentally led into believing she wanted him. "Steven isn't a stalker either, he just likes you a whole lot."

"Bet he'd change his mind if he knew I got ready for our date last night by doing another guy."

Courtney straightened in her chair, blue-green eyes wide. "I thought you told Ty you were through with casual sex?"

"What makes you think I'm talking about Ty?"

An astute smile settled on Courtney's lips. "You're grinning like you went a round with the vibrating toilet seat."

Candy felt the endorphin rush that always surfaced the day after she slept with Ty, and knew a euphoric grin would be on her face just as her friend claimed. If the office only *had* a vibrating toilet seat . . . then maybe she could satisfy her sexual itch before she went home each night and risked running into him. "I told him. He didn't buy it. And I, apparently, have all the willpower of a whore where he's concerned."

Courtney studied Candy's face so intensely she felt like an even uglier bug than she had since twisting up her hair and putting on the full-coverage dark green pantsuit this morning. "What if there's a reason for that? You want a guy who will take you seriously, but how do you know Ty isn't that man?"

"I want a guy who loves what's inside the package as much as he does the package itself. Ty has never cared to learn more about me than which nipple is the most responsive."

"He knows what your favorite meal is," Courtney pointed out.

"Only because it's a creation of his own making."

"He knows you have a cocoa allergy."

"Only because I didn't want him cooking dinner for me and accidentally killing me in the process."

"He knows you have a thing for going down while he's going up."

"Only because—" Courtney's words registered, and Candy stopped her excuse to laugh out loud. She most definitely *did* have an affinity for going down on Ty while he was going up in his airplane. "Very funny. And it just proves what I've been saying for weeks now—everything with Ty is about sex. Good for him, but I'm past that point in my life."

She was also past the point where having this conversation with Courtney seemed worthwhile. Her coworker had been singing the praises of her four-month relationship with Blaine Daly, Pinnacle's hottie construction manager, the last few days and was obviously wearing rose-colored glasses because of it.

"I should get back to work. Tom has me putting together a promo piece for a trade show tomorrow and he wants it ready for review by three." Candy slid off the edge of Courtney's desk and started for her own cube.

"You know, Jake's proven that he never meant to scare me. He's honestly turned out to be a good guy."

Candy halted at the entrance to Courtney's cubicle and swiveled around with her shock. "You want me to date your ex-stalker whose divorce has been final less than a week?"

"He's *not* a stalker, and of course not. I'm saying that I was wrong in thinking my flirtatious behavior put me in harm's way. It didn't, not really, so your claim that the fear the same thing could happen to you is the reason you're dressing and acting like a nun and dating guys who couldn't be more wrong for you feels like total crap."

"It's not total crap." Courtney's eyebrows rose with her "yeah, right" look, and Candy amended, "It's just partial crap." She retraced her steps to her coworker's desk and sank back down on the edge. Quietly, she confessed, "I have a medical condition."

Concern replaced Courtney's skeptical look. "Oh, God. How serious?"

"I'm not dying or anything. Technically, I don't even have it yet. But the odds are favorable I'll get it."

"What is 'it'?"

"You really want to be bored with the details?"

"Do I look bored?" Courtney sat forward in her chair, interest alive in her eyes along with continued worry.

The truth was until Courtney came to her earlier this year and asked for her help in outing her inner sex diva, Candy didn't have any gal pals. She'd spent the ten years prior to that moment surrounding herself with men. Having so many guys in her life was a blessing when the urge for an orgasm struck, but men weren't exactly primed for listening to female problems. Her mother made for a good chat companion, particularly when it came to her current health concern, but she also lived halfway across the country. Lately, too, both of her parents' time was wrapped up in expanding their Southern cuisine franchise.

Suddenly anxious to share, Candy scooted a little farther down the desk so there would be no risk of eavesdroppers. "The women in my family have a tendency to develop uterine fibroids at a young age. Each generation, that age goes down. Considering my grandmother was thirty-eight when they first showed up and my mother was thirty-four, I figure I'm due for a visit from the Fibroid Fairy next year."

"Ouch. I don't know anything about them, but I'm sorry to hear it. You're just speculating you'll get them at this point though, right?"

"I can hardly afford to do anything else. Once the little suckers hit, I'll be lucky to have a handful of essentially pain-free childbearing years ahead of me. That's if they don't grow too fast and medicine can work to shrink what does develop. If they don't, I'm looking at a hysterectomy. I don't even know if I want kids, but I'm not going to give up the opportunity to decide so I can continue playing fuck friends with Ty. I need to find a responsible guy for the long haul before it's too late."

Courtney frowned. "Ty doesn't know about this?"

"No, and he never will."

"You're going to want to hurt me for suggesting this, but maybe the problem isn't that he doesn't care enough to learn about you beyond from a sexual standpoint. Maybe it's that you've spent so many years leaving men while things are still going good, that you're afraid to risk doing anything else where Ty's concerned."

Candy had left a lot of men happily behind. Even so, the idea seemed ludicrous. "Let's say you're right—"

Courtney drew back in her chair. "About wanting to hurt me?"

"About me not opening up to Ty. Why would it be any different for me to open up to Steven, because *that* I've been doing plenty of?"

"So much that you're convinced he can't possibly love you when he doesn't know a thing about you?"

"He knows some. Enough, maybe." Courtney's mouth quirked, and Candy ground out, "Just answer the question already."

"All right, here's a guess. In your head you think Steven's a good choice for the long term, but in your heart you know you'll never see a relationship through with him. He's grapes. You're mangoes."

Steven was more routine and, yeah admittedly, stuffier than her. But then, better they be mismatched fruits than the nut Courtney was starting to sound like.

Ty hadn't spent the weekend peering out his condo's front-door peephole. He'd just spent the last five minutes doing it. He'd happened to overhear Candy return from her date with

Steven the other night and just happened to look out in time to see the guy laying that puny, pathetic two-second lip brush that didn't even deserve to be called a kiss on her. Just happened to hear they were doing dinner with his folks today.

What kind of friend would he be if he didn't take the time to meet Candy's man? See if the guy was deserving of her. See if Ty had anything to worry about where the stiff was concerned. Going back to that feeble kiss, the odds were next to nil.

Speaking of the stiff, Steven's familiar figure appeared through the fisheye lens and proceeded to knock on Candy's door. Ty stepped out into the hallway, purposely letting his door bang shut, and Steven turned around.

Oh, yeah, he looked like a total stiff. A regular poindexter with his closely cropped brown hair matted to his head just so, fancy smancy black suit and designer dress shoes, and a black and gray striped tie done up with a perfect double Windsor.

Ty could look like that, tie a knot just as well. But why the hell would he want to?

For one thing, it was damned uncomfortable. For another, the polished look wasn't even close to what Candy wanted in a man.

Smiling, he extended his hand. "You must be Steven?"

The schmuck looked first surprised and then pleased as he accepted Ty's hand and gave it a firm shake. "Candy's been talking about me?"

"Sure has. All interesting stuff." Ty considered letting the handshake continue, adding a little more muscle to it in the meantime. He went easy on Steven in the end, because the poor guy was probably already operating under the belief Candy was head over heels for him and this visit with his folks meant she was ready to make a commitment.

It was possible some part of Candy thought that way herself, but the rest of her had to know better. "I'm a longtime friend of hers. Fly airplanes for a living—do some aerial photography, but mostly sky cruises. You should let me take the two of you up sometime. Knowing how much she loves it, I'll give you a steal on the price."

Steven's eyes warmed with the invite. He flashed a set of capped teeth that had to cost serious mint. "I'd like that."

Candy's door opened with the last of his words. She stepped out in a long-sleeve, ankle-skimming black dress, which showed off next to zilch in the way of curves. Her hair was back up in one of those damned clips. They looked like they were attending a funeral instead of dinner.

Of course, they might as well be attending a funeral—of the end of their relationship. It was inevitable. All a matter of time.

Candy narrowed her eyes Ty's way while she laid a hand on the stiff's arms. "Steven, hi." Rising up on tiptoe, she kissed his clean-shaven cheek. "I see you've met Ty."

Steven placed a hand over hers. "Actually, we never got around to names. Your friend was just offering to take us flying sometime."

"He was." Cynicism laced her voice.

"I was," Ty confirmed. Then, because he did feel bad for the guy, but not bad enough to let Candy continue to date him when he was clearly not right for her, he added, "Did Candy tell you she's a five-star member of the Mile-High Club?"

Awe registered in Steven's eyes. "I had no idea. She's so modest."

Yeah, she was so modest she waited until Steven glanced his way to give Ty the finger. "That's Candy for you. Little Miss Modesty."

Steven looked back at her, and Ty took advantage this time by blowing Candy a kiss.

Grinning with the fury sizzling in her gaze, he stepped back toward his door and twisted the knob. "You two kids have fun. I know I will be. Twins." He waggled his eyebrows. "Cute, blonde, and identical. Does it get any better than that?"

* * *

Candy hadn't spent the four hours since she'd gotten home from her dinner date with Steven peering out her condo's front-door peephole. She didn't have to since the walls were thin enough in her bedroom she could hear the ding of the elevator as it reached the top floor. Only she, Ty, a married couple who were gone for the week, and an older guy who worked nights lived on the third floor, so it was safe to assume the ding that came shortly after nine thirty was the one announcing Ty's return.

She didn't bother to waste time checking the peephole, just threw open the door and prepared to land into him for being a jackass this morning. He was lucky that Steven missed the Mile-High Club crack, or she'd be greeting him with her fist.

Ty stepped into view as her door crashed back against the wall. Looking over, he had the gall to grin. And her poor deprived pussy, which really shouldn't feel so deprived since he'd just satisfied it a handful of days ago, went damp.

From a grin.

Not even a nice grin. But a sinful one that had his hazel eyes shimmering with heat, making it clear he had naughty thoughts going on.

She refused to fall victim to that grin, or the decadent way the hem of his plain green sweatshirt hugged his lean hips, looking way better than any thousand-dollar suit could. Unless that suit happened to be on Ty. Well, then . . . Then she must be dreaming because he never dressed up without an unavoidable reason.

Crossing her arms, Candy bit out, "You're home early."

"It's Sunday. I had the twins in bed by nine. The one was a little fussy, so I had to rub—"

"Oh, God! Spare me the details."

Amusement shone in his gaze. "Never had a problem hearing details before. Matter of fact, it used to make you hot." His grin took on a devilish quality as he came closer. Close enough she could see the tiny flecks of green in his eyes and all but feel the warmth radiating off his body. "You always liked to hear about the time I walked in on my college roommate doing that sorority chick. She had these huge tits—a lot like yours, come to think of it. Anyway, it was pretty obvious he couldn't decide what to stick between them first: his face or his dick.

"He went with his dick right about the time they realized I was standing there. Of course, they were just drunk enough not to care. And I was just drunk enough to yank my cock out of my jeans and treat it to a first-rate hand job. So did you and Steven have a good night?"

"I . . . it, ah, was fine. Great. We had a great time." Jesus, he moved into her personal space and broke out a dirty story she'd heard a dozen times, and she turned into one big quivering hormone who could only think of sex.

She could think about more than that, though. If she concentrated on the small white scar that ran along the skin over his upper lip and prevented the hair from coming in quite right there.

His skin was more sensitive in that spot than on any other part of his face or neck. Incredibly ticklish. Incredibly huge turnon point. One lick and he'd be sporting a semi. Two licks and his cock would be stiff as a board. Ready for her to jump on and go for a nice long, wet ride.

O-kay. So, apparently, focusing on his scar wasn't working either.

Apparently, she needed to go back inside since she'd forgotten her reason for coming out into the hallway in the first place. "I have an early meeting. See you later."

" 'Night, Candy, baby." Ty blew her a kiss just before he disappeared inside his condo door and the lock *snicked* into place.

He'd never had that annoying air-kiss habit until earlier this week. He'd done it again this morning, followed it up by shutting his door in her face. The similarity of that time and this time had Candy recalling why she'd come out into the hall. Because she'd been pissed. And with one grin and a few naughty words, he'd made her forget all about it.

Well, she wasn't going to give him the satisfaction of knowing he'd addled her by pounding on his door and yelling at him. She really did have an early morning meeting, so she was going to go to bed and indulge in a full eight hours of sleep.

After making hasty work of her bedtime cleanup routine, Candy climbed into bed and snuggled face first into her pillow.

And was immediately met with visions of Ty standing with his hand on his cock while he watched his college roommate fuck some big-chested girl's tits. Only, it wasn't just some big-chested girl. She'd heard the full version of the story enough to know the woman's name was Alyssa and that she was a natural redhead, going by the shade of her pubic hair.

Ty liked to remind her of that part right before he stroked his fingers along her naked mound and said he'd never know if she was a natural blonde and was damned happy for it. Then he'd slide one of those big fingers into her pussy and work her body until she was gasping out breaths and feeling the slow burn of orgasm rippling through her.

Then the best part came, when he brought his dick to her tits and proceeded to glide it between the valley of her cleavage until he was coming hard, right up into her mouth. Filling her throat while she eagerly sucked back all he had to give.

The vision evaporated, and Candy groaned with the incredibly aroused state of her body.

Ah, hell, she was never going to sleep now.

She'd made the mistake of leaving panties on, and they were damp and pressing against her stimulated slit. Rolling onto her back, she brought a hand down between her thighs. The pink mini tee that doubled as an incredibly small nightshirt rubbed against her straining nipples with the move, and she gasped.

Thank God she hadn't given up self-induced orgasms along with casual sex.

Self-induced orgasms that involved fantasies of Ty's magical hands sliding along her damp body? Those were probably taboo, but she closed her eyes and let them surface.

His shaggy golden brown curls and devilish grin entered her mind. Imaginary hands massaged and soothed every muscle in her body, somehow managing to simultaneously bring her nerve endings screaming to life with the caressing pads of his fingertips.

She sank her own fingers into her sheath, petting the slick swollen flesh, able to almost feel his fingers there as well. Her other hand pushed beneath the tee, up over her belly to her breasts, tugging and pinching at her erect nipples.

Liquid heat pooled in her sex as the nipple play bordered on painful. Warmth coursed through her body. She brought her fingers from her pussy to grab the vibrator from the top drawer of the night stand.

The red plastic dildo whirred to life with a twist of her fingers, found itself a home, nice and snug between her breasts. Her free hand traveled back between her thighs.

Candy twisted and plucked at her engorged clit the same way she'd been doing with her nipples. Wet her finger with the cream pooling in her sex and used them to get the vibrator nice and juicy. In her mind, Ty's cock replaced the plastic device. Recklessness flashed in his eyes as he pushed his shaft between her tits. Fucked the mounds with long, luscious strokes while his fingers worked inside her cunt, up and down, circling.

Blistering heat through every inch of her.

Heat that crashed into her as a searing orgasm as the Ty of her mind came with an upward thrust and his cum jetted against her lips.

Moaning for more, she opened her mouth.

The next loads of imagined salty fluid met with her tongue and teeth, coasting delightfully downward as she rocked her hips and pumped her finger and rode out her climax.

Feeling weak and weary and wonderfully satiated, Candy kept her eyes closed, kept the vision going until it morphed into a dream and she slipped into contented unconsciousness.

3

With the aid of nightly orgasms, made sinful by the reappearing role of Ty as her fantasy lover, Candy made it through date six and seven and still no real tongue kisses from Steven.

But now it was time for date eight and things weren't looking so good.

Seated beside her in Ty's plane, in the first of two rows of passenger seats, Steven grinned so huge you would have thought he'd just shot his first wad.

Candy kept a smile glued on, when what she wanted to do was cross the couple feet to the cockpit and beat Ty upside the head for not telling her Steven had arranged this evening sky cruise.

In all fairness, she'd been going to great lengths to avoid Ty everywhere but in her dreams and fantasies the last week and a half. It was possible he'd wanted to let her know about the flight but couldn't track her down.

Then again, he could have called her condo and left a message.

Then again, too, he probably didn't realize how hard it was

for her to sit in this seat and not remember with panty-wetting clarity the time he'd bent her over the top of it and fucked her from behind.

Bullshit, he didn't. This was *Ty* she was talking about. It was almost a certainty he knew exactly what sitting here was doing to her.

Steven leaned across the narrow aisle between their seats. He took her hand and gave it a squeeze. "I'm glad Ty didn't ruin the surprise."

"Me, too." *Liar.* "The color along the shoreline should be stunning this time of year."

His grin went from loopy to lustful. "*You* look stunning."

He let go of her hand to move his fingers to the clasp of his seatbelt. Releasing the lock, he shifted in his seat and inclined the top half of his body toward her.

His mouth swam into view. So close. So . . . open?

Holy shit, Steven was actually going to kiss her like he meant it!

Candy's heart picked up, beating a wild tattoo that suggested there just might be something to the whole building anticipation thing. Holding her breath, she unhooked her own belt, turned in her seat. Waited. And there it was. After more than a month of dating.

Contact.

The hot press of his soft lips against hers.

The damp slide of his tongue into her mouth.

The sound of Ty's deep voice coming through the overhead speaker system. "Sorry for interrupting, but we're cleared for takeoff. I need you to sit back in your seats, put on your belts and headsets, and relax."

Like a perfect gentleman, Steven did as instructed. Breaking the kiss off short, he straightened in the tan leather seat, slid the safety belt into place over his lap and the headset over his ears.

Candy did the same, but added glaring at the portion of Ty's head she could see past his seatback to the list.

He was damned well *not* sorry.

Unfortunately, neither was she. Steven really wasn't much of a kisser. Of course, he hadn't had much chance to prove himself either.

The Cessna gave a lurch, rolling into action. Steven focused out the rectangular left-side passenger window as the twin engines roared to life. She followed his move again and looked out the right-side window, watching as the small airport's three-runway tarmac unfolded beneath them and then slowly receded with the ascent of the plane.

Minutes passed where the sound of the engines continued to fill the plane, loud even with a headset on. The noise quieted some then and the plane evened out.

Ty's voice came through the headset earpiece. "We've reached our flying altitude. You can take off your headset."

Candy placed her headset beneath her seat. Steven followed suit, then looked over at her incredibly hopeful. "Can we take our seatbelts off?"

"We can, but probably shouldn't." If he was free to move around, he was liable to try another tongue kiss. She did want to give him a real chance. Just not while Ty was in viewing distance and likely to intrude on her thoughts as much as via the speaker system. "Ty hates to fly with passengers moving around in the back of his plane," she improvised.

Steven frowned. "Is that normal for a pilot?"

"To want your customers to be safe? I would think so."

He looked unconvinced but turned his attention back out his window.

The view really was breathtaking at this distance. Autumn in all its glory melded as dazzling shades of red, orange, yellow, green, and brown against the Lake Michigan shoreline. They flew beneath what little cloud cover dotted the evening sky, and the sun shone brightly on the calm water beneath, turning it in to an arresting shade of blue.

"This is incredible," Steven voiced her thoughts.

"It sure is."

The flight continued to be incredible for the next twenty minutes while Steven forewent talking to take in the sights. Then the view got even better as the sun started to dip toward the horizon and the sky became dusted with brilliant streaks of red, pink, and orange.

Apparently, he wasn't into sunsets though. He quit looking out his window to turn to her. "Mom and you hit it off the other day."

"She was nice," Candy said truthfully. "Your dad and sisters were, too."

Happiness edged into his blue eyes as he took her hand back in his. "I'm really glad you like them, because I was hoping you'd start spending more time with them."

"Oh. Doing what?"

The really huge smile he'd worn before takeoff returned. "Wedding preparations."

She sucked in a breath as her belly twisted with the implication that seemed to fill those words. Probably, she was jumping to conclusions. Even so, her voice shook in a completely uncharacteristic manner as she asked, "Who's getting married?"

"We are. I just haven't asked yet." Letting her hand go, Steven unbuckled his safety belt to go down on one knee in the cramped space between the seat fronts and the cockpit. "Will you do me the honors, Candy?"

The whole knee thing was bad. But when he pulled a diamond-encrusted ring out of his coat pocket, she was thankful to be sitting down since she'd never felt this woozy in her life.

"Oh my God!" Candy screeched so loud flight control could probably hear her back on the ground.

Ty definitely heard her. He looked back, around the edge of his seat, and assessed the situation. Lips pressed in a hard line, he met her eyes.

Do something, she silently begged him. *Anything.*

"I know it's only been a little over a month since we met," Steven said, bringing her attention back to his face, "but when something feels this right it can't be wrong."

Oh, hell, yes, it could!

Besides, this didn't feel right. She'd wanted it to, but it didn't.

"Sorry to interrupt again, but we're losing air pressure." Ty's voice came through the speakers with a tremble too practiced-sounding to be authentic.

Thank God Steven didn't know him better. He bought in to that tremble, and his gaze went from anxious to alarmed. "Is that bad?"

"It's not good." Candy didn't need to fake her unease—Steven's proposal took care of that nicely.

"I need you both in your seats ASAP," Ty ordered. "Scratch that, I need Candy up here to copilot." Steven sent her a wary look as he pocketed the ring and sat down, quickly doing up his safety belt, and Ty explained, "She's logged hundreds of flight hours and knows what to tell them back on the ground to help see we get there in one piece."

She gave Steven an apologetic look. "I'm sorry, but I need to get up front."

"Go. He needs you."

Technically, she was the one who needed Ty, but she didn't quibble over Steven's assumption as she unbuckled her seatbelt and hurried into the copilot seat next to Ty.

He handed her a headset identical to the one he wore. A headset he'd obviously set to a private channel since his voice came through the earpiece the instant she put it on. "Problems in paradise?"

"Why would he propose to me, Ty? Why? He doesn't even

know me." She'd told him stuff, as she'd claimed to Courtney, but very little that mattered. Instead, she'd focused on sharing those G-rated facets of her personality and life that would make her look wholesome and staid and sophisticated. And, hell, nothing at all like she was.

"That's why. You acted like the woman he wanted, and now he's paying you back by giving you what he thinks you want to get."

"I don't." Not from Steven. Not from any guy this fast.

"You're preaching to the choir, Candy, baby."

The desire to beat Ty upside the head returned, but this time she knew he didn't deserve it. He was acting arrogant but it was warranted. "Now what?"

"Now, I'm gonna set this thing down and you're gonna break the bad news to Steven that you can't marry him because he's a missionary-style kind of guy and you need a man who's not afraid to take you in the ass." He glanced over to flash a wicked grin. "Once the heartbreaking's over, you know where to come for the good stuff."

Focusing out the windshield, Ty flipped the switch for the overhead speaker. "Put your headset on and hang on, Steven. I'm going to set this bird down. I don't think there should be any problems, but you might want to pray just in case."

The reason Candy had always lived by the rule of ending things while they were still going good had just become blatantly obvious. Ending things on a happy note meant not having to face the guy's anger when she said they were through.

Or, in Steven's case, beaten look.

She reached across the Lexus's armrest to give the back of his hand a reassuring stroke as he merged off I-96 onto the city street that led to her condo. "I'm truly sorry, Steven. You're a nice guy, but things are moving too fast for me."

A portion of the fury she would expect from any other man moved into his eyes as he glanced from the four-lane roadway to her face. "Your friend doesn't like me, does he?"

"Ty doesn't *not* like you." Ty didn't *not* like anyone. There were just some people he would rather leave than take, and she could guess Steven would rank high up on that leave list.

"But he told you I wasn't the right man for you?"

"Not in so many words."

"Another man's jealousy is no reason to end a relationship."

Actual assertiveness clung to the words, raising Candy's regard of Steven—just not enough to change her mind. "Ty isn't jealous. Our friendship is based on sex not emotions."

The Lexus jerked to the right. A horn blared from somewhere beside them and, as Steven settled the car between the lane lines again, a red minivan flew past with the driver's hand out the window, middle finger raised.

Firmly gripping the wheel, Steven looked over at her, a mix of astonishment and aversion on his face. "He's your *lover*?"

She bit her tongue. Really, those words should not have left her mouth. "That came out wrong."

"So he's not your lover?"

"No." Aside from in her nightly fantasies and dreams. And, oh yeah, in her condo a couple weeks ago. But they were talking about the present. And at the present, this very moment in time, Ty was not in this car doing her.

Steven looked appeased if not like he was completely buying into her claim. "If you're not seeing anyone else, why not give us a chance? You don't have to marry me right this second, but why not keep dating?"

"We don't have enough in common. I'm mangoes. You're grapes."

"That makes no sense."

She hadn't thought so either, when Courtney spoke the

words, but now they made perfect logic. Now, Candy realized trying to forge a relationship with Steven would be like trying to fit her Double Cs into a barely B cup. Painful.

Her condo was less than a mile ahead, so she let her response linger until he pulled into the parking lot and stopped the car. She unhooked her seatbelt and grabbed her purse. With her hand on the door handle, she smiled at him. "I had a good time. Really. But this is the end of the road for us. Good luck, Steven. I hope you find a great woman who deserves such a nice guy."

"I know you're on a timeline of sorts, but I seriously doubt taking a few days off from the good girl gig to scratch your need-to-be-laid itch with Ty would hurt anything," Courtney said as she stepped into Candy's cubicle.

Candy turned in her chair to frown at the advice. Much the same advice Ty had been giving her since things went so far south with Steven two nights ago. Thankfully Ty had stopped at advice.

If he'd tried to coerce her with his body . . .

Yeah, thank God. Right now she was liable to be well rested and well fucked if he'd done that.

Candy sighed. Appealing as that sounded, the second of the two items was not going to aid her cause of finding a man for the long haul. One who waited at least a few months and gave her more than a ten-second tongue kiss but less than full-blown sex before proposing. "I appreciate the concern, but I don't have an itch in need of scratching."

Courtney's expression called Candy the liar she was, but she kindly ignored pointing it out verbally. "You'd sleep much better at night."

Not that pointing out the bags under Candy's eyes was any better. "Are you suggesting I look like hell?"

"You look a little tired." She sent her gaze the length of Candy's body. "And a lot overdressed. A muumuu would be perfect if we lived in Hawaii, or if it were at least warm out. It's October and that dress is about four sizes too big."

"I *like* this dress, and it doesn't have a tropical thread in it." It also wasn't too big.

The midnight blue sheath dress was curve-hugging hot when paired with a chunky black belt that naturally lifted the otherwise knee-length hemline up to mid-thigh. A couple stitches on the wide straps pulled them into tiny little lines that barely marred the fine bone structure of her shoulders. Black stilettos and sheer thigh highs with black runners turned the sizzle factor up several steamy notches.

Of course, right now she wasn't wearing the belt, the stitches, the stilettos, or the sexy stockings. Right now, she had on basic black pumps and the dress flowed loosely along her body, which was a good thing only from the standpoint that the haphazard fit detracted from the fact that her face really did look like hell from lack of sleep.

Courtney let loose an incredulous laugh. Sympathy entered her eyes then. "I'm sorry, but c'mon. A year ago I might have believed you. But that was before you taught me your sex-diva secrets and how to recognize when someone's full of crap."

Candy gave in to her own laughter, because frankly she needed a good stress reliever and laughter worked as well as anything. Sobering, she admitted, "I would love to give the good girl gig a hiatus for a couple days, but I can't do it. I cannot sleep with Ty for two nights and then go back on the celibacy wagon. Sex is like chocolate. If you haven't had it in a long time, you forget how good it is and how hard it is to give up."

"Considering you've only had chocolate once in your life and it put you into the hospital, that's a bad analogy. But, okay, I see your point. Maybe you could try counting horses. That worked well to get me to sleep as a kid." She seemed to remember that Candy was a lifelong city girl and amended, "On second thought, how about Prada handbags?"

"That I'd be willing to try."

"Good, then—"

"Morning, ladies." Pinnacle's fifty-something redheaded admin stepped into the hallway outside of Candy's cube with a wide-mouthed crystal vase bursting with pink orchids in her hand. She slipped into the cube past Courtney, and set the vase on the end of Candy's desk. "I was starting to think the flower shop forgot where you worked."

Candy's gut tightened as she eyed the vase. Back when she'd been fulfilling her pussy's every desire by sleeping with whatever man appealed to her, she'd received flowers on a regular basis. It had been months since she'd operated that way, longer since she'd gotten flowers. The odds these ones came from Steven were strong enough to make her stomach go queasy.

She feigned an appreciative smile. "Thanks, Sherry. They're beautiful."

The admin left and Courtney plucked the business-sized card out of the flowers and handed it to Candy. Candy opened the card and pulled out the note within, reading it aloud. "I found a great woman who deserves me. Give us another chance and I'll prove it. Love, Steven."

Courtney fingered the yellow-stemmed labellum at an orchid's center. "Do you think he gets the erotic implication?"

Candy moved her thumb away from the remainder of the writing. "P.S. I know what the flowers symbolize."

"Maybe he isn't such a stiff, after all."

"What, he was just holding back because he thought that's what I wanted?" Not likely. Not a guy who applied so much of whatever it was he put into his hair that it didn't even budge in a strong wind. Or maybe it really was a rug. She never did get around to checking.

"Could be."

"It could, but I doubt it." Discovering if his always immaculate hair was real wasn't nearly enough motivation for Candy to go out with him again either.

Candy closed her condo door, slid the lock into place, leaned back against the wood, and breathed a sigh of Friday freedom. Then the phone started ringing.

She ran into the kitchen and grabbed it off the wall-mounted handset. "Hello?"

"Welcome home, beautiful. Did you like the flowers?"

Steven. Shit. That's what she got for not checking caller ID. Her mind had been swept up in the fact that she'd made it inside without Ty spotting her and either trying to seduce her or blowing her another one of those damned air kisses that had begun to make her want for the real thing.

She hung her keys on the brass wall holder just outside of the kitchen while she mulled over an appropriate response. "They were nice."

"You always say that about me. That I'm nice. I'm not always, you know? I can be bad if you want me that way."

Whoa! Steven sounded upset. And like Courtney might have been right today, that he wasn't such a stiff. Even so, Candy didn't want to go down the dating road with him again. He'd never gotten a good shot at a tongue kiss, but the sample in Ty's plane was enough to say they wouldn't work out physically. "I just want you as a friend."

"Can I take you out to dinner as a friend?"

"I have plans tonight."

"With Ty?" Steven speculated, the edge of anger back in his voice.

"With a girlfriend from work." Another lie, a bad habit she'd developed lately, but she didn't care for his tone.

"What about tomorrow?"

"Working late." Remembering tomorrow was Saturday and

that she'd told him she didn't go into the office on weekends, she quickly asked, "How about I call you when I'm available?"

"No need to do that. I'll just stop in and surprise you sometime."

The call disconnected without a good-bye and an eerie shiver chased along Candy's spine.

By "sometime" could he have meant right now? And how did he know she'd just gotten home? Following work tonight, she'd stopped at the day salon to have her eyebrows waxed and a shoulder massage, which hadn't come close to Ty's all over body rubdown. Steven couldn't have known her schedule, unless he'd been following her the entire time.

For the most part what happened to Courtney, with the guy at work behaving as if he was stalking her in response to Courtney's too friendly flirting, didn't bother Candy. Didn't make her fear the same thing could happen to her. But for a little part, it did.

Right now, it actually did a whole lot.

She didn't want to be here alone. Stupid since the condo had great security and visitors needed to be buzzed into the building. Still, she didn't.

She could call Courtney and make good on her going out with a girlfriend allegation. They hardly ever did things outside of work, but now was as good a time as any to start getting together more after hours. Only, Courtney had mentioned this morning that she and Blaine were going up to her parents' blueberry farm for the weekend.

That pretty much just left Ty.

He probably wouldn't be home on a Friday night. Although, it wasn't quite seven yet, so he could be.

Dare she go over there? It would be the equivalent of walking out of the ashes and into the flame.

Unsure of her plan of action, Candy unlocked and opened

her condo door. The yellow glow of the elevator's up button caught her attention a short ways down the hall.

What if Steven was in that car?

Well, then, she would just have to make him go away.

But what if he wouldn't go away? He'd sounded so much more intense than she'd ever realized he could be, both on the flower card and on the phone.

The elevator pinged as it moved from one floor to the next.

She sucked up her better judgment and knocked hard on Ty's door. "Ty? Open up!"

His door opened an instant later. Her heart wedged in her throat at the sight of him in low-slung black boxer shorts and nothing else. Before her brain could be overtaken by the glory of his solid stomach and scrumptious chest, she pushed past him into the condo.

Shutting the door, he raised an eyebrow at her. "Need to borrow a cup of sugar?"

"No. Your bed."

4

Candy crossed her arms over her chest and took a step back, looking like even more of a priss than her shapeless dark blue dress and the stuffy upsweep of her hair accomplished.

She could hide her curvy figure behind tasteless clothing, but that wouldn't stop Ty from remembering what she looked like out of those clothes. Wouldn't stop him from inhaling her sexy fresh apple scent. It wouldn't end the knowledge that if he kept eyeing her breasts, as if her arms and two layers of clothing didn't cover them, her nipples would poke to hungry life along with the stirring of her pussy.

A flush crept up her exposed neck, and she narrowed her eyes. "I'm not here for sex, so stop looking at me that way."

He grinned at her tone: accusation underlaid with arousal. "How am I looking at you?"

"Like you want to bend me over the arm of your couch and make good on your offer from the plane."

Mmm . . . That did have a nice ring to it.

Ty glanced down the hallway to where it opened up into a living room and the left side of a couch was visible. He looked back at Candy to find her attention had wandered down the hall as well, her breathing picking up in the meantime.

He could definitely talk her into sex . . . if sleeping with her didn't work against his plan to bring her back to the easy living, easy loving side of life, and if he didn't have chicks waiting in his bed.

He lifted his gaze to her face. "Having nice-guy problems again?"

She met his eyes, visibly relaxed by his serious tone even if she did keep her arms twined around her breasts. "Maybe. Steven can't seem to accept we're through and it's starting to creep me out. I'd feel a lot better staying here tonight."

"I only have one bed."

"I know, but we're adults."

"I just wasn't sure if there would be room for all four of us."

"Four?" Candy's eyes went wide as the words gasped from her mouth.

Ty laughed. "Yeah, four. You, me, and the chicks I left in my bed so I could get the door."

Her mouth hung open before she slammed it shut and glanced across the entryway to his bedroom door. "You have . . . chicks . . . in your bed?"

Crashing erupted behind the partially closed door before he could respond. "Shit. I better see what they're doing."

Candy watched in dazed wonder as Ty disappeared behind the door. Throughout the years they'd been sleeping together, they'd often also been seeing others. It shouldn't bother her to think he had another woman in his bed. It might not if it were just one woman. But it was two. Most likely, the cute blond twins from Sunday night.

"Candy?" His voice carried out to her, sounding a little winded, like already he was in there working up a sweat. "We could use your help back here."

What? Was he serious? Did he honestly believe she would join them? "I'm leaving. I'll be fine at my place."

"Quit being a—Ow! You little bitch." Ty muttered something she couldn't make out and an odd sort of twittering noise followed. "Candy, get in here!"

She should follow the voice of logic screaming in her mind, telling her to face whomever might have been on that elevator, just so long as it meant getting out of this condo. But her damned curiosity had her crossing the entryway toward his bedroom instead. "I'm not crawling into some fuck fest with you and . . . chickens?" She blinked to be sure she hadn't made the peculiar scene up, but it remained the same.

One little fuzzy yellow chicken sat in a shallow metal pan in the center of his bed, basking beneath a heat lamp that dangled on a long cord from the ceiling fan. Ty sat on the edge of the bed, holding another fuzzy little yellow chicken while it wiggled its birdie feet and pecked at his hands. Next to Ty's feet was a small upturned dish that chicken number two must have somehow managed to knock off the bed, judging by the water trail along the side of his bedspread and the visible dampness of the beige carpet beneath the dish.

"You have chickens in your bed," she stated the obvious. "Why do you have chickens in your bed?"

"They're chicks. And I got them as a present for the twins. We were getting along just fine until you knocked and scared this one." He held up the bird in his hands. "Now, she's suddenly discovered she has a beak and, apparently, a taste for my hand."

"The twins are into chicks?"

"They're into anything that makes a lot of noise or freaks out my sister when it gets out of its cage."

"The twins are your nephews? *That's* who you had a date with on Sunday?" Really, she should have known. Twice she'd had to break their Sunday plans this last year and both times Ty ended up spending the day watching his sister's eight-year olds.

"Who'd you think I meant by the twins?" Amusement warmed his eyes as he placed chicken number two in with the other and then set the pan in front of the lamp on his nightstand.

Oooh . . . he thought he was so funny.

Candy rolled her eyes. "Exactly who you wanted me to think, perv."

"Me, the perv? You're the one who got it in your head I was spending Sunday afternoon doing twin sisters."

"Because you made me."

"Because you were jealous."

"As if I have a reason to be jealous. I can have you anytime I want."

Snorting, Ty stood from the bed. "Think pretty highly of yourself, don't you?"

What she thought is that, in the course of discovering chickens on his bed, she'd managed to forget he was only wearing boxers. The snug-fitting kind that grew even snugger as she eyed the obvious bulge of his cock. That he was getting aroused by their conversation went to show how accurate she was in believing he was always eager to do her. That she was getting equally aroused went to show how badly she really was itching for his brand of scratching.

Maybe she *could* handle taking a couple days off from the good girl gig, as Courtney called her quest to find a long-term man before the Fibroid Fairy struck. After all, she'd made a decent comeback to the celibacy wagon after Ty forced himself on her the week before last.

Forced, right. There was definitely a lot of forcing on his part when she'd been straddling him and jerking his clothes off at warp speed.

Right now, Candy wouldn't have to jerk much of anything off to get to his body. One little tug and his boxers would be around his ankles. Another little tug and her panties would be around her own. A final tug would have her dress out of the way. Then all it would take was a single push and he would be inside her, his dick grinding up against her cervix. His lips locked on hers, tongue in her mouth, kissing her with an expertise Steven had no shot of ever attaining.

Yep, that sounded pretty damned good. Enough to step forward and slide her fingers into the front of his boxers.

Hooking her thumbs on the opposite side of his underwear, she tipped back her head and unleashed her most seductive smile. "Like you'd turn me down if I asked you to do me right now."

"I would." His hands remained at his sides, his voice even.

Playing hard to get. How completely un-Ty-like, and so incredibly tempting.

Candy kicked off her pumps and lifted up on bare toes to brush his ear with the damp flick of her tongue. "Do me, Ty." Whispering the words on a hot breath, she rubbed against him. "Right now. Fuck me."

"Not gonna happen." He remained motionless, but his eyes were growing unfocused. His breathing picked up.

He was close to giving in.

And she was having the most fun she'd had in months.

Pulse pounding with excitement, she moved back a couple feet and started to ball the sides of her dress in her hands. "I'm undressing." The hem caressed her upper thighs: She let go of the dress to push her hands beneath and grab the sides of her paper-thin panties. "Tell me when I'm naked and wet for you, you won't give in."

His gaze latched onto her hands as she brought the translucent white panties skimming down her legs. He swallowed audibly, but his voice hung on to that steely note. "I won't."

Lifting the dress back up to mid-thigh, she climbed onto the bed. "I'm going to lay back and fondle myself. You're going to want me in a way you can't deny."

"We'll see." Ty looked at the chicks peeping from the nightstand.

Go ahead and pretend you care more about the birds than watching me masturbate. You won't be able to pretend in a second.

She lay back on the bed with the dress's skirt pooled around her waist. The heat lamp was a foot away and yet close enough she could feel it warming her feminine flesh as she spread her thighs. The thought of getting his cock in her had her pussy slick, and it made a delightfully erotic sucking sound as she slid a finger between her labia and deep into her channel.

Candy moved her free hand beneath the dress. Squeezing her breast through the cotton and lace of her bra, she pushed a second finger into her sex and pumped them together. The sucking sound intensified. The smell of her arousal lifted into the air.

She clamped her muscles around her fingers and sighed with the next thrust. Liquid heat sizzled in her veins and leaked out as juice from her cunt. "You want me, Ty," she moaned. "You know you do. Admit it."

Finally, he averted his face from the chicks to look at her.

He glanced at her crotch for all of a second—just long enough to have his erection giving a noticeable jerk against the front of his boxers—then he turned and started for the bedroom door. He turned back when he reached it, bypassing her fondling to meet her eyes. "I want you. I'm just not going to have you. My sister's dropping by to pick up the chicks in fifteen minutes and I promised to have their cage set up and ready to go."

"Oh." The smile fell from Candy's lips. Her fingers stilled

with her disappointment, the deliciously building tension going with it.

She should have known something was up from the second he segued into that hard-to-get routine. But then, he'd done almost the same thing the other week when he left her wet and panting in the shower, so how the hell was she supposed to read him right anymore?

"You know where I keep the nudie mags. Help yourself to some reading material, and I'll be with you just as soon as I can."

Ty put the finishing touches on the chick's cage, which, considering he'd spent the afternoon building it, required less than five minutes. He used the next five to get his body under control and then talk with his sister who called to ask if he could bring the birds by the house instead of her coming to pick them up. Since it fit well with his plan to continue to get Candy hot and bothered and then leave her wanting, he agreed.

Ty returned to his bedroom, expecting to find Candy indulging in porn the way he'd suggested and the way she'd done when they'd been interrupted in the past. Only, she hadn't gotten out the porn. She lay half naked on the bed in nearly the same revealing position he'd left her. Instead of enticing him with her fingerplay, she was snoring.

He'd noticed how tired she looked when she'd rushed into his condo. If he didn't need to deliver the chicks to his sister as promised, he would leave her to sleep. He could head over to Denise's by himself and be back within the hour. But, just in case Candy was as creeped out by Steven as she'd let on, he didn't want to risk leaving her here to wake up alone.

After pulling on jeans and a sweatshirt, so he wouldn't be tempted to take advantage of her helpless state by finally granting her Sleeping Beauty fantasy, he sank down on the bed next to her and gave her shoulder a gentle shake. "Time to wake up."

She didn't budge, just kept on with the snoring. He gave the shoulder shake attempt another few tries then quit with the gentle approach to roll her to the side and swat her bare butt. Her eyes snapped open instantly, bleary and disoriented.

Ty straightened, grinning as he lifted his cell phone off the dresser and hooked the back clip to the waist of his jeans. "Amazing the good to be had in a little ass paddling. Have a nice nap?"

Frowning, Candy scooted up to a sitting position. "I wasn't sleeping."

Yeah, and she hadn't been snoring either. Letting it go, he grabbed the scrap of white cotton she called underwear off the floor and tossed them to her. "There's been a change in plans. Denise called and she needs me to bring the chicks over to her place."

"I didn't hear the phone."

"It was my cell," he lied, because God forbid her wrath if he pushed the sleeping issue. "I have it set to vibrate because it feels so good when it rings." He unhooked the phone from his jeans and tossed it to her. "Stick it in your pussy and I'll give you a call."

She attempted to give him a revolted look only to end up laughing. "You're demented."

"You're tempted."

Without responding, Candy hopped off the bed and handed him the phone. She turned her back to him to work the panties up her legs, like he hadn't seen every inch of her countless times. "When does she want the chicks?"

"I said we'd be over in twenty minutes."

She spun around, the hem of the shapeless dress falling to her knees. "*We?* What if I don't want to go?"

"I figured you wouldn't want to stay home alone with Steven liable to track you down. Besides, Denise wants to see you."

Hesitance passed through her eyes, but in the end she nodded. "Fine. I'll go."

Ty's sister had asked him to deliver the chicks to her place on the outskirts of the city because his brother-in-law was working late with his survey crew and the bird's cage, built to fit them until they were full size, would never fit into her hatchback. Only, when they arrived at the ranch-style house, Brad's burgundy work truck was parked in the drive.

Ty grabbed the cage out of the back of his own truck and started up the stone walkway to the front porch. Candy followed behind with the chicks in the metal pan. Before he could knock, Denise opened the door, wearing a pale pink sweatsuit with her long, brown curls pulled up into a ponytail. "Brad's in the shower. The guys changed their mind about working late, but it was too late to call you back by the time I found out."

She stepped back and held open the door as Ty passed through with the cage. Candy moved inside, stacking the pan on top of the cage, and Denise gasped and pulled her into a hug. "God, it's been ages!" She set her at arm's length to grimace at her ugly dress and hairdo. "What happened to you?"

Laughing, Ty made his way down the hall to the twins' bedroom. He would have liked to stay to listen to Candy's response, but his sister and her unintentionally uncouth personality were bound to get Candy talking more without them.

The twins were staying at a friend's for the night, so Ty was able to make fast work of settling the chicks into their new home. As he was finishing up, Brad stepped into the bedroom with an open can of beer in either hand.

He handed a beer to Ty. "I haven't seen Candy in months. Thought maybe you two called it quits."

Ty grabbed the can and took a drink. "She did. I didn't."

"What's she doing here then?"

He smiled. "Being sexually frustrated."

Brad sank down on the bottom bed of the boys' twin-sized bunks. "You've got my attention."

"She decided she wanted to call it starts again tonight. Thing is, I know damned well if I take her up on it and jump into bed, she'll change her mind in another couple days. So I'm working at her slowly, letting her have a taste of what she wants, and then leaving her hanging."

Surprise registered in Brad's eyes. "You're trying to lure her in for the long run?" Beneath a dark blond mustache, he smiled approvingly. "I never thought I'd see the day you made a commitment. Denise is going to be thrilled."

"Christ, no, this isn't about making a commitment," Ty snapped back with the unexpected and way-off-base speculation. "I just want to see Candy happy and having fun again. Get that damned clip out of her hair."

Brad's smile took a downward curve. "What if her being happy and having fun involves making a commitment?"

"It doesn't. If she wanted to be married so damned badly, she would be engaged to the schmuck who proposed to her Wednesday night."

The elevator doors pinged opened on the condo's top floor. Candy stepped out and grabbed her keys from her purse.

Ty sent her a questioning look as they walked the short distance to their facing doors. "What happened to spending the night?"

That plan fizzled out about the time Denise got over her less-than-sexy appearance to share how elated she was to see Candy and Ty together again, because she'd always known Candy would be the one to get him to settle down. Candy liked his sister too much to build her hopes up by falling back into bed with Ty for a night or two, and then walking away.

Reaching her door, she slid her key into the lock. "It's late enough Steven shouldn't be an issue."

"Sure about that?" he asked behind her.

Her pulse picked up with his tone. Genuine concern seemed to fill his voice, like he might actually care about her beyond a sexual standpoint. Of course, it was probably just Denise in his head, making him ask the question. In defense of her appearance, Candy had told his sister about Courtney's could-have-been stalker and how earlier tonight Candy had feared Steven could be up to something similar.

Veering away from the serious, she turned around to meet Ty's eyes and focus on the physical. "I'm sure that I no longer want to screw, if that's what you're asking."

"It wasn't. But it doesn't hurt my feelings either." The corners of his lips hitched up in the same slow, sexy, devilish grin she'd seen in her mind every night this week while she masturbated. "I have a date with a sure thing tomorrow."

The heat his grin brought to her belly died with his words. Not because she was jealous of him seeing another woman, but just because she was jealous of him having actual sex while she relied on her vibrator.

If he *was* having actual sex.

She smiled knowingly. "Does this sure thing happen to have feathers?"

"Oh, no, Candy, baby." Ty brought his hands out, using them to carve the shape of an extremely curvaceous woman out of the air. "Tonya's *all* woman."

5

"I'm thinking about moving to Orlando," Candy called over her shoulder loud enough for Courtney to hear across the cube-farm hallway.

"*What?*" Courtney gasped back.

Candy swiveled in her chair. "I hate how cold and long the winters here are. I spend half the time whining and the rest of the time in bed, covered up to my nose."

Eyebrows knit, Courtney charged across the hallway to plunk down on the edge of Candy's desk. "Where is this coming from?"

Candy took a sip from her morning latte. Setting the cup down, she turned to nod at Pinnacle's Intranet site displayed on her computer screen. "The monthly internal job postings just went up and they're looking for a PR specialist for the southeast region." She scrolled through the postings page. "I bet they could use a kick-ass tech writer, too. What do you say? Want to pack up and head to the land of sunshine? Find us a couple of rich retirees looking for some sweet young things to love up and spoil to the max?" *Get the hell away from Ty.*

And Tonya.

Candy had seen the buxom redhead, who looked way too much like the sorority chick from Ty's college days, for the first time last night when she'd stepped off the elevator as Ty was letting the woman into his condo. She'd felt slightly nauseous and like beating the crap out of him ever since.

Courtney gave her a get-real look. "I love snow. Even if I didn't, like you think I'd move away from Blaine?"

Closing the postings page, Candy smiled tauntingly. It was so much more fun to spend the morning teasing her friend than accepting her jealousy of Ty had morphed from him having sex while she wasn't to him having sex with another woman, period.

Unless he and Tonya weren't sleeping together.

As if!

Knowing Ty's vigorous sex drive and how much he loved big boobs, they probably hadn't stopped screwing for more than a few hours since their sure-thing date two days ago.

Keeping the smile frozen on her face, Candy goaded, "I thought maybe things were getting boring. It *has* been a while since you and Blaine hooked up, and I know how afraid you are being tied down with one guy will turn you into the average Courtney of days past."

"No boredom." Courtney's face lit up with her wide, naughty smile. "Our recent adventure into public indecency could have something to do with it."

"Doll, it's only indecent if you get caught. Which is liable to happen with Mr. Florida Retiree Man. That whole not-so-fast-as-he-used-to-be thing at work."

Courtney's smile vanished. "You can't seriously move! Not only are you one of my closest friends, but I'm getting married next summer. I need to start thinking about wedding planning very soon. You're supposed to guide me through it."

"I look like I know about weddings?"

"Together we can figure it out. Besides, you're my maid of honor."

"What about Gail?" Candy asked about her coworker's ex-roommate. "Things still bad between you?"

"Not bad, really, just different. We've accepted our lives are taking two separate paths. I still plan to see her, do lunch or have an M & M night once a month or so, but she's not going to do the butt dance at the reception with me. Probably no chicken dance either. Electric slide is definitely out." Pleading entered Courtney's eyes as her red-painted lower lip pushed into a mew. "Don't go, Candy. Please. I don't want to be a one-woman locomotive."

Candy laughed, a lot harder than the moment warranted but she needed to expend some of the stress and frustration eating at her over the whole Ty situation.

Why now, after three years of spending the time they weren't together dating and doing others, did she hate the idea of him with another woman?

Going solemn, she pressed a hand to her heart. "I don't know yet if I'm going anywhere. If I do decide to transfer, I swear to take the two weeks off before your wedding so we have plenty of time to practice our dance moves. By the way, you forgot the twist. Any self-respecting sex diva knows how to work it to the ground."

"Sex diva?" Courtney questioned hopefully. "Does that mean you're going to quit with the staid, sophisticated lady routine?"

"I've already quit with some of it." Candy glanced down at her red turtleneck and black slacks, which were still body covering but also moderately figure revealing. Her gaze skipped to her guilty indulgence of three-inch black spikes, and she smiled elatedly. "For the night of your wedding, I promise to quit with all of it."

"What if you're engaged by then?"

Candy's smile evened out. She wanted to find a long-run

man by summer—needed to—but, truthfully, what were the odds when the pickings were guys like Steven and guys like Ty? "Mr. Fiancé is gonna have one lucky night."

"Do you think it's a coincidence a man named Chubby was involved with a dance that gives people the opportunity to grind up against each other in public?"

Candy laughed out loud as her weighty thoughts lifted with the abrupt change in topic. Thank God she and Courtney had become friends, because she seriously needed her on days like this one. "I'm fairly certain most people twist alone. And that if Chubby had any idea you just suggested that, he'd be taking the first flight into Grand Rapids to kick your ass."

Steven could be more than the sedate man she'd gotten to know the month they'd been dating. He could be a closet mango.

Candy reminded herself of that fact as she stepped out of her car onto the streetlight-brightened driveway of his two-story home. A potential bad-boy side and the possibility that he might hold the power to make her stop caring who Ty slept with were the reasons she'd chosen to look past his hasty proposal and her Friday-night freakout session following his call to give them another chance.

With skepticism leading the way, she started up the brick steps toward his front door. He opened the door before she could . . . and sent her doubt into a tailspin and her heart soaring with hope by pulling her into his arms and planting a big ol' tongue kiss on her.

They both came up panting for air a minute later.

Stepping back, he smiled. "I've missed you."

She returned his smile, not quite certain she'd missed him, but not exactly sorry she'd come here either. The forceful style of his kiss had the makings of a bad boy. The tight-in-the-ass-and-thighs fit of his casual jeans and the flash of curl-dusted skin past his partially unbuttoned black dress shirt added to the idea. The almost rumpled appearance of his hair was promising enough to have Candy taking his hand and letting him lead her into his house.

They moved through an open foyer and beyond the door to a massive great room before they stopped in a dining room. A long oak table was set with glasses of red wine, decadent-smelling platters of food covered with square silver lids, and flickering red pillar candles.

Steven pulled out a chair and waited for her to sit. Her attention caught on his manicured fingernails against the seat's deep blue paisley fabric, and she was hit with nice-guy flashes.

Then those flashes evaporated, as his free hand journeyed to her ass and copped a feel of butt cheek through her skirt.

Well, thank you, God. Coming here might just be the best move she'd ever made.

Curbing an anxious laugh, she sat down. After pushing her chair toward the table, he rounded the head of the table and sat opposite her.

With a megawatt grin, he lifted the lids off the serving platters to reveal a pepper-crusted beef roast with complimenting dark gravy, red-skin potatoes in butter sauce, and asparagus dusted with oregano and parmesan. "I hope you like dinner. I cooked it myself."

"It smells incredible."

He filled her plate, ladling the rich-looking sauce over the beef. She waited for him to fill his own plate before she took a bite. And then it was as if sheer decadence had entered her mouth to seduce her taste buds. It was all she could do to stop her blissful moan as she forked another heavenly bite between her lips.

Mmm mmm mmm . . . Ty had nothing on this new version of Steven.

He could kiss. He could cook.

"Eat up." His blue eyes flashed with wickedness. "I have a long night planned."

He could speed up her heart with anticipation. "I can hardly wait."

Candy savored each bite of food, thrilled in the tartness of the red wine on her tongue. Exchanged suggestive glances with Steven while silently praying her expectations would not go unfulfilled. That tonight would be the night she stopped caring if Ty was doing Tonya or any other woman on this planet. If that meant forgetting the good girl gig and jumping Steven, so be it. He'd already proved he liked more about her than her breasts with his marriage proposal.

Her sex clenching with expectancy, she dusted off the last of her beef and crossed her silverware over her empty plate. Scratching her arm, she sat back and watched him sip at his wine.

There was a definite sensual quality about the way his lips fit to the edge of the glass, how his throat worked with each swallow. The flash of his tongue as he moved the glass away to frown at her.

Frown? Where did that figure into the sensual angle? "What's the matter?"

"Do you have a rash?"

"No. Why?"

He nodded at her left arm. "You've been scratching your arm for the last five minutes."

"No, I haven't." But even as she said it, she felt the urge to scratch. She also felt warm. A little off kilter. Her face sort of achy and numb.

Candy looked down at her arm to the telling raised red rash.

Ah, fuck!

She jerked her gaze back to Steven's face, demanding, "Did you feed me cocoa?"

"There was some in the gravy. That's what gives it the rich texture."

Texture? He was talking about texture and she was about to puff up like a balloon.

God, she'd actually believed he had the power to speed her heart. From the first bite, it had been the cocoa at work. "I'm allergic to cocoa! How could you not know that?"

"The question is how could I have?" His sensual front vanished with the snap of his words. "You don't exactly share a lot of truthful information on yourself. Hell, if it weren't for your ex-lover's Mile-High Club comment, I'd probably still be convinced you're a prude."

He'd caught *that*? And wanted to marry her even knowing she was a farce? Or maybe learning she wasn't so innocent was an impetus for his proposal.

Damn, she couldn't have this conversation now. Couldn't think nearly straight enough.

She shoved back her chair and stood. "I *need* to go. I *need* my inhaler."

"I can drive you," Steven offered, but it was the kind of offer that rang with clear obligation and, frankly, she didn't want to get in a car with a guy she obviously didn't know any better than he knew her.

Frankly, she was already regretting this night and it wasn't even over yet.

That her reaction to the gravy really wasn't his fault had her annoyance relenting to a weak smile. "Thanks, but I can drive. I'm okay for now. Fifteen minutes from now things might not be so pretty."

Candy retraced the path they'd taken through the house until she was seated in her car, facing the lighted vanity mirror. Lumps were beginning to emerge on her cheeks and forehead. She hadn't eaten straight chocolate or solitary cocoa. Still, depending on how much cocoa he'd used in the gravy and how soon she could get to her medicine, the inflammation could grow worse until she would be lucky to see past her bloated eyelids.

Shit, she couldn't risk driving.

She needed Ty.

Grabbing her cell phone from her purse, she stabbed the first number in memory. The phone started ringing and then the sound cut short as it picked up on his end. "I need you to come get me," she rushed out before he could say hello.

"I'm on a date," he said dryly.

"So am I." Her heart sped faster and panic quavered into her voice.

"Where are you?" He sounded suddenly concerned, like he'd detected her unease.

Or maybe he was pissed and she was too delirious to hear it.

She *had* to be out of her mind to have called him. Why hadn't she tried Courtney? Or anyone but him. Why wouldn't he leave her freaking head?

"Candy?"

"Steven's," she supplied, because she had called Ty and, damnit, she did want him to come get her. Only him. "I'm at Steven's place. He lives off West Alpine."

"You're seeing that schmuck again? What happened to him creeping you out?"

Nothing she had the mindset to consider right now. Now, she said to hell with everything and resorted to the typically unthinkable. Pleading, "Come get me, Ty. Please."

"I'm already walking out to my truck."

"Thank you." After rattling off Steven's house number, she tossed her phone into the passenger's seat, locked the car doors, and sat back.

Last year, she'd never have had to face this panic. She'd always carried an inhaler and allergenics in her purse. But then, last year she'd switched to a smaller purse and the inhaler and medicine had been the first to go since she hadn't needed to use either in well over a decade.

Now, she needed them. Now, she closed her eyes and counted Prada handbags while she prayed for Ty to hurry.

Either Courtney's suggestion had worked and she'd fallen asleep as a side effect of the counting, or Candy had zoned out as part of her reaction, because she opened her eyes and screamed when Ty knocked on her window.

Pulling in calming breaths, she hit the door locks and opened the driver's door.

"What went wrong this—" His gaze zeroed in on her face and, in the low lighting, she could see his expression go murderous. "Where is the bastard?"

"Steven didn't hit me. He fed me cocoa."

"Son of a—" With a glare at the house, he balled his hands into fists. "Why the hell didn't he know you were allergic? You told me the first time I cooked you dinner."

Because Courtney was batting two for two tonight. Candy was too much of a mango for Steven, and the two of them had never stood a chance.

She wasn't too much of a mango for Ty, though. Right now he even seemed like he cared about more than her tits, like he wanted to plant a fist in Steven's face for causing her misery.

Or maybe she was still delirious. "I need to get home, Ty. I *need* my inhaler."

Sympathy replaced his glare. "Christ, I'm sorry." He uncurled his fingers to reach into the car and help her out. "You're barely breathing and I'm acting like an asshole.

"Is your inhaler enough, or should I take you to the ER?" he asked when she was standing unsteadily in the driveway next to him.

Maybe it was just her mind making up his concern, but it sounded good anyway. And he felt damned good as she snuggled up tight against his side and let him walk her to his truck. "Home's fine. I'm mostly okay right now, but my head could swell to the size of a watermelon and my throat close up, if I don't get my inhaler and medicine soon."

6

Walking away from what promised to be the first of many nights of scorching sex with Tonya to rescue Candy shouldn't have him feeling so good.

Ty did feel good as he changed into sweatpants and a T-shirt in his bedroom. Damned good, and just a little like a perv when he returned to the living room to consider Candy lying naked on his couch. A thin blue sheet covered her but, with the way it outlined her curvy body, it was more of a temptation than a true concealer.

He sank back on the recliner kitty corner from her. "Feeling better?"

Finally free of the clip, the dirty blond waves of her hair slid alluringly along the mottled brown fabric of the couch with her nod. "I don't think I'm going to burst into flames or scratch my arms off anymore." She lifted her head off the couch pillow far enough to meet his eyes. "Sorry I ruined your date with Ms. Tits."

The swelling of her face had begun to subside. Even so, he wanted to treat Steven to his fist. Maybe the stiff hadn't purposely given Candy cocoa, but he'd obviously been an ass about her reaction to it, that she'd called Ty to come pick her up.

"I'd rather be with you," he admitted.

She flopped her head back against the pillow. "Doubtful."

"Truthful." He grinned. "You have big tits *and* put out on the first date."

Instead of laughing, as he'd expected, she lifted her head back up and eyed him in astonishment. "You haven't slept with her?"

He shrugged. "Turns out she's into guys who want her for more than her boobs."

"I like her better already." She gave a weak smile, but her expression didn't match her tone.

She sounded detached, like she wasn't into the conversation. The medicine had to be working its magic on her system, making her sluggish.

"I'm moving," she said softly.

Definitely the medicine at work. Candy was neither soft-spoken by nature nor, aside from the subtle head movements, had she budged since he'd helped her undress and lay on the couch a half hour ago. "It's just your mind playing tricks. You're lying perfectly still."

"I'm moving," she repeated, louder this time and stone sober. "To Florida."

Ty's breath sucked in. Pulse racing with the bombshell news, he shot forward in the recliner. "Why would you?"

She laid her head back on the pillow. "A better-paying job in a much friendlier climate. You know what a baby I am when I'm cold."

Bullshit. If this was just about a job, or even her aversion to cold weather, she wouldn't have looked away to respond.

He pushed to his feet and crossed to the couch, towering over her so she had no choice but to look up at him. With her face still lumpy and red, he felt guilty pushing the issue. Just not guilty enough to stop. "*Is* it a job? Or the chance to get me out of your life?"

She rolled her eyes. "Your ego never ceases to amaze me."

"And your ability to deny the truth never ceases to amaze *me.*"

A slow, catty smile curved her lips. "The thought of not having to contend with you did cross my mind."

"Contend, my ass. You love that you're a hallway away from feeling good." He raked his gaze downward, stilling on the thrust of her breasts against the sheet. Her nipples beaded, pressing as rigid circles against the thin blue cotton, and he barked out a knowing laugh. "Your body doesn't lie."

Candy crossed her arms over her chest. "My *body* loves fucking you. My mind is unimpressed with my body."

Ty's cock roused with her harsh talk. He sank down on the edge of the couch and slipped his hand beneath her arms. Past the sheet, the warmth and weight of a breast filled his palm and warmed his blood. "Then how about I appeal to your body?"

"Jesus, Ty, my face looks like a camel. You can't honestly want me."

But he did. And she wanted him, too, going by the way she uncrossed her arms and arched her back with the stroke of his fingertips over an erect nipple. "Didn't you ever hear beauty's more than skin deep?"

Sighing, she lifted his hand from her breast. He figured he was up against more denial—rejection that he'd accept if she gave any sign she was still in discomfort. She didn't give any sign of discomfort.

She took hold of the edge of the sheet and pushed it down to her navel.

Feisty, fun-loving Candy emerged, flashing an openmouthed smile ripe with the carnal promise of her tongue. Taunting warmed her soft brown eyes as she gathered the generous globes of her breasts in her hands. "Guess you don't want to see this skin then?"

She squeezed the twin mounds, circling her thumbs over the deep pink skin of the areolas before hiding the stiff buds beneath her fingers.

Ty groaned with the bucking of his cock. Shit, she drove him nuts with her hot and cold attitude lately. She was flashing siren hot in his face now, but there was nothing to say she wouldn't go ice cold again in two seconds. There was also nothing to say she wasn't sincere about moving out of state. In which case, he had no reason to continue in his quest to bring her permanently back to the easy-living, easy-loving side of life by teasing her to the brink of orgasm and then leaving her hanging.

He might as well screw her start to finish and make his dick's day. "I could be persuaded to touch if you asked nicely."

Lowering her lashes, she said in a dirty sweet voice, "Pet my tits, Ty."

With a rough laugh, he brought his hands over hers. "Very nice." Her fingers parted, exposing the tips of her nipples peekaboo style. He bent his head, inhaling her sexy apple scent as he petted a tight crown with the flick of his tongue. "Tasty, too."

Gasping out a hot breath, Candy returned her fingers to the sheet. "There's more skin where that came from." She started to ease the sheet down. "Right down here."

He lifted his head, waiting with his breath wedged in his throat. Waiting for her hairless pussy to come into sight. Waiting to bury his tongue inside her cunt and eat out her honey for what could be the last time if she had her way.

Christ, he didn't want her having her way, ending all chance of future fun between them. But what could he do to stop her if she really did have a new job lined up? Or, hell, just if she wanted away from his advances, even if she appeared red hot for them now.

Best not to think about that. Best to enjoy the show.

No sooner did he get his mind back on the show than the sheet's descent stopped an inch north of revealing her mound. Ty's shaft gave a disgruntled throb. He looked up to find her eyes closed and her mouth lacking the fuck-me smile.

The same gut-level concern he felt upon seeing her swollen face back in her car slammed into him, speeding his pulse. He brought a hand to her cheek, stroking the backs of his fingers across the fading lumps. "Okay?"

Opening her eyes, Candy smiled. "Uh huh. Just counting handbags."

Handbags? What the hell . . .

Narrowing his gaze, he pulled his hand away and sat back. "Your mind must want me out of your life damned bad if it can't even stay with me long enough to screw."

Amusement bled into her smile. "Shockingly, it isn't quite that sick of you yet. The red wine I had at dinner just rendezvoused with the medicine and made me a little dizzy."

Not her mind rejecting him, then, but the reality wasn't much better.

His glare let up while his cock silently sobbed. "In that case, you can count the sex off. I'm not about to make you feel worse."

"I'm fine now." She looked to where her hands restarted the downward slide of the sheet. "Nice and wet."

The sheet cruised to her upper thighs and the shimmering lips of her sex came into view. She was extremely nice and wet. Still, he wasn't sleeping with her. Not when another dizzy spell might be lurking just around the corner. "And not getting fucked tonight."

"Oh, c'mon!" He shook his head, and her lips pushed into a pout. "Fine. If you're too concerned about my health to do me the right way, you could at least finger me for a while."

Right, because they both knew how good he was at stopping

once he had his fingers inside her. "Nice try, Candy, baby, but it's not gonna happen. Roll over and I'll give you a massage."

"All right." Discontent clung to the words. "If that's as good as I can get." She kicked the sheet to the floor and rolled onto her belly, resting her face in the crook of her arms.

Ty shut out the hungry pulsing of his cock and took a few seconds just to look, just to savor every inch of her pale, rounded butt cheeks, the dip of her sides at her waist, the sweep of her silky blond hair as it cascaded around her shoulders and onto the couch pillow. Just in case she really was serious about moving away.

Just in case she was serious, he poured every ounce of concentration into his hands as he brought them to either side of her head and worked them in slow circles. Gradually, he applied pressure and moved his hands down around her ears, then lower to the base of her neck. He worked out the kinks in those muscles with the circling of his fingertips, and Candy melted into the couch with the same helplessly throaty whimper she always gave at this point in his rubdowns.

The routine moan followed as he brought his hands to her shoulders and kneaded. And the routine throbbing of his dick followed that low, husky sound, bringing his attention right back to his shaft's rock-solid state. Bringing his focus to the cleft of her ass and just how easy it would be to straddle her from above and slide inside the tight hole.

"Ty?" The lone word murmured against her folded arms.

"Mmm . . . ?"

"Do you want to get married someday?"

His hands froze on her shoulders, his gaze moving from her butt to the back of her head as he considered just how unroutine that question was.

The day that Candy met Steven's folks, Ty had thought she might be after a commitment, or at least believe in some part of her mind that she wanted one. But then, she'd turned Steven's proposal down flat. He'd thought that meant the whole concept was out of her head. Was he wrong? Was a commitment what it would take to keep her around? He liked her one hell of a lot, yeah, but he was barely into his thirties and taking great pleasure in the single life.

"Sure," he said casually as possible. "Someday. Like when I'm forty."

She jerked with his response, or maybe it was just because she was getting cold lying around buck naked and his warm hands made for a startling contrast. Whatever the reason, his hands slipped downward with the move and his fingers ended up on her breasts, caressing along the soft sides plumped up with her position.

"Oooh . . ." She writhed beneath his touch. "That feels sooo good. Don't you *dare* stop!"

"Not a chance." When she was purring that way, he didn't want to stop all night. That his handling made her drop the marriage subject was a much-appreciated extra.

Flushing the subject from his own thoughts, Ty stroked and rubbed and toyed with the supple mounds, and his shaft steeled against the front of his boxers and sweatpants a little more with each pass.

He gritted his teeth against the tension flaming high in his lower spine, snugging his balls in their sac.

Screw the tension. He could hold it together. Save what might truly be a final fuck for another day. One when he didn't have to worry she would be too dizzy or disoriented to remember.

Or so he thought he could, until Candy lifted her ass a few inches in the air and ground her cunt against the couch's rough fabric. With a breathy moan, she segued into another wriggle, pressing her sex down hard and rocking her hips back and forth.

His dick jumped with the erotic move. "What are you doing?"

"My pussy's really tense. Just trying to ease the ache." She sounded neither dizzy nor disoriented. Rather, sexy and sultry and like she was dying for him to ram into her from behind.

He might be imagining that last part, but then, knowing her lusty appetite and how seldom she'd fed it the last months, probably not.

Even so, he didn't give her his cock. Just traced a finger down the crease of her ass to end an inch from the opening of her sex. Her legs moved apart, revealing her plump pussy lips from behind and silently welcoming him inside her slick body, right where he said he wouldn't go tonight.

Drawing a finger across her slit, Ty groaned, because he knew damned well he was going there.

His cock gave another anxious buck as he eased a finger into her sizzling hot channel and parted the moist flesh. Moving deeper, he rubbed and coaxed and caressed. And nearly cried like a baby with his body's relief when Candy shifted on his fingers, spinning her lower half around on the couch until her knees were on the floor in front of him, her belly and breasts flat against the cushion and her lush ass right up in his face.

"You're slipping." He brushed his fingers over the backs of her thighs, a barely there caress that had her butt pushing higher in the air and her legs spreading invitingly wide.

"Am I?" she asked, all coy and innocent-like.

"When I started, I could only see your ass," he returned in the same tone while he brought his hands to his sweats and shoved them, along with his boxers, down his hips. "Now your cunt's on full display. All spread out and pink and juicy."

"And still tense. I bet it would help if you fingered me with your cock."

He released a coarse laugh. "Pretty sure there's another word for that."

He didn't hedge over the particulars, though. He also didn't waste any more time worrying over her health or feeling guilty, but worked the sweatpants and boxers off his body the rest of the way, took his cock in hand, and brought it to the rear of her sex.

"My, what big fingers you have," Candy gasped as he pushed inside, rocking his balls up against her slit.

Her pussy clenched around his shaft, and wave after wave of raw sensation spilled through him. Grinding his teeth, he stilled his rocking. As little loving as she'd gotten lately, she was damned tight and his control was already thready.

Bracing one hand on the edge of the couch, Ty slipped the other around to her front. He used his fingers on her clit, twisting and teasing the bundle of nerves, pressing against it with the pad of his thumb. Wanting her walking the tightrope of orgasm just as fast.

"That a latent Big Bad Wolf fantasy coming out?" The words hitched out, rough and raw, as he worked his hips into a slower rhythm.

"You won't do me Sleeping Beauty style," she spoke in between mewling pants. "Might as well give wolfie style a try." Bringing her hands to her butt, she gripped a soft cheek in each and pulled them apart to expose her puckered anus. "Look, another tense spot."

Feeling like his dick would spurt at any moment, he shoved it hard into her pussy. Candy let out a throaty giggle. If her hands weren't in the way, he would have swatted her ass for acting like such a fucking tease.

Shit, she knew he couldn't resist it when she got nasty like that.

He brought his hand back around from her clit to run a finger the length of her crack. She increased the pacing of their joined bodies. Groaning as the tension barreled forward again, he dipped a finger partway inside her damp, silky passage. "My, what a tight asshole you have."

She shoved backward, taking his finger inside the rest of the way. "The better to feel you fucking it. I want your dick in my ass, Ty."

His shaft spasmed with anticipation. Pulling from her sex, he brought the tip of his cock to her asshole and coated the puckered skin with her pussy juices. "Sure you're up to it?"

Without words, without hesitation, without giving him a second to hold on, Candy rammed back, sucking his shaft deep inside, nearly blowing it for him then and there.

"Oooh, yeah," she moaned, already moving forward again, gripping the couch cushions white-knuckled as she worked her hips into a quick and dirty rhythm. "So sure."

Ty gritted his teeth with the feel of her taut skin clenching around him. The wetness building up. The nearly unbearable strain pushing through his body, drawing every muscle and tendon snug as shit.

Palming her tits, he pulled her back to his front. Burying his face in her hair, he bit down on her ear, nibbled at that sweaty, salty skin as he shoved his cock inside her ass again and again. She turned her face with his next nibble and their mouths met, opened, clung as their tongues sought out and found each other in a hot, wet, needful kiss that shook him head to toe.

The burning tightness in his balls intensified, along with the knocking of his heart against his ribs. He broke the kiss to punish her neck with a bruising bite. Squeezing her breast, he growled, "You *can't* leave this behind."

"A good job can last a lifetime," she shot back, her ass muscles squeezing him tight.

"A good fuck can last the night. This one isn't gonna." Not when their breathing had gone ragged and coarse. Not when one rub of her clit was all it took to send her pussy spiraling into a shuddering orgasm. Not when her ass pumped back against his dick and balls so forcefully with her release he couldn't keep his eyes open.

They snapped shut and his control snapped off.

Bellowing as he came, he emptied his cum into her. He took her mouth in another fierce kiss as he pounded wildly to the last drop.

A half minute passed, and Candy eased back on the couch, separating their bodies. Turning around, She went up on her knees and eyed him through hazy brown. "You're right."

Ty's grin came fast and furious and smug as hell. Mindblowing as that orgasm had been, this news was a thousand times better.

She wasn't leaving. She wasn't ending their fun. "You finally get the message."

"I get it." She crawled to the side of the couch and stepped off. "I'll never be happy with a guy who's afraid to take me in the ass. Mr. Florida Retiree Man's either going to need a strong heart or a first-rate pacemaker."

7

Courtney strolled into view of Candy's cube, peered inside, and smiled so wide the curve of her pink-painted lips took up the bulk of her face. "Someone slept with Ty."

Tossing aside the graphics magazine she'd been thumbing through, Candy groaned. Damn this endorphin rush that always came the day after doing Ty. And damn the perma-grin that accompanied it. She didn't want to think about last night. With Courtney pointing out her grin, she had no choice but to both think and talk about it.

Or maybe she could avoid it by bringing up a topic sure to consume Courtney's mind.

Candy grabbed the almost-empty cup of latte from her desk. She swallowed down the lukewarm remains while Courtney shook off her black leather pea coat and hung it in her cubicle across the hall.

Courtney returned to Candy's cube, and Candy said soberly, "Someone's moving to Orlando."

"Someone's full of crap." Humor tinged her words.

"Someone's dead serious," Candy returned without a hint of amusement.

Courtney's smile fled. "No." She sank onto the edge of Candy's desk, crossing her legs beneath a short green corduroy skirt before leaning close to ask, "What happened last night? You have night-after-boinking-Ty glow, but I thought you were having dinner with Steven?"

"I saw Steven. And he fed me cocoa."

"Oh, shit. I guess you realized it fast since you're not in the hospital."

"I didn't ingest a lot. Just enough to make me miserable until my medicine kicked in." Just enough to have her heart rate kicking up and her believing she was aroused by the revamped version of Steven. Just enough to make her face lumpy, her body rashy and feverish, and Ty still hot for her.

Relief flashed in Courtney's eyes. "Thank God for that. So how does Ty figure in?"

Candy sat back in her chair and bridged her fingers over her belly. Obviously they were going to have this conversation whether or not she wanted to. "I was afraid to drive with not knowing how my body might react, so I called him to come get me."

"You were so thankful, you repaid the favor by setting aside the good girl gig to let him scratch your need-to-be-laid itch?" Courtney asked skeptically.

Candy shrugged. "He left a date with Ms. Tits to pick me up. I figured I owed him."

"Yeah, right."

"Okay, fine. That wasn't how it went down. He picked me up and insisted I go back to his place, after I got my inhaler and medicine, because he wanted to make sure I was okay."

"And you say he doesn't care."

"Anyway, things were going fine, and then I told him I was moving to Florida."

"He doesn't want you to go, does he?" Courtney's smile returned wide, vivid, and lovey dovey. "Because the thought of you not being next door is too much to bear."

Candy did a mental eye roll. Seriously, she was happy for her and Blaine, but Courtney had to lose the whole rose-colored-glasses thing.

Which wasn't to say Candy disagreed. After the way he'd left a date with Tonya to pick her up and watch over her last night, she did believe Ty cared about her beyond her body. He'd miss her when she left. Would he be brokenhearted? She couldn't see it. Another woman would move into her condo, move her way into Ty's bed, and take over whatever spot Candy currently occupied in his thoughts.

Yeah, it sucked and, yeah, she was jealous as hell thinking of that other woman, with his hands on her body, his cock pumping inside her, his teasing words and looks bringing fun to her life in a way no one else had ever been able to accomplish. But that was the way of it.

"What guy *would* want their next-door fuck friend to leave?" Candy asked dryly.

"You honestly can't still believe that's how he feels. You've only slept with him once in the last three-and-a-half months. Twice if you count last night."

"He cares—"

"Heck, yeah, he does."

"But it doesn't matter."

"Of course, it does!" Courtney gasped. "How could it not?"

Candy sighed. Something told her no matter what she said, Courtney wouldn't agree. But then, Courtney didn't have health concerns forcing her to make choices she would otherwise put off at all costs. Candy's attempts at finding a reliable guy for the long haul by dressing and acting the part of the staid, sophisticated lady might have been overkill; still, the point remained that she did need to find that guy and soon.

Much sooner than what Ty's nine-year plan allowed. "Last night I asked Ty if he ever plans to get married and he said sure, when he's forty. You know I can't wait that long."

Courtney eyed her assessingly. "Does he know about the Fibroid Fairy?"

"I told you I have no plans to ever share that with him."

"Does he know that you love him?"

"I don't love him. Hell, half the time I don't even like him." Okay, so the second half of that was yet another lie. The first half . . . didn't matter.

She would move on, just as Ty would. Head down south and find a long-term guy. Not an old geezer, the way she kept joking, but a guy her age. One ready to settle down and spend his days as a family man and his nights taking her in the ass, or wherever else appealed.

"Does he know you've developed a chronic lying habit?" Courtney persisted.

"It doesn't matter how either of us feel, Court. I'm going to miss you, and admittedly Ty, but I'm going. I met with HR this morning, while you were out for your dentist appointment, and the transfer paperwork's in progress."

Ty hadn't seen Candy since she'd left his condo three nights ago, right after she made it clear she really was moving to Florida. He'd spent the last few days doing aerial shots for his brother-in-law's survey company, and by the time he got home she was already out for the night. On dates or just getting ready for the move, he didn't know.

What he did know was that she was standing outside his door now. If the view through the peephole was accurate, then she wore her hair down in thick, blond, finger-pleasing waves, a red-painted seductress's smile, and a silky-looking white robe that parted to expose the bulk of her breasts and barely covered her crotch.

Her expression went anxious as she knocked a second time.

Did he really want to subject himself to the kind of white-hot sex that was bound to leave him hungry for more, when he knew damned well he would probably never get that more?

Hell, yeah, he did.

Grinning, Ty opened the door. "Looking for a cup of sugar?"

The seductress's smile returned. "That depends." She poked her head inside and glanced around. "Do you have company?"

"Like chicks that kept me from answering the door the first time you knocked?"

"Like a woman."

"What if I do?" His grin went cocky as he glanced toward the partially closed bedroom door. "What if I have hot blond twins tied up in bed, waiting for me to return and make good on their Sleeping Beauty fantasy?"

Ice entered Candy's eyes with the mention of him doling out her fantasy to others when he'd never done so for her. "In that case, I won't come in for a good-bye fuck." Her voice came out chilly. "I took the job in Orlando. I leave Sunday morning. Have a nice life."

She started to turn away. Ty grabbed her by the front of the robe, gaping the sides to free her breasts in full as he yanked her inside his condo and shut the door.

His attention zeroed in on the twin beauties inches from his fingertips, and his cock stirred to throbbing life. Shit, he was going to miss them. He was going to miss her as a whole, but it appeared she was already all but packed and on the first flight out.

Leaving his fingers to play along the sides of the robe, he lifted his gaze to her lips. No frostiness here, but fire-engine red. He bent his head for a taste, just one hasty brush. The kind of puny, pathetic kiss he'd seen Steven give to her last week.

Only the brush didn't feel so puny or pathetic with Candy's warm breath cruising across his lips, her tits arching toward his hands as he straightened again.

Maybe Steven knew a thing or two about seduction, after all.

He met her gaze to find heat in place of the coolness. "How can you be ready to move out of a condo you've lived in for years in less than three days?"

"I'll take what I need for the first couple weeks, then come back for a long weekend to take care of the rest of the stuff."

"I won't be here in two weeks."

Her eyes narrowed, some of the coolness flashing back into them. "Don't be pissy just because I'm not going to hang around and play fuck friends anymore, Ty. Besides, what makes you think I want to see you when I come back?"

"I *really* won't be here in two weeks." He also hadn't been being pissy, but blindsided by how happy he'd been to get to see her again only to be deflated when he realized her return wouldn't fit with his schedule.

Not that it mattered, since she'd made it crystal clear she didn't want to see him.

Three years they'd been friends. Three years they'd been lovers. And this was what he got? Essentially shit on.

Aversion eating at his gut, Ty released her robe to grab her around the waist. "I have a family reunion that I already promised both Denise and my parents I'd go home for. If you don't want to see me, there's no point in worrying about it."

He lifted her off the floor a few inches. Candy's breath sucked in. Her eyes went smoky and unfocused, eradicating the chill. Her upper half started to sway toward him, like she thought he planned to cart her off to his bed for a long hard night of loving. He would have, too, if she'd kept her mouth shut.

Since she hadn't kept her mouth shut, since she'd made it clear that after today she never wanted to see him again, he opened his door and set her down outside of it. "Screwing you tonight would also be pointless. Have a nice life."

Blowing a last kiss, he let the door crash shut in her face.

* * *

Candy's mouth fell open as Ty's door slammed closed inches from her face. She curled her fingers into fists, silently seething.

Three years they'd been friends. Three years they'd been lovers. And this was what she got? Just another damned air kiss.

The fury left her on a sigh.

She deserved his rejection. Not only had she been mostly ignoring him for weeks now, but she'd let him believe she was sincere about not wanting to see him again. She'd acted like a jealous bitch the second he insinuated he had twin blondes in his bed waiting for their fantasies—make that *her* fantasy—to be fulfilled. She knew he'd been taunting her, and still she'd taken the bait, gobbled it right up, and spit it back in his face.

It was for the best their relationship ended stormy. As much as she prided herself on always leaving men on a good note, it would have to be easier to forget him this way.

Pulling the gaping sides of her robe together, Candy returned to her condo. She'd acted like being ready to move in three days was a breeze. In reality, there was a buttload of packing to be done. People to call. Mail to have forwarded.

Ah, hell, she was going to bed.

It was already after nine, and she wasn't feeling calm enough to pack right now, let alone make nice with another person.

Her heart was still beating hard from when Ty brushed that shockingly tender kiss across her lips. Her body still flushed with the idea he was going to carry her to his bedroom and spend the rest of the night pleasuring her in a way that would be forever branded on her mind. Her pussy still moist with the want for one last night of ecstasy in his arms.

Her pussy was SOL.

After a quick cleanup routine, she shook off her robe and climbed into bed. She'd left off her tee and panties with the idea she could ease the sensual ache between her thighs at least a little. Only, now that she was lying down, masturbation didn't appeal. Not when she knew it would be Ty's shaggy curls and cocky grin in her mind when she came.

Pulling the covers up to her chin, she closed her eyes and counted handbags.

Obviously, it worked. The next time Candy opened her eyes, she was flat on her stomach and the alarm clock showed it was a little after midnight.

Twelve . . .

The edge of her pillow blocked the view of the last two glowing red digits. She tried to reach out and compress the pillow's soft down. Her hand didn't budge. Her entire arm remained still. As did its mate. And her legs.

Holy Jesus, she couldn't move! She was paralyzed!

Panic shot through her, clawing at her belly. Her heart skipped into her throat. She whimpered and wriggled on the bed. Then she realized she *was* wriggling. She wasn't paralyzed.

She was bound.

Sucking in calming breaths, she forced her eyes to make out shapes in the nearly pitch-black bedroom. Some big shape that didn't belong moved on her right. Her ears pricked, her hearing intensified with the virtual loss of sight.

She could hear the breathing now. *His* breathing. "Ty?"

He moved toward her like a panther, quickly and gracefully until his fingers were shoved into the back of her hair, clenching the strands, jerking her head up off the bed. "I don't know who the fuck Ty is, Beauty"—the words grated out as a harsh breath near her ear—"but if you say his name again, you're going to have it washed out of your mouth with my tongue."

Beauty?

As in Sleeping Beauty. Oh, hell, yes. He was finally going to deliver her fantasy.

It was so much better than either a sappy good-bye or the stormy one from several hours ago. It was the perfect ending to their friendship. Maybe he'd always known this day would come. Maybe he'd saved her fantasy on purpose.

Whatever the case, Candy's anxiety was gone, replaced with the burning need to be taken, to be ravished like he was some feral animal with a raging blood lust for her and her alone.

She attempted to turn her head to make out his face in the semidarkness. Between the tautness of the bindings around her wrists and ankles and the crude way he gripped her hair, she couldn't move an inch. She could feel his eyes on her body, though, wild and intense, probing her intimate flesh, stroking along her slit and singeing wetness deep in her pussy.

One of his thighs pressed against the backs of hers. Coarse hair tickled her bare skin and she knew he was naked, too. Naked and undoubtedly hard, liable to push inside her at any moment. Her sex contracted with nerves of anticipation.

"Yes, sir." Her voice came out low and throaty. "Who are you?"

The fingers in her hair tightened, dancing shards of deliciously dizzying tension through her scalp. Then they let go, and he took the press and warmth of his thigh from hers. "No one you need to worry about."

"Y-you aren't going to t-touch me." Very real fear shook her words with the idea he'd changed his mind. That he was about to leave.

He couldn't leave, damnit. She needed contact. Needed his touch one last time.

"I'm going to touch you, all right." The press of his leg stayed away, but his fingers returned, coming down this time on her inner thighs, trailing in feather-light circles, up, up, almost to her pussy. Her sex went molten as his fingers skimmed higher. Her muscles clamped down. She held her breath. Waited.

Almost there.

Almost.

His fingers lifted, leaving her body completely, and Candy cried out in sexually frustrated misery.

A dark, dangerous laugh rolled from Ty's mouth. "Cry all you want, Beauty. I'm still going to paddle your ass and fuck you stupid."

Relief and arousal jetted through her body in tandem. His fingers returned, on her ass now, smoothing across her cheeks. Petting, massaging. Driving her mad with their torturously slow movement.

One finger stroked her crack, dipping shallowly inside. Sucking in a breath, she squeezed her anus and waited for penetration.

Only, he didn't enter her. He lifted his hand and brought it down across her ass. Hard.

The crack of skin against skin filled up the silence of the bedroom. She thrashed in her bindings as pleasure-pain erupted throughout her soft cheeks. That pain doubled with the next slap of his big hand against her bottom. Sensation burst around to her front, pooling cream in her sex and tingling her clit with lustful ache.

The ache didn't get better but worse with the next of his swats. Tension and emotion sparked through her entire body, her entire existence. Her breath exhaled in short pants. Fierce need balled in her pussy like a heavy weight.

Candy attempted to squeeze her thighs around the building strain of orgasm. But she couldn't clench them the way she was spread out. She could only rely on Ty.

He chose that moment to lift his hand away.

She thought to speak, to offer to beat him upside the head if he didn't finish the damned job, to ruin the fantasy façade if that's what it took. His hand returned before she could, paddling her ass with a smack so intense it had her whimpering.

She thrashed in her bindings again, grinding her soaked cunt against the softness of the sheets as tears of ecstasy stung her eyes. Oooh, yeah . . . Her tender little ass had never been happier in its life. One more swat and she'd be lying in a puddle of her own juices.

"Please. Stop. Let me go. I can pay," she pleaded in a thin voice, all the while smiling like a mad woman because she knew the begging would incite further spankings.

At least, she thought she knew.

No more swats followed. The press of his body didn't return. She could hardly hear his breathing now, like he'd moved far away. Like he was leaving for real this time.

He couldn't. He wouldn't.

He did. Separated her wet folds and shoved his finger into her from behind. "How much is it worth for me not to ram my dick into this pussy?"

Relief sagged through her followed by a shuddering quake of rapture as Ty pumped his finger inside her sheath. "I . . . I just remembered I don't get paid again until next Friday. I only have a couple hundred dollars."

"Sorry, Beauty. That ain't gonna cut it." His finger jerked from her cunt.

A heartbeat later the wet tip of his cock brushed against her lips. Not those of her pussy, but of her mouth. "Open up and suck me."

Pulse racing, Candy parted her lips eagerly, greedily. His shaft pushed inside, just an inch. Pre-cum met with her tongue, and she murmured her elation as he fed her another inch.

Ah, yeah. It had been way too long since she'd tasted him. He was so big and hot. His taste salty, silky, his own.

She wrapped her tongue around his stiff member, working her mouth up and down the bare inch of movement her restraints allowed. He fisted her hair again and forced her mouth beyond that inch, gliding his dick deep inside.

Moaning, she licked his length, turned her tongue on the corona, circling the way he'd done as he'd massaged his hands and fingers over her flesh countless times. His rod pulsed in her mouth. The grip on her hair increased with his primal groan.

Blood pounded between her ears as she waited for the pummel of his cum against her throat, the hot taste of it on her tongue.

He jerked her head back and his cock out of her mouth before she got a drop.

Candy groaned. "I want—"

Ty's hand fell across her ass, shooting deliciously fresh fingers of pleasure-pain through her. "I don't give a shit what you want." The bed dipped. He came over her, straddling the backs of her thighs with the heavy muscles of his own, running the head of his cock along her opening. "This is *my* show. *My* time to drive into this pussy."

He filled her in the next instant, sliding into her drenched body, taking her breath away with the complete magnitude of her helplessness and his savageness.

He took her ass in his hands and lifted her hips off the bed as far as the restraints would allow. "Christ, you're a hot one. Dripping all over my cock. Feeling my dick in you makes you want to come, doesn't it?"

His shaft pumped into her wildly. His rough voice raked over her, demanding, arrogant. Complete and total Ty.

How would she ever forget him? How would she ever replace him?

"Doesn't it, Beauty?" His fingers moved beneath her prone body, finding a breast and pinching its nipple tight.

She cried out as emotion flooded her. Orgasm sizzled in her belly. She wanted to explode. Wanted to rub the skin off her wrists and ankles if that's what it took to liberate them of the bindings so she could stroke her clit, free her pleasure.

But, no, she didn't. She didn't want to be the one to free her pleasure. She wanted only Ty doing that, when he was along for the rapturous ride. "Yes, sir."

"Yes, sir, what?" he growled.

"Your dick makes me want to explode. It feels huge in me. Big and stiff and throbbing. It tastes so good. I've never wanted to suck a dick as bad as I wanted to suck yours." It was the truth. Always would be the truth.

"You're not getting it back in your mouth so you can quit with the whining. Maybe I won't give it to you anymore at all." He yanked out of her, lifted his fingers from her nipple.

Candy strained in her bindings, writhing beneath him, seeking out his cock with her sex alone until her limbs burned with the effort. "Please don't leave me."

"Begging again. Always begging with you. All right, Beauty. Just this once I won't go."

Just this once. One more time. One final good-bye to her pussy's favorite plaything.

Only, he wasn't just her pussy's favorite plaything. He was all of hers.

He lifted her hips back off the bed a couple inches and his dick returned, pumping into her with the slap of his balls against her ass. His fingers moved to her clit, circling around it, twisting it, pressing against it mercilessly. Freeing her finally to the throes of orgasm.

Scorching white light erupted behind her eyelids and deep in her core, bursting to her toes, to her fingers. Taking away her breath. Making her too dizzy and weak to move. Not that she could have moved much anyway. Not that she wanted to go anywhere but straight to this mind-numbing nirvana with Ty.

"Fuck, I'm going to miss you, Candy." His cry was hot rage, pure animal, utter perfection as he drove into her one last time and then filled her with his cum.

The heaviness of their mingled breathing and the scent of their loving filled the bedroom. Her muscles screamed from being drawn out for so long. Candy ignored the ache to bask in the glory of her name on his lips and the feel of his big body draped over her one last time.

Too soon, Ty pulled from her body, breaking that final connection. The glory turned cold as emotion charged through her, stinging with its bittersweet clarity.

It was over. Everything was over.

He sat back on her lower thighs, bringing his hands to her shoulders, massaging the tight muscles with intimate familiarity. "Yeah, I know your name's Beauty, but you remind me of candy. Hard candy. The kind you could suck on for hours and never get tired of the taste."

Hope speared through her, lightening the ache that fanned from her belly to her heart and had nothing to do with the physical. By hours did he mean he wasn't going? That it wasn't over?

In answer, his chest pressed against her back, hard and sweaty and delicious. His mouth found her ear, licking at the lobe. "So sweet. So good."

He took the soft, sweaty skin between his lips, nibbling and sucking while his fingers journeyed down, back between her thighs, back to her clit. Still so fresh from the last orgasm, with just a few strokes she was flying off the handle again. Flying fast and furious into another soul-gripping climax.

Ty's fingers slid into her hair as spasms tore through her. This time his touch was easy, gentle, caring. He turned her head to the side and his lips settled over hers, just as easy, gentle, caring. He kissed her soft and long and then a little harder, but still so sweet, so perfect, so lovingly.

And then so sinfully as he pulled his mouth away and brought his hands to one of her wrist bindings. The first binding came undone, and then the second. Even before he moved to free her ankles, there was no denying this time it really was over.

The bed dipped as his weight left it. "I'm outta here."

The ache returned, spearing at Candy's middle as she rolled onto her back. She wanted to demand he stay. *She* couldn't. Beauty could. "You don't like me, sir?"

"I like you, Beauty." His voice was low, distant, and she could see his faint outline half in, half out of her bedroom door. "But I still have a lot of other bedrooms to break into."

With a weak smile, she lay back on the bed and accepted that not even Beauty could stop him. Not when he had nine more years worth of bedrooms to break into, women to screw. Not when she heard her front door close and the lock *snick* into place seconds later, like he couldn't get out of her condo and on with his life without her fast enough.

8

"I expect an e-mail every day. And pictures of Mr. Florida Retiree Man." Courtney released her death-grip hug on Candy to wince. "Just not in a thong, please. Old guy and exposed butt cheeks seriously do not go together."

Standing next to them in the airport's passenger screening line, Blaine groaned. "I knew I should have waited in the car."

Candy laughed. "Don't worry, Mom. I'll call as soon as the plane touches down."

"You'd better." Hopefulness entered Courtney's eyes. "Or you could just not go."

No, she couldn't. Her luggage was already checked and she'd turned in her auto lease over a month early so she could buy something more sporty and suitable to the Florida sunshine. If she stayed now, she would be naked and carless. She wouldn't dare leave her condo. Unless, of course, it was to cross over to Ty's and indulge in the kind of sex that left her with an ecstatic smile and two nipples up.

And a pitiful ache in her heart.

Candy kept her smile plastered on while inside her belly churned. "I need to go. Maybe not forever, but for now."

"I know. It still sucks."

Blaine wrapped an arm around Courtney's shoulders. Wiggling his eyebrows, he grinned. "Since when is sucking a bad thing?"

Courtney punched his arm. "Not funny. Not in a moment like this." Even so, when she looked back at Candy it was with an impish smile. "On second thought, maybe I won't miss you. I would never be engaged to this idiot, if not for your helping me reveal my inner sex diva."

The whole rose-colored glasses thing was a bit much at times. Still, seeing Courtney and Blaine like this, so obviously in love, Candy couldn't be happier for them. Or more envious. "Yeah, you would. He was checking out your butt long before you put on the hoochie clothes."

"The woman has a point." Blaine's hand slipped from Courtney's shoulders to give her backside a playful swat. "No man could resist an ass this fine for long."

Emotion bubbled up as a lump in Candy's throat with the exchange, too reminiscent of Ty's handling two nights ago. Of the way he'd almost ruined her Sleeping Beauty fantasy by using her real name when he said how much he'd miss her. Of the tender way he'd kissed her before slipping out of her condo. Of all the fun they'd had together and never would again, because he'd given her what she wanted, just the way he always had.

Swallowing back the lump, she glanced forward at the passenger screening line and nearly wept with relief. She nodded at the sign indicating they'd reached the point where nonfliers weren't allowed to follow. "Looks like this is where you two get off." Blaine's eyebrows rose with the play on words, and she laughed out loud. "You're such a perv."

Turning to Courtney, she pulled her into a quick hug. "Thanks for keeping me company, doll."

"Anytime." Unshed tears glimmered in Courtney's eyes as she stepped back. "Have a good flight."

"Keep the vibrating toilet seat warm for me." Candy forced back her own tears and the resurfaced lump with the teasing words and a sassy smile.

Until Courtney, she'd never had a gal pal, and up until this very moment, she hadn't realized the extent to which she would miss her. They'd do e-mail, exchange calls on occasion, but it would never be the same. Nothing would ever be quite the same again. Though it didn't seem possible just now, she could only hope that meant it would be better.

"There comes a time in every man's life when he has to suck it up and admit he's wrong." Brad delivered the unsolicited advice to Ty across the table of the tiny mom-and-pop shop where they met every Sunday morning for coffee and donuts. "After that man gets married, that single time is increased by about six thousand."

Ty stuffed a last bite of cream cheese Danish in his mouth, swallowing it down, before pointing out, "I didn't do anything wrong."

His brother-in-law's mouth quirked beneath a blond mustache. "That why Candy's on her way to Florida while your sorry ass is sitting here, looking like someone shot your dog, totaled your truck, and spilled your beer all in the same hour?"

"I don't have a dog." He also didn't want to have this conversation.

Ty had managed to keep busy enough to mostly keep Candy from his thoughts. If he let her back into them now, he was bound to remember how damned hard it was to leave her condo after delivering her Sleeping Beauty fantasy. He was bound to recall he'd brought that fantasy into the flesh, after swearing he was through with her, in the hopes it would cement him in her mind in a way she couldn't forget. He was bound to point out her plane didn't leave for another forty-five minutes, because he was a sorry ass indeed and had checked into the airport's flight schedule.

"Her plane doesn't leave till ten." Shit. He'd gone and done it.

Brad's eyes lit with optimism. "You could be there in fifteen minutes. Twenty if traffic's heavy."

Ty gripped his coffee mug, wishing the turbulent emotions pushing through him would somehow transfer to it. "What do you suggest I do when I get there? Tell her I don't want her to go, but I don't know how to get her to stay?"

"You know."

What he knew was that he'd never really believed Candy was afraid for her safety, following what went down with her friend, and ending her easy-living, easy-loving lifestyle because of it. As for what Brad was pushing at—the commitment thing—he couldn't figure why she would want one so suddenly. "I'm not ready to settle down."

Brad sat back in his chair, chomping down the last few bites of an apple fritter while he eyed Ty with disgust. "I stood up for you when Denise said you were an ass this morning, but that's only because I was sticking to the man code. You *are* an ass."

"Because I don't want to rush into marriage?"

"Because you've got this woman who's a knockout and perfect for you, yet you seem to think there's someone better out there. Only, if you believe that, why do you keep bringing Candy by the house? All you're doing is getting Denise's hopes up."

"I don't think there's someone better." After going out with Tonya last night only to end the night by turning down her offer to come inside for a nightcap in the form of her naked body, Ty wasn't even sure he wanted to see or do other women, period.

Hell, things had always been so simple with Candy. They had fun together without having to mince words for fear of hurting each other's feelings. Why'd she have to go and throw the zinger of all curveballs by changing the rules?

Glaring at his coffee mug, Ty pushed out a sigh. "I don't know what I want."

"You're gonna have to be an ass alone while you figure it out." With an eager smile, Brad stood. "I promised the boys I'd take them to see my folks. Then I promised Denise I'd come home without them for a few hours for some body worship time."

Candy's belly pitched as she handed the flight attendant her ticket to check before boarding. She hadn't taken a plane in years, always choosing to take the sightseeing approach and drive the sixteen-hour trip to her parents' Baton Rouge semiretirement home.

She hadn't taken an *air*plane, that is. She'd ridden in a private plane plenty, and thoughts of all the naughty fun she'd had with Ty in his Cessna haunted her now.

Taking the ticket, the woman scanned her information. Her gaze stilled on the passenger name area, and she looked up to question, "Candace Masterson?"

"That *is* what it says." Candy winced at her snarky tone. Shutting out her completely unwelcome thoughts, she gave an apologetic smile. "Sorry. Flying makes me nervous. And cranky, obviously."

"No problem." Returning her smile, the woman handed her ticket back. "There's a gentleman who asked to see you before you board." She nodded past several rows of connected waiting-area seats to the glass-windowed wall. "He's over there."

Ty?

Candy's breath came out shakily as she followed the direction of the attendant's nod. If it was Ty . . .

Her heart stuttered and hope sailed out the airport's seemingly endless supply of windows. The guy stood thirty feet away with his back to her. Even from this distance, the flawless style of his dark brown hair and his stiff attire were too memorable to mistake.

Shit, she didn't want to see Steven. How did he even know she'd be here? And why had he reverted to black slacks and a sport coat when he'd looked so much better in casual clothing?

"The doors will close in ten minutes," the attendant said.

"Thanks." Feeling like the spikes of her black stilettos were made of lead, Candy plodded slowly over. "Steven, what are you—" She gasped as the guy swiveled around. As she discovered it wasn't Steven, but Ty. "What happened to you?" Not only was he dressed like a total stiff, right down to his tie, but his curls were gone. Styled straight, his hair appeared darker, more refined, far less sexy. "You look like—"

"Steven," he supplied soberly.

"Yes."

"I thought maybe that was what you wanted."

She thought it had been, for a short while. But now she knew better. Knew she needed a bad boy—just one who was ready to settle down. Unlike Ty. "I appreciate the gesture, but we both know we'll never work. We have such different needs right now."

His eyebrows rose as he took in the swell of her breasts above the low-cut V-neckline of her black sweater. Heat charged through her—the kind of carnal heat that stabbed straight to her pussy and left her blood boiling with arousal—and she amended, "Mostly different needs."

Ty's gaze lifted to hers. "I love you."

"You . . ." Had he said that? Had he *really* just said that? "*Why?*"

A deep, delicious laugh rolled out of his mouth. She had to fight not to laugh, too, not to smile. Not to throw herself in his arms. "You love me, too, Candy, baby. You know you do."

Always so arrogant. Only, this time he wasn't. His words might sound certain, but there was hesitance along with desire in the depths of his hazel eyes. Still, she couldn't give in. She had to be feisty, plucky, and, yeah, even pissy.

"What if I do?" Candy asked tersely. "You planning to follow me to Florida so we can pick up the fuck-friend game down there?"

Ty's expression went stone sober. He stepped toward her, right into her personal space, right where she could see the little white scar just below his nose and the flecks of green in his eyes. "We're not just fuck friends. And, yeah, I'll follow you. I can find work in Florida as easily as in Michigan."

The air lodged in her throat. The breathless sensation let up then, as her heart sped a mile a minute.

They weren't just fuck friends. She'd known it for a while now, but to hear him say it . . . That still didn't mean he was ready for a committed relationship, and she couldn't settle for anything less. "The reason I took the job in Florida is to get away from you, Ty."

His lips curved in a smugly knowing smile. "What happened to it being a higher-paying position?"

"It is. But not any higher than what I'd make working here, after my annual raise kicks in next month."

"And the weather?"

"Part of me hates the cold. The rest of me thinks warming up is a great reason to screw."

"Just any guy will do for the job, right?" She nodded, and he shook his head, his smile going rueful. "Then I guess I shouldn't have fast-forwarded to someday."

Candy frowned. "Someday?"

"You asked if I wanted to settle down someday. I said sure, like when I'm forty. Forty's a ways off. Someday's right now."

The air lodged in her throat a second time, staying there this time as she tried to digest his words. What exactly was he saying? That he was ready to commit to her?

"Excuse me. Ma'am." The flight attendant tapped her on the shoulder. "The doors will close in two minutes."

"Thanks," Candy said, refusing to pull her attention away from Ty and the raw honesty that filled his eyes.

"I don't have a ticket. I tried, but the flight was already booked." A slow smile tugged at the corners of his mouth. "I do have my own plane with a first-class seat for the Mile-High member of a lifetime."

"I just . . ." *What?*

She hadn't been expecting this. She'd spent the last three days getting him out of her head and all the while accepting he never would leave it, because she finally knew why he was there to begin with. Somewhere deep down she'd always believed the same as Denise. That when the time came for her to settle down, Ty would be the guy by her side.

His hands reached out, grabbing her upper arms and pulling her close. She went like a rag doll, like a woman awestruck by the pure affection that seemed to fill his eyes.

"I don't need sex to feel complete, Candy. I need you."

His lips came over hers, so slow, sweet. Then harder and intense, drugging, so good. Yes. She wanted this. Wanted him forever, if that's what he was offering.

"Ma'am. The doors—"

Candy broke the kiss off short to wave away the attendant. "Close them."

Hoped flared in Ty's eyes, emerging on his face as a wickedly delicious smile. "Really?"

"That plane can't take me anywhere your Cessna can't."

The smile faltered. "You're still taking the job in Florida?"

"It would be easier, considering I have a temporary lease agreement worked out down there and my car already turned in here." She let her own smile out to play as the euphoria she always felt after doing him filled her through. Without them even having sex first! Well, what do you know? There might just be something to the whole rose-colored glasses thing, after all. "Of course, if I did stay, Courtney would probably be so happy she'd do my work for the next month."

"I'd be so happy, I'd do *you* for the next month. Make that the next fifty or sixty years."

"You'd honestly forget about the nine-year plan, to marry me?"

"I really *would* be an ass if I didn't. You're the perfect woman for me." His eyes warmed with a mix of humor and lust as he set her back far enough to eye her cleavage. "Like I said before, you have big tits *and* put out on the first date."

Candy wanted to sink back into him, rub her breasts and the rest of her body against him. First, she owed him the truth. "I should probably tell you about the Fibroid Fairy."

"Is that the one who flies around leaving fibroids under your pillow?"

"Close. The one who flies around implanting fibroids in my uterus."

Ty's expression went first deadpan and then filled with concern. "You're sick?"

"No. There's a good chance I could get that way in the next year or so, though. Not sick, really. But I'll probably be in pain that won't go away permanently until I have a hysterectomy. I won't be able to get pregnant after that."

The worry left his eyes slowly, though not completely, with his nod of understanding. "You had to fast-forward to someday, too."

"Not by choice."

"Not like my someday." He pulled her back into his arms as his lips reclaimed their smile. "It took a while, and admittedly Denise and Brad calling me an ass, but I finally figured out wherever you are is where I want to be."

The emotion she'd spent days fighting off—hell, months—barreled through Candy with her grin. She lifted a hand to his tie and loosened it from around his neck. "This isn't you. We both know it's not me either. I like my guys simple, easy on the eyes, a little cocky, and rough around the edges." Letting her grin go dirty, she brought a hand lower, between their bodies, and stroked his shaft through his slacks. "Make that a lot of cocky."

"What do you want, Candy?"

"To give the good girl gig a permanent hiatus. Will you be my mango, Ty?"

Humor returned to his eyes and he released a boisterous laugh. "Christ, you're strange."

"Me? I'm not the one who sits around on my bed stroking chicks." A gasp sounded beside Candy with the too-loudly spoken words. She looked over to find a sixty-something couple glaring her way. "Chicken," she clarified. "He was stroking his chicken."

Outrage flared in the woman's eyes. "How completely—"

"Yep," Ty cut her off. "That's me. Lying on my bed, enjoying a nice hard stroke."

"His nephew's chicken," Candy tried again while tossing Ty a sidelong murderous look. "Chickens. There were two of them. Ah, hell, I'll never see you people again." Forgetting about onlookers, she turned back to Ty and flicked her tongue across the small scar lining his upper lip, knowing even before lust burned into his eyes it would rouse his cock. "The point is, you're tempted."

"No, I'm not." Holding her close, he circled his groin and a very obvious bulge against her belly. "There's no tempted about it. I'm ready to take you home and let you stroke my chicken all night long."

Her pussy went liquid with the promise. Lifting her mouth to his, she teased, "Does this chicken happen to have feathers?"

"Oh, no, Candy, baby. This chicken's all meat, all man, and all yours."

All aboard!

Here's a preview of P.F. Kozak's
sizzling new book

DO IT TO ME!

Coming soon from Aphrodisia!

1

Charlie really needed a shower. His eight-to-twelve shift in the engine room had wrapped up at midnight. He wiped his grimy hands on his white boiler suit, now covered with the grease, soot, and sweat. He wasn't fit to be seen, let alone enjoy some female company. Nonetheless, he made his way to the Monkey Bar at the stern of the ship, to see if his mate Morgy had come through for him again.

As he thought would be the case, the crowd at the bar had thinned. After midnight, most passengers inclined to late night partying drifted to the Twilight Bar, where they could disco until the wee hours. The Monkey Bar closed at 1 A.M.

Morgy spotted him and waved him over. Charlie could tell by the expression on his face that the barman had a bit of business to share.

"Hey there, mate. How about a pint to wash the taste of soot out of my mouth?"

"Bloody hell, what happened to you? You're filthy!"

Charlie propped his foot on the rail in front of the bar and watched Morgy draw his pint. "I had a run in with a fan on the number four soot blower. Fuckin' thing got stuck. I got it unstuck and lubed, but not before I got covered with soot and grease." He gartefully took the glass, and then looked around. "Good thing there aren't many passengers left. I shouldn't be in here looking like this."

"Especially with your coveralls open to your navel." Morgy eyed Charlie's hairy chest. "There's dirty sweat sliding down your treasure trail."

"It's hot as Hades next to the boiler!" Charlie chugged half the pint in one long drink, and then wiped the foamy mustache on his sleeve. He noticed Morgy still looking at him. "You're going to burn a hole in my chest if you keep staring at it."

"You're making me wish I'd lined up a bit of company for myself tonight."

Charlie laughed. In a low voice, he poked some fun. "What, you couldn't find yourself a boyfriend in the crowd tonight?"

"No, I was too damn busy sorting out a Sheila for you."

Charlie smiled broadly. "Which one of the ladies did you reel in?" Charlie had given Morgy a list of candidates before he started his shift in the engine room. He'd hoped one of them would come into the bar tonight.

"The one I want to be like, of course." Morgy then did a spot on impersonation of the stacked blonde Charlie had seen by the swimming pool that afternoon. "What is your name again? Yes, of course, Morgan. I do remember seeing that delightful young man earlier today. Meet with him? Goodness, is that allowed?"

Charlie held up his hand to stop Morgy's performance before any of the remaining passengers heard him. "All right, Miss Oz! I know which one it is. Sandy blonde hair and a great body. I saw her again this avro on the Lido deck by the pool." He smiled as he remembered the crimson bikini she had on. "Her togs gave me a throb in the knob."

Morgy winked at Charlie. "You do the same for me."

Charlie shook his head. "Jesus H. Sufferin' Christ, you're such a friggin' queen."

"Yes, and proud of it. Can't show it too much in here. It's bad form."

"You're shit out of luck getting a chubby from me. I like women."

"Can't blame a girl for trying. One of these days, I'll get you drunk and give you a head job." Morgy tapped his lips with his index finger. "Or maybe, you'll have your way with me."

"Not bloody likely, mate. Never have, never will."

Morgy smiled. "I've heard that before."

"Now you're hearin' it again." Charlie took another drink and waited. "Well, you going to tell me about the Sheila you set up for me?"

"This one's on the prowl. You were right, her name is Petula, but she says her friends call her Pet. Came in here looking over every man in the bar. Seemed happy she hooked up with someone she fancies."

"You think she fancies me?"

"I know she does. She asked me if you're married, and what you do on the ship. You'd best be finishing that pint PDQ. I told her to meet me here at one, and I'll take her to your cabin. If she sees you looking like a brown-eyed mullet, she'll turn around and go back to her first class cabin."

"First class? Not too shabby! Think she has money?"

"What do you care? It's not her money you're after."

"You got that right, mate." Charlie finished off his pint. "Gotta go and wash up. You got your key?"

Morgy patted the pocket on his red vest. "Right here. Don't worry, you'll have a naughty tonight."

"I know I will. Thanks, mate. I'll see what I can scare up for you next time."

"Promises, promises." Charlie left Morgy finishing his cleanup. He would be closing the bar directly, and then escort Pet to Charlie's room.

Charlie took the authorized route back to his cabin, walking through the verandah and crossing the Lido deck to the stairs that led back to the engine room. Just as he thought they would be, the swimming pools on the Lido deck were deserted at this hour. Again he remembered seeing Pet that afternoon in her swimming togs. His mates called this the Libido Deck with good reason.

From the engine room, he took the stairs that led to the crew's quarters on the starboard side of the ship. As he walked down the alleyway on C Deck toward his cabin, Charlie glanced at the locked door that separated the passengers' quarters from the crew's. In about fifteen minutes, Morgy would be opening it with his contraband key and bringing the sexy Sheila to his room.

He didn't have much time. After skimming off his soot covered boiler suit, he jumped into the shower. With a woman coming, he made sure he scrubbed all the nooks and crannies thoroughly. He paid particular attention to his nuggets, hoping this sexy lady would do some teabagging.

Once he quickly dried, he put on some black trousers and a white shirt. He didn't bother with shoes and socks, figuring he wouldn't have his clothes on for long. He straightened his bunk, and unearthed his stash of gin. Just as he set two glasses on his desk, someone knocked on his door.

When he answered, a curvaceous blonde in a sexy, low-cut blue halter dress stood there. Morgy was nowhere in sight.

"Charlie?"

"You're Petula, right?"

"Yes. Morgan unlocked the door, and then pointed down the hall. He told me cabin 169. I'd hoped he wasn't mistaken."

"Nope, Morgy knows my cabin. We're best mates. He wouldn't steer you wrong." Charlie stepped aside. "Please, come in."

"Thank you." Petula came into Charlie's small cabin. He gave her a once-over from behind. He almost whistled when he saw that the back of the dress dipped open nearly to her bum, and then it flared at her waist into a full skirt. She obviously didn't have a bra on! Charlie could see most of her bare back.

He managed to get his wits. "Make yourself at home. Would you like a drink? I have some good Gordon's Gin. I can make you a gin and tonic."

"That would be lovely. And please call me Pet." She laid her clutch bag on his desk and sat down on the edge of the bunk. "They don't give you fellows much room in these cabins, do they?"

Charlie smiled. "They save the good cabins for the paying passengers. We're just hired help." He noticed Petula studying his old, scratched up desk.

"Are those initials carved into the wood?"

"Yeah. When my mates come in here for a drink, they leave me an autograph. That desk has history. Some of those initials are from other engineers who had this cabin before me."

"You're an engineer?"

"I'm a third assistant engineer. I just got off my watch. I do eight-to-twelve twice a day."

Petual took the glass Charlie offered her. "That's how you could be on the Lido deck this afternoon. I wondered about that."

Charlie pulled out his desk chair and sat down. "I saw you this avro." He gestured toward her with his glass. "Couldn't help but notice what a good looking woman you are."

"How sweet of you to say that. I also picked you out of the crowd."

"Did ya' now? You weren't put off by my being with the crew and not a passenger?"

"Quite the contrary." Petula checked him out as he had her. "Most of the men I've met are old, married or pansies. You aren't any of those."

"Now, how would you know that?" Charlie moved from the desk chair and sat on the bunk beside her.

"It's quite obvious you aren't old, or a pansy." She sipped her G&T before she added, "And I asked if you were married."

"Who'd you ask?"

"The lifeguard at the pool. I pointed you out today. He told me your name and said he didn't think you had a wife, but to ask the barman at the Monkey Bar."

"So that's how you met my mate Morgy. I wondered why you showed up there tonight." Charlie considered telling her more, and decided it wouldn't hurt. "I described you to him and told him to keep an eye out for you."

"It did seem quite a coincidence that he offered to bring me to your cabin without my asking."

"No coincidence. I wanted to meet you, but I had to be careful. It's against the rules for me to be socializing with the female passengers. I could get my arse in deep if anyone finds out you've been in my cabin."

"Don't worry. I won't tell anyone I know you, or that I've been in your cabin." Petula pointed to his poster of a topless dark skinned woman, who seemed about to peel off her panties. Charlie had hung it over his desk so he could see it from his bunk. "Charming picture."

Not the least bit embarrassed by his choice of artwork, Charlie explained his fantasy Sheila. "I found that picture in a small shop in Sydney and snapped it up straight away. I call her Yooralla."

"I never heard that name before."

"It's an Aborigine word that means love. Knew a girl once called Yooralla. Don't know what ever became of her, but she was even more beautiful than that Sheila. I think of her sometimes when I'm alone." Charlie's voice trailed off. He hadn't meant to say that.

"That picture reminds you of her, doesn't it?"

"S'pose so." Not wanting to sound so serious, he set his glass on the floor and again pointed to the poster. "Figured she would keep me company on these long, lonely nights at sea."

"Does she? Keep you company, I mean."

"When I need her, she does. But tonight, I don't need her." Petula suddenly stood up, set her glass on the desk, and picked up her bag. Charlie got up and grabbed her arm, afraid she had decided to leave. "You aren't going, are you?"

"No, dear Charles. I have something for you in my bag."

Charlie relaxed his grip on her arm. "Bloody hell, you gave me a start. I thought I had done something to put you off."

"Not at all. Truth be told, you're the only man I've met on this long, boring trip that interests me."

Charlie grinned. "Is that a fact!"

"That is indeed a fact. That's why I want to give you this." Petula opened her clutch bag and gave Charlie a key.

"Is this what I think it is?"

"That's an extra key to my cabin. I'm on Deck B, Cabin 232."

"Hell, Pet, B232 isn't a cabin, that's a suite with a balcony. Those digs cost a friggin' fortune!"

"I can afford it, so why not?"

"I know you're British. What are you, royalty or something?"

"No, not royalty, just lucky."

Charlie gave her back the key. "Don't know why you're givin' that to me. I'm an engineer on the *Ortensia.* You're a first class passenger on her."

Petula put the key on his desk. "Your mate Morgy told me about you, about how you know more about a ship than anyone else he's ever known. He also told me you're good at making keys."

"He told you that?"

"He told me you're the one that copied the special key that

opens the door between the passenger cabins and the crew's. You could copy my extra key, and then give it back to me."

"Your knowin' that could get my arse put off the ship, let alone your being in here with me."

Petula wrapped her arms around Charlie's neck. "Getting cold feet, Charles?"

"Why me, Pet? Why are you keen on me?"

"I could ask you the same thing."

"That's an easy one. You're a good looking woman. You gave me a boner this avro, and you're giving me another one now." Charlie cleared his throat. "I'm sorry. Don't usually use such coarse talk with a woman."

"And I don't offer the key to my room to just anyone. I saw you the other day. I made it a point to find out your name when I saw you again on the Lido deck this afternoon."

Charlie slid his hand up Petula's bare back to her neck. "I don't remember seeing you before today."

"You were busy checking the lifeboats."

"Friggin' 'ell, you watched the lifeboat inspection? You must have been bloody bored."

"I was. You entertained me."

"Is that what I'm doing tonight?"

"I hope so. I need to be entertained."

"I can see that." Charlie leaned over and kissed her, hoping Petula would return the kiss. Not only did she return his kiss, but she held onto him like a drowning woman clinging to driftwood.

When he pulled away, she whispered, "What are we waiting for?"

Charlie reached under her hair and tugged at the string that held her halter top in place. "Not a damn thing. Let's get on with the job." The tie came loose. Just like a bib falling from a baby's neck, the halter top covering her breasts fell to her waist.

Without Charlie having to ask, Petula unbuttoned his shirt.

"Do you remember how hot it was the day you inspected the lifeboats?"

"Sure I do. It was cooler in the engine room than it was on deck."

Petula pulled his shirt open. "Your coveralls were open like this, and I could see your chest. I wanted to touch it so much." She rubbed his pectorals with both hands.

"Well, Pet, when I saw your bathing togs today, I wanted to rub yours, too." He filled each hand with a soft breast. "And that's not all I wanted to rub."

"Tell me what else."

"Better to show you, I think."

He stepped backward toward his bunk, taking Petula with him. "I don't want to muss up your dress. Maybe you should take it off."

"Perhaps I should. Will you help me? You're an engineer, you should be able to manage a zipper." She turned around and waited.

Knowing his way around an engine didn't help him one iota in this situation. All he saw were folds of poofy blue chiffon. He didn't see even the slightest hint of a zipper. "Where exactly is it, Pet?"

"It's back there. You'll find it."

Charlie sat down on the edge of the bunk. He figured the easiest way to find it, and the best way to get things rolling, was feeling under her skirt. He heard her breath catch as he slid his hands up the back of her legs, but she didn't stop him.

When his fingers grazed the bare flesh of her bum, he nearly pulled his hand away, startled that she didn't have any underpants on. He paused, and got his bearings. This one wanted it as much as he did. It had been a while since he'd had a Sheila so willing, and ready for it.

Letting one hand rest on her bare arse cheek, he reached up

with the other to feel the inside of her dress. He felt the zipper teeth with his fingers, but still couldn't see the damn thing.

Reluctantly, he pulled his other hand out from under her dress and felt for the zipper from the outside. After he traced the line of the teeth, he finally discovered the small tab wrapped in blue cloth at the waist of the skirt. He slid it down in one smooth motion to the bottom of her bum.

"Christ, Pet, it's easier to tear an engine apart than it is to open this friggin' zipper."

"That's why I asked for help. I knew you'd figure it out."

The dress hung precariously on her hips, her bum crack now partially visible. On impulse, Charlie leaned forward and licked her lower back. Petula shivered.

Not wasting any time, he pushed the dress down her legs to her ankles. As he suspected, she had nothing on underneath. He kissed each arse cheek and then reached around and tickled her pubic hair. Petula sighed.

"Pet, you shouldn't walk around the ship wearing nothing underneath your dress. My mates are good blokes, but not one of them would think twice about reaching under and copping a feel, and maybe even doing a private lifeboat inspection with you."

"Charlie, maybe that's what I've been hoping would happen."

He gently lifted each foot, took off her shoes and untangled her dress. Then he turned her around, and tickled her pubes again. "You want it bad, don't ya, Pet?"

"You're the first man I've met on this ship who seems to be more than just talk. Yes, Charlie, I want it bad, and I want someone who's man enough to give it to me."

Even with is erection throbbing in his trousers, Charlie decided not to take her just yet. He wanted to make her want it even more. He pulled her closer and buried his face in the golden curls between her legs. Petula gasped when his tongue connected with her sensitive flesh, and moaned when he sucked her clitoris into his mouth.

Charlie sucked his prize until he had Petula squirming to get away. She pushed at his head and gasped, "I can't stand it. Stop!"

When he let her go, he fully expected Petula to collapse on the bed beside him. She didn't. Instead, she knelt between his legs. Before he fully grasped what she meant to do, she leaned forward and licked his knob through his trousers. "Pet, aren't you ready to get a leg over?" He wanted to screw her, badly.

"Not yet, dear Charles. It's your turn." She tried to undo his trousers. Not wanting to get his willy knicked in his fly, he stopped her and undid it himself. He'd never had a Sheila go after him like a hungry wombat. He rather fancied it.

Charlie lifted his arse so Pet could drag his trousers down and off. He doffed his shirt and tossed it onto the floor. That left them both naked.

He reached down and squeezed her tits. "Christ, Pet, you're built. You should be a model."

Much to his surprise, she started to laugh. "I used to be. I design clothes now. I designed the dress I was wearing."

"Shoulda done a friggin' better job on the zipper."

"Says you, Mister Engineer."

Then she shocked the shit out of him. She grabbed hold of his donger, and took him full in her mouth, sucking him like a vacuum pump.

"Oh, yeah, Pet, that's the way. Shit, yeah!" Petula sucked him hard, and licked him all the while. Charlie remembered he'd hoped for some teabagging. He tapped her on her blonde head. "Pet, do my knackers."

Without missing a beat, Petula released his cock, and moved her mouth lower. First she licked his balls, and then she sucked the whole sack into her mouth. Charlie thought he had died and gone to heaven. She rolled his testicles in her mouth like lollies, licking them as she would yummy sweets.

Charlie let her play with him as long as he could stand it. When he knew he wouldn't last much longer he stopped her. "I'm ready to shag, my Pet. Let's do it."

"Wait, I've got condoms in my bag."

"No worries. I have some right here." Charlie reached under his mattress and pulled out a small package. Petula watched as he ripped open the wrapper and rolled the rubber onto his prick. "Sailors, and engineers, are always prepared."

"So are women looking to get laid." Charlie grinned and pushed her backward onto the bunk. "Well, Pet, you're about to get it good."

With no preamble, Charlie pushed his cock deep into Petula's body. She gasped and lifted her pelvis to meet his. "Fuck, yes, Charlie, do it hard!"

She didn't have to ask him twice. He frigged her harder than he had any Sheila on the ship. He had only ever fucked a woman this hard during the few visits he made to a whorehouse in Hong Kong. Petula stayed with him, slapping her pussy against him just as roughly as he pounded her.

Charlie didn't know how long he could hold on, but she seemed close. He growled at her, "C'mon, Pet. Come for me, I want to feel you come."

"Jesus, yes, I'm so close." He wiggled his fingers between them just enough to reach her nipple. Then, he pinched it as hard as he could. Petula yelped and then began to shudder.

"Oh yeah, Pet, that's it, let it fly."

Charlie continued to bang her as she shook underneath him. Before she stopped shaking, his balls clutched and he sprayed into the rubber. Petula dug her fingernails into his back and scratched him down to his arse. Another spasm gripped him as he squirted again.

He heard her whisper, "Oh, yes, you're definitely man enough to get the job done."